THE SAN JUAN REPRISAL

Otis Morphew

Trafford rev. 01/06/2014

 www.trafford.com
North America & international
toll-free: 1 888 232 4444 (USA & Canada)
fax: 812 355 4082

PROLOGUE

Mike and Nora Zant, along with their son, Mitchell and his friend, Reno Cortez were all avid hunters and gun enthusiasts. Reno's family owned and operated the Membreno/Cortez Gun Club in Albuquerque, . . . and all were the best of friends, their sons were God Sons to both families.

In the Summer of Nineteen and fifty-six, Michael and Nora, as well as the two boys were all invited to attend an out of season Black Bear hunt in the San Juan Mountains of Southern Colorado, an area they hunted in every year anyway. Michael wanted a bear rug for his den and readily accepted, only this time the boys could not go with them, . . . and as it turned out, this hunt should have been rejected altogether.

The two of them were only just starting their hunt when they were brutally abducted and taken to a secret location in the northernmost area of the mountains where they were immediately disrobed and given jobs in a drug lab, deprived of their dignity, their clothing, and threatened with a lashing should they protest, or not follow the rules set down by a ruthless drug Cartel.

Michael could see immediately that their chances of being found were slim, to none at all. The compound could not be seen from the air and the landscape was too treacherous to search. Men and women alike were abused almost daily as they were all underfed and overworked, chained at night to their cots, and closely guarded by day. Mike and Nora were only two of another twenty-three abductees, and most of those worked in the forty acre Marijuana field, while the two of them and several others worked in the cave.

By all reason, Mike and Nora Zant would have vanished for good, because the F.B.I., as well as the National Guardsmen and the Sheriff's Department's trackers had given up on ever finding any trail the kidnappers might have left, . . . and had not young Mitchell Zant, and Reno come looking, that would surely have been the outcome! But they were up against a Columbian Drug Cartel of unimaginable proportion, and like all Crime Organizations, it flourished by using fear and brutality as its tools of trade.

CHAPTER ONE

Albuquerque, New Mexico is the second oldest city in the United States and lays sprawled along the banks of the Rio Grande River. A city steeped in Indian tradition and lore, Albuquerque thrived on that heritage from the onset, it's mild climate and agriculture made it the major city in the state of New Mexico. New industry was moving in at a record pace, and still is, . . . home construction was rampant due to population growth.

The city's major lifeline is known as the Rio Grande Research corridor, a large installation belonging to the Government, a massive constellation of high technology, . . . and all coming to light in the wake of nuclear research during and after the second world war. The area's major employers were, and are a part of this complex. Sandia National Laboratories for research and development is here, as well as Kirkland Air Force Base, which is involved heavily in weapons research. The entire facility was cloaked in secrecy and self contained, boasting the tightest security known to exist in 1956, and this security network covered the all of the complex, . . . with the exception of Zant Industries, located in a separate part of the city.

Zant Industries was an outside contractor and was responsible for the design and development of a totally new concept in navigation and guidance systems in use by the Government as well as the Nation's airlines, under different guidelines and design of course. Therefore, because of the Government contracts and product secrecy, very strict security measures were also in place. Michael Zant, owner and CEO of Zant Industries had become a millionaire several times over by the age of thirty.

Michael Robert Zant's mother and father de-boarded the immigrant ship at New York's Ellis Island in the spring of 1900 from Oslo Norway, and for some reason disliked what they saw there. They stayed just long enough to earn enough money to travel westward and after several months, to finally to settle in Albuquerque in 1902, . . . and it did not take long for the senior Zant to begin work as a brick mason, or to learn the English language. Mrs.

Zant, being a barber and hair stylist began work at a local salon where she also learned to speak fluent English.

They were happy here and soon were able to purchase a small house along the river and a year later, Juliette Zant was born, and had she lived would have grown into a dark haired beauty, like her mother. But some things are not meant to be, Juliette was three when she contracted influenza and died. They quit trying to have children for a time after that, but in 1910, Michael was born, and was an exceptional child. He was able to read complete sentences, and do addition and subtraction at the early age of three. It was known from the onset that young Michael had an extraordinary mind, and a memory that one old sawbones called photographic, and quite amazing for a child of any age.

He did not prove them wrong, Michael Zant went through lower school, high school and college, graduating with top honors at the age of only sixteen, and with a degree in Mathematics, Electronics, English lit, Science and Mechanical engineering. By his seventeenth birthday he was working as an Electronics Engineer for the Sandia Corporation where he designed wiring assemblies for automobiles and passenger trains which for Michael Zant, was not what he wanted to build his career on. He was bored most of the time, considering his job too routine for a mind that was constantly reaching for other things. It was here that, after a couple of years, he decided to put his brainchild to the test.

He already knew that the Government was using guidance systems in their aircraft and ships at sea, sonar, radar, etc. But he also knew, or believed that these technologies could be improved on. He believed that it should be possible to electronically direct a vehicle's destination without having to constantly monitor the instruments. A pilot should be able to set those instruments only once and forget about them, take a nap even, . . . then be awakened when he arrived. This would be impossible to accomplish with an automobile, he knew, . . . but with airplanes and ships it very possible. He believed he could improve on the existing guidance technology, why? . . . Because it had been proven that the current systems were not totally fail-proof. Oh they were accurate when working right, but far too sensitive to totally depend on!

He was 22 years old when he proposed the updated version of his new guidance system to the United States Air Force, and it was not easy, getting an appointment with the right people was next to impossible. So he started with the facility right there in Albuquerque, the Government Weapons Research Center. One Engineer viewed his new circuit board, understood it's properties and saw the possibility of using something of this design to direct missiles to their targets a long distance away, . . . and with the Engineer's help, young Michael was able to present, and demonstrate his smaller updated version of guidance control to the Government. A short two years later in a rented warehouse, and under Government supervision, Zant Industries was born. Government contracts were signed, and Government money supplied for research and development.

Michael Zant found, and hired the brightest electronics minds he could find from those not already employed by Uncle Sam. New buildings were constructed around the newly purchased warehouse and property, new offices and state of the art laboratories installed. Michael Robert Zant was on his way and he dove into his established career with all the zest and vinegar of a whiz kid. He had succeeded, but he knew that any and every balloon can pop at any given time and so, kept each and every development and research under his personal supervision, . . . and all the while hoping that someone in his employ would step up and become his trusted man in charge.

Some time later, Michael found himself becoming friendly with, and liking one of his senior engineers, a man with a superior knowledge of electronics, and who was teaching him things even he did not know. They became very good friends, and to the point that Michael began putting him in charge of certain projects. This was the man he needed and so, after several months of observation, Sean Webster was put in charge of overseeing all operations of his research labs, making them even closer friends, however, there was still something missing in Michael Zant's personal life, . . . someone to share that life with.

None of the young women had yet seemed to fill the void and after a date or two he would politely bow out. They were all pretty enough, and some even drop-dead beautiful, and he could have had his pick of any of them, after all he was Michael Zant, and he was loaded! None of these were what he wanted, well, other than sexually, . . . and he found them all willing and able. Actually, wanted was the wrong word to use in this situation, . . . they were not what he needed! He knew this, because afterward he would realize that the void was not filled, the emptiness was still there. But then one day, out of the blue, Sean came to his office and invited him to a gun club to shoot his collection of firearms. Michael's first impulse was to decline but then again, he had nothing to look forward to but another empty weekend and so accepted his invitation.

The Membreno/Cortez Gun Club had been in business for as long as Michael could remember, but he had never had the urge, or even considered the possibility that he might enjoy the excursion. When he arrived, however, he was very impressed with the entire layout of the shooting range. The targets were state of the art, electronically notifying a shooter of his accuracy. Golf course style, evenly cut green grass adorned the areas between shooter and targets. Each shooter would stand behind waist-high tables, with walls on either side of them for privacy, and each stall was provided with ear and eye protection. It was one beautiful place, he decided, and huge! There were several shooting ranges in the facility covering several acres, and almost as many buildings. Pistol ranges were both, inside one of the buildings, and outside. The inside ranges were mostly for police qualifying and, or for Government qualifiers. But there were also inside ranges for citizen shooters, and to one of these ranges was where Sean took him, . . . and when the older man opened the heavy carrying case of handguns, Michael was avidly impressed. Sean had guns from the civil war era, and some used by the gunfighters, Colts, Derringers, smiths.

Michael Zant fell in love with guns that day and as it was his way with all that he does, after studying the dynamics of shooting, bullet trajectory, etc. became quite the marksman with both handgun, and rifle. He quickly purchased handguns of his own, some were new, some replicas of the past, but he began spending his weekends off at the club, and was now an upstanding member, fast becoming friends with the owners, an Apache man and his Mexican wife, both very knowledgeable and sophisticated people, . . . liking them at first sight.

Having all but forgotten the void in his life, having filled it with his newly found love of shooting, he was unprepared the first time he saw her. It was on his third weekend at the range. He was firing his Winchester Rifle at an outside range when he saw, rather he heard the electronic monitor on her target as it registered center shot after center shot and curious, left his stand and moved out onto the range far enough to see the shooter, and was never the same afterward. He was mesmerized, and found himself watching her intently as she fired her weapons, noting that she could not be any older than he was, if as old. The way she moved stirred him the most, and the way her long, dark hair flowed back from her head in the breeze as she fired. It did not take long for Michael Zant to form a conclusion, . . . he was in love!

He tried very hard to concentrate on business that next week, but found it next to impossible, he could not erase her from his mind. But he was, after all, a man that possessed an extraordinary mind, and it did not take him long to realize that the only cure for what he was now going through was to initiate a meeting, maybe then he could concentrate on his business. Yes, he thought, that was the solution, and he would do it. After all, he had never found it hard to approach a girl before. But then again, he somehow knew that this one was different than all the others, her upbringing, everything about her was different.

He was on the range the next weekend and he had thought she was not coming as she had not arrived yet, and had just began firing his rifle when she fired her own. Gathering his courage, he placed his rifle on the table, left his booth and walked the short few steps to move into her booth beside her as she was about to fire again, startling her, . . . and as their eyes met he knew she was the one and evidently, so did she. They were inseparable after that, and it was in disbelief that when she told him her name, and that she was sole owner of the Salon where his mother worked, he was speechless. He knew that a Nora Prescott owned the Salon, his mother had said so, and she knew that Mrs. Zant's son was Michael Zant, owner of Zant Industries! Such a small world and they never knew the other existed, or that they would fall in love.

His mother of course was ecstatic, as was his father when he was told, and it was the exact same with her folks. Nora Loralee Prescott, and Michael Robert Zant were now an item, and inseparable for the next three wonderful years. They wanted to wait until their dream home could be built, and a future planned before getting married and in June of 1929, all the pieces were in place, they were married in the old Mission Church and moved into their new home. Everyone at Zant Industries was there, as well as the senior Zants, the Prescotts and Mister and Mrs. Cortez. The celebration at the new Zant home's extremely large rear garden and pool area was written about for a week calling it the biggest blowout in decades. There were most of a hundred people there, and enough gifts to fill Michael's enormous, western style den.

The Zant Estate was a sprawling one-story structure that lay amid large elm and oak trees that almost cloaked it from the view of traffic along Paradise Boulevard. The house, was nestled between rolling hills on two sides, the front drive accessible through double wrought iron gates anchored between two tall, four by four brick pedestals with wrought iron eagles adorning the tops, and twisted it's way through the trees up to the house. A wrought iron framework, with an insertion reading Mike and Nora stretched between the two pedestals above the gates, along with the street address.

*   *   *

Having decided to wait a while to have a child, Mike and Nora continued their heavy workloads with a renewed vigor and of course, continued their weekends at the Membreno/Cortez shooting range and on occasion accompanied by Sean Webster, who by now had become a very close friend of the family. It was Sean who, soon after that invited them on their first month long hunting excursion to Colorado. They were undecided at first, but when Sean convinced them that it was a chance to test their shooting skills in the wilds they finally agreed to go, . . . and it was an outing both were thrilled with, each bagging their first Elk. This was the beginning of an every year hunting vacation that continued for the better part of the next ten years, right up to the point when Nora became pregnant with Mitchell Robert Zant, and for the next five years they were both content to be nothing more than a family.

Young Mitchell was five years old in 1945, the war was over and Zant Industries had continued to grow to enormous proportion. Michael Zant was considered one of the wealthiest men in New Mexico. This was also the year they agreed that young Mitchell was old enough to go hunting, . . . and hunting they did go.

These new hunting ventures continued every year since, during Mitchell's summer vacation from school of course, and they even began taking Mitchell's best friend along with them, . . . an adventure that both boys took to avidly.

Young Reno Cortez was the only son of Nakito and Melissa Cortez, owners of the Membreno/Cortez Gun Club. Nakito was a full blood Membreno Apache Indian who was a teenager when found starved and severely dehydrated by a Mexican family migrating from Arizona to New Mexico. The Mexican couple had a daughter slightly younger than Nakito when they took him in and needless to say, Melissa fell in love with the boy at first sight. Nakito stayed with the family, adopting them as his own, even taking the last name of Cortez. Not long after establishing themselves in Albuquerque, Nakito and Melissa were married. The Apache Indian language closely associated it's self with Spanish anyway, and it was not hard for Nakito to make the adjustment, nor was it hard to master the English language, . . . both Nakito, and Melissa enrolled themselves in school and though married, no one even knew.

Nakito was a boy with a hunger to accomplish something with his life, and his love for weaponry of any kind gave him the idea for a shooting range. His belief was that people would come and pay for the privilege of shooting their guns on a target range. He had been right and now, Nakito Cortez was a very prominent citizen in Albuquerque, as were his family. Reno Cortez was the same age as young Mitchell Zant in 1945 and had been playing games together at the gun club for three years while Mitchell's parents fired their weapons at targets. Reno, however, had a slight head start on young Mitchell when it came to weapons, Nakito began teaching Reno the skills of the Apache Indian at the age of three, and by five he was able to follow the almost invisible tracks of mice in the wooded areas. He was also taught to use a modified bow and arrows, and to clean fish and small game for consumption. This schooling went on until Reno started school at the age of six, and his studies took over his spare time. Reno Cortez was eight when he was invited to go hunting with the Zant's and by then, he was adept with both bow, and knife, . . . and having been taught on weekends to fire a rifle, had become quite a good shot with one. Nakito and Melissa had great respect and trust for Michael and Nora Zant, otherwise they would not have allowed Reno to go along. Reno became a regular on the Zant hunting excursions after that and by 1950, both boys had bagged their first Elk in Southern Colorado. This was a thrill that would repeat it's self over and over again, and did so until 1956 . . . . This was Graduation year!

CHAPTER TWO

Graduation was over precisely at ten, and by ten-forty Michael and Nora exited the building, having been jostled and all but mobbed by an exited crowd of more than four hundred, . . . and by eleven were leaving the parking area in bumper to bumper traffic on their way to the celebration.

"You ever see a crowd that size?" Asked Michael as he maneuvered the Fairlane through traffic, . . . and when she didn't answer." "I haven't, not even at my graduation. Unruly is what they were!" When she still didn't answer, he glanced across to see her staring forlornly through the car's side window,

"Why so quiet, sweetheart, . . . you okay?"

"What?" She said, startled by the question.

"You haven't said a word since leaving the Civic Center."

She smiled warmly at him and shrugged. "I'm just a little overwhelmed, I guess, . . . and a little nostalgic. Graduation seems so, . . ." She frowned at him then tearfully turned to look out the window again while she quickly retrieved a wipe from her purse and dabbed at her eyes. "It just seems so final to me." She looked back at him then.

"It's like, . . . I don't know, . . . like, . . . I just feel like this is the first step in losing Mitchell, Michael! Almost like he won't be needing us much longer!"

"I wouldn't worry about that," He smiled. "That boy will always be part of our lives, besides, he's all set and determined to take a job with me after college, . . . if that ever happens?"

"Now, why did you say that?"

"You know why, . . . he could have, and should have graduated two years ago, he had all the credits, and more, too! I graduated college at his age."

"That's not what he wanted, Michael, you know that! Didn't you listen?"

"Of course, I did!"

"He didn't want to grow up too fast, that's all, . . . and I'm glad! He should have time to be a kid, grow up with his friends, . . . and he should have fun doing it!"

"I know, sweetheart." He sighed. "And I guess I know why he did it! . . . I was just never a kid."

"Maybe you didn't want to be one."

"I think you're right . . . . I don't think I ever lived at all until I met you." He smiled then steered the sedan into the crowded parking lot. "But I guess dad was right. You don't miss something you never had, . . . and I never really had a childhood." He found a parking spot and pulled in to park. "But I'm still so proud of him that I could pop, . . . yes sir, that was a very nice graduation." He turned the ignition off.

"And not to worry, darling, . . . the lifeline with our son will never be severed, it will only grow stronger!"

"Thank you for saying that, Michael, I love you."

"Ditto, Mrs. Zant." He got out of the car and went around to open her door. "And you are stunning tonight, my dear."

"Thank you, darling." She smiled at him. "You're not so bad yourself."

"I know!" He grinned and closed the door before ushering her to the sidewalk, and hand in hand walked up the walkway to the doors of the steakhouse.

"Oh, look, here they come, Michael."

They both watched, having been alerted by the squeal of rubber on pavement, as Mitchell's bright red, 1934, fat-fender Ford Coupe entered the parking lot and parked.

"Boy knows how to make an entrance, doesn't he?" He grinned widely, and they watched as him and his friend Reno got out of the car and walked toward them.

Mitchell Zant was only five feet-eleven, slender, and with a well developed body, not muscular, but definitely not a weakling. He had a full head of wavy, dark brown hair, well kept and handsomely trimmed. An oval face and a mouth that seemed to always smile to show his even white teeth, . . . and eyes of brown that showed his intelligence, always darting about, taking things in and storing them away in his memory. He wore his clothes well, always neat in appearance and his shoes always shined with what old vets would call a spit-polish. Mitchell, called Mitch by his friends, was a well-groomed young man.

Reno Cortez was slightly shorter than Mitchell, with olive colored skin that reflected his Apache Heritage, a strong, rugged face and full lips that were also smiling most of the time. His hair was inky black and also wavy and well groomed. Reno possessed the body of an Apache warrior, wiry, strong and sinewy. His movements, the way he walked, all gave the appearance of a stalking puma that seemed ready to spring into action at the slightest provocation. Reno's dark eyes were always alert and flashing, but never seemed to mirror his emotions. To a stranger, young Reno Cortez would appear to be someone not to tamper with, . . . and he was, as a few of the bullies at school could attest. A ruggedly handsome young man in his own right, Reno also wore his custom suit very well.

"Aren't they handsome, Michael?" Sighed Nora as they approached.

"Fine looking young men, especially ours." He replied. "We did okay, darling." He nodded. "Very well indeed!"

"My word, Mitchell!" Gasped Nora as Mitch and Reno joined them, and she was smiling broadly. "Where in the world is your robes and cap, . . . you looked so handsome in them, both of you?"

Grinning, Mitch reached and pulled his mother against him in a hug. "Graduation is over, Mom, . . . the thing was hot, and it made us feel a little self-conscious."

"Yes ma'am," Grinned Reno, looking through the glass doors at the crowd. "Besides, all those other grads in there look alike. Can't tell who they are with them robes on." He smiled wider as he looked back at them. "We'll be the only handsome men in the place." He tilted his head at Michael then. "Present company included, Mister Zee!"

"Thank you, Reno." He laughed and looked back toward the parking lot. "I expected your mother and father by now, have you seen them?"

"Oh, mom and dad are already here, Mister Zee, the car is parked next to the curb out there. They'll be inside already."

"Then why are we standing here?" He pulled the heavy door open, allowing all of them to file by before following them into the crowded interior, . . . and once the hostess arrived, gave her his name and all followed the girl into the noise and bustle of the dining room, finally to join Nakito and Lisa Cortez at their reserved table.

*   *   *

Michael Zant wiped his mouth with the table linen and leaned back in his chair to observe the others, listening to the overly crowded noise of the room, which made it next to impossible to hear the conversation at his own table. His eyes fell on Nakito as the Indian finished his dessert and he thought back over the years that he had known the Apache and his Spanish wife, and also thinking that if not for the shade of his skin no one would ever take him for an Indian. Nakito Cortez was as refined as any man he knew. His suit and tie was impeccable, and the shade of his clothes fully complimented the color of his skin.

He smiled to himself, Nakito Cortez was as fine a man as he had ever met and he was proud to call him friend. Of course, him being a somewhat wealthy man in his own right placed him right up there amid Albuquerque's elite. He had come a long way from his heritage, that's for sure, starting a shooting range at the right time took planning, and the Gun Club was a smart thing to do. Only a man with keen foresight could have accomplished it, because now the Membreno/Cortez Gun Club was the most popular and well-known club of it's kind in the southwest, catering to many National Events and tournaments. Michael smiled slightly as he watched him and knew that a better friend he would never find.

Nakito pushed his plate away and turned to Michael, flashing his even white teeth in a wide smile. "I am a proud and happy man tonight, Mike!" He looked across at Reno and smiled even wider. "My son is no longer a Bambino, he is a man, and," He looked back at Michael. "He is going to college. He is going to be someone of importance!"

"He already is, Nakito." Grinned Michael. "You have done well, my friend, believe me. I have never known a finer young man."

"Thank you so very much, Mike, . . . nor I, your son. Mitchell is like a second son to me, also."

Smiling, Michael picked up his wine glass. "Here's to the two finest sons any two men, or women ever had!"

"Here, here!" Voiced everyone around the table, and they all sipped at their drinks.

"Am I mistaken here, Nakito," Grinned Michael, looking across at the boys. "Are they agreeing with us?"

"Why not, Dad?" Laughed Mitch, nudging Reno in the arm. "No truer words were ever spoken!"

"Amen!" Agreed Nora, reaching to grip Mitch's arm lovingly. "And we love them dearly."

"I love you, too, Mom, Dad."

"Well," Boomed Michael, clearing his throat. "You boys about ready for the big hunt, we leave in a couple of days, you know?"

Mitch glanced at Reno before looking back at his father. "I'm afraid we can't go this time, dad."

"What? . . . May I ask you why?"

"Yes, why not, sweetheart?" Gasped Nora. "I don't understand, we've been looking forward to this for weeks, and so have you!"

"I know, Mom, . . . but for some reason they moved the college entrance exams up a month. It takes place in two weeks."

"And over a period of several days." Added Reno.

"Why didn't you tell us, sweetheart?" Asked Lisa.

"We only found out tonight, ourselves, mom." Shrugged Reno. "If we don't take the exams now, I may not be accepted for this fall's classes, they are almost all booked solid." He shrugged then. "Mitch won't have a problem getting in, but I might."

"Don't say that, buddy." Responded Mitch. "I'll have to take those exams like everyone else."

"That's not what I meant." Said Reno. "But we both know I have to study harder than you do, . . . and I'm not complaining about it, it's just a fact!"

"I know that!" Sighed Mitch. "But we are in this together, buddy."

"Well," Sighed Michael. "I guess we could postpone it for a month, or all together, for that matter. This is more important than a hunting trip . . . . No big deal!"

"It is a big deal, Michael." Said Nora quickly. "Carrie Bowman called me yesterday to verify the reservations. They are booking up solid for this bear hunt. She said they were already turning down bookings, Michael. They are such good friends, sweetheart, it wouldn't be right and besides, Cato is waiting to guide us."

"Well, I guess it wouldn't be right at that." He nodded and looked across at Mitch. "We'll miss you two going with us, son. We were looking forward to it."

"Sorry, dad, . . . so were we."

"Okay, . . . what about you and Lisa, Nakito, the room is reserved? . . . It's been a couple of years since you two have gone with us, what do you say?"

"I wish we could, Mike." Shrugged Nakito. "But the Southwest Archery Tournament is ten days away. It's the biggest event of the year . . . . Maybe next year we can all plan on going."

"I can handle the tournament, pop, if you and mom want to go?"

"I know you can, son, . . . but the Governor is coming to this one, and he expects me to participate in the award ceremony." He sighed and looked back at Michael.

"Tell you what, though, . . . next year we will load up my old Silver Streak and all go hunting. I have got a new Chevy, two-ton ordered, that should pull that big camper to Colorado with no problem. What do you think?"

"That's a deal," Nodded Michael. "We'll plan on it." He looked at Mitch then. "You be okay while we're gone?"

"Of course, dad." He grinned. "Next week will be full anyway, graduation parties you know. But don't worry, we don't drink!"

"I know, . . . but I still worry about it."

"He's exaggerating, Mister Zee." Laughed Reno. "In fact, Chief Carma invited us out to celebrate the Laguna festival with them next week, . . . be a lot of fun."

"Looks like we won't be missed then." Sighed Nora. "Be careful you two, whatever you do. And Mitch, check on your Grandparents."

"Don't worry about us, mom, just concentrate on bagging that black bear."

"If she sees it, she'll bag it, son." Nodded Michael.

"Bear?" Queried Nakito. "I thought I heard you mention that . . . . Isn't it a bit early for bear season?"

"It's a special hunt," Responded Michael. "Seems the black bear population has grown a little too out of proportion, some of them are venturing into areas populated by people, . . . becoming a menace, I guess. Sooner or later they could become aggressive . . . . Anyway, I wanted a bear rug, and that's why we're going this early. But, if I had known the boys weren't going, we'd have waited until September."

"When are you leaving, dad?"

"Monday morning, I think, . . . and since you boys aren't going, I think we'll fly up there. I haven't taken the Cessna up in a while . . . . I always liked that twin engine plane. We can fly into the Durango—La Plata County airport, be there in about three hours, four tops."

"Fly?" Gasped Nora. "I wouldn't have thought of that, it's a great idea! . . . We'll need to rent a car though, once we're there."

"No we won't, I'll call Mister Bowman in the morning early, he'll have a car waiting to take us to the lodge."

"That's quite a ways," Said Nakito. "Must be sixty or seventy miles, one way."

"It is, . . . but there's no place to land a plane near the Keyah Grande Lodge, . . . and I don't think I would attempt one if there were. Terrible wind currents in the San Juan Mountains!" He looked across at Mitch then.

"What are your plans for tonight, boys?"

"Aww, I don't know, dad, . . . guess we'll cruise around for a while downtown, maybe find a party or two, I won't be too late."

Nodding, Michael took out his wallet and looked at the others. "Are we ready to go?"

"Yes," Nodded Nakito, also taking out his wallet. "But this celebration is on me tonight, I insist!"

"Then, be it far from me to deny you that privilege, Sir!"

"Thank you very much." Nodded Nakito and raised his hand for the check. When the check arrived, he looked it over, added gratuity then placed money on the tray she was holding, thanked her for impeccable service and all got up to thread their way back and outside onto the sidewalk.

Michael placed a hand on his friend's shoulder, getting his attention. "As always, it's been a pleasure, my friend." He gripped Nakito's hand warmly.

"Yes," Nodded Nakito. "As well as you, my friend. It has been a most wonderful day! . . . Will we see you at the range tomorrow?"

"Not tomorrow, I think after Church, I want to check out the plane, maybe call in a mechanic or two to go over it, I haven't flown it in a while . . . . And we have to stow our gear on board."

"I understand." Nodded the Indian. "Then fly with God as your Co-Pilot, my friend. Watch those ill-winds aloft, . . . and do not worry about your son, my home is his, should he desire."

"I know that, Nakito, and I will do that, thank you. You, too, Lisa." He pulled the Mexican lady to him in a hug. "We love you guys."

"Yes," Voiced Nora, moving to embrace Nakito, and then Lisa. "We love you both very much."

"As we love you, darling." Sighed Lisa. "Be very careful, please, . . . I do not trust airplanes."

"We will." Nora smiled then allowed Michael to steer her toward the car. "Don't stay out too late, son."

"I won't, mom!"

"Well," Sighed Nakito, turning to the boys. "We are so proud of you boys." He hugged them both, as did Lisa before stepping off the sidewalk and allowing Nakito to usher her toward their own car.

Mitch turned to watch his father close his mother's door and waved as he came around to get in himself, and was watching as his father backed out and maneuvered the Fairlane Ford toward the exit, . . . and it was then that he suddenly frowned and shivered inside. "Wow!" He muttered.

"What's, WOW, Mitch?" Grinned Reno. "What's wrong?"

"I have no idea." He shrugged then and shook his head. "I was watching mom and dad drive out and I had a chill, . . . that never happened before! . . . It was weird, I know that! . . . Do you think it was an omen or something?"

"I don't know," Shrugged Reno. "Maybe, . . . Dad believes in that sort of thing. Says his ancestors lived their whole lives guided by omens, or visions . . . . I wouldn't worry about it too much, Mister Zee is an excellent Pilot, and that Cessna is a great plane, we've flown in it, remember? . . . I didn't like it much, but we've flown in it!"

"I guess you're probably right, but it unnerved the hell out of me for a second!" He shivered again then. "So what do you want to do, cruise, . . . it's a bit too late for a movie? Unless you want to see one of them midnight horror flicks, I hear Frankenstein is showing at the Plaza?"

"Get real, Mitch!, Cruise a while, I guess, I don't feel much like a party."

"Makes two of us, of course we'll have to visit the Pig Stand, right?"

"Well, that goes without saying!"

"When are you going to ask Jennifer out, man?" Asked Mitch as they stepped into the parking lot. "You wait too long, some hard dick is going to whisk her away from you."

"Yeah, she is a knockout." Sighed Reno. "But I would rather see her as a knockout, than me getting her knocked up. That's what would happen, too! . . . The way she looks on them roller skates, and in that mini skirted uniform, man, . . . that would make any man's pecker hard!"

"They all make mine hard, Reno, . . . come on, let's go."

*   *   *

They were all three a little somber as Mitch stopped the Fairlane at the control post, inserted and turned the key to activate the heavy gates and then drove out, . . . and after stopping again to close them, drove out onto Paradise Boulevard and headed East toward I-25 and the airport.

"I sure do wish you were going with us, son." Sighed Michael.

"Me, too, honey." Added Nora. "It won't be the same without you, sweetheart!"

"Thanks, . . . but I sort of wish you weren't going at all." Returned Mitch, but then added quickly; "Don't get me wrong, Dad, I'm glad you're going, I want you and Mom to enjoy yourselves, . . . it's just that, . . . well, I'm a little uneasy about this one."

"What do you mean, son," Queried Michael curiously. "Did something happen?"

"No, sir, not exactly."

"Then what is it, sweetheart?" Chimed in Nora. "You're not coming down with something?"

"No, Mom, I'm not sick."

"Then what, son, tell us?" Urged Michael.

Mitch was quiet for a few long seconds. "Okay, . . . while you and Mom were leaving the parking lot Saturday night, I was watching you drive away and, . . . well, I had a chill, Dad, I shivered inside! . . . It was just for a second, but it scared me. Anyway, . . . all I could think of was that it was an omen or something. Do you believe in that sort of thing?"

"Don't think I ever thought about it! . . . But tell me, do you think this uneasiness, or omen had something to do with our hunting trip? . . . Because something like you just described happens to me from time to time, . . . but I never considered it an omen, and nothing ever happened that I could associate the feeling with?"

"I don't know, Dad, but it was a dark feeling."

"Well, I don't know, either," Said Nora. "But it's a little scary!"

"I've never felt anything like that before, Dad, . . . so I don't know if it was because of the trip, the fact that you're flying this time, or what, . . . just be careful, that's all!"

"We will, sweetheart." Soothed Nora. "And you shouldn't worry, your father is an excellent Pilot, and a more than excellent hunter, . . . and so am I, I might add."

"I know, Mom . . . . It's probably nothing anyway."

"Tell you what, son . . . . I will call both you, and Sean the moment we arrive at Durango airport, well, maybe not there, but for sure when we get to the lodge, how's that?"

"It would help a lot, thanks, Dad."

"You can count on it, Darling." Added Nora.

"I will!" He made the turn onto Interstate 25 and headed South, and twenty minutes later was turning through the gates at the West end of the airport's row of hangars and shortly after, stopped the car at the open hangar doors of the one bearing the name of Zant Industries.

The twin engine Cessna plane had already been rolled out, gassed up and was waiting for them, and as they exited the Ford, Michael's Chief Mechanic came out to greet them, carrying a smile across his face, and a clipboard with papers for Michael to sign in his hand. They took a few minutes to go over the checklist of final instructions, shook hands, and the Mechanic headed back to his office inside.

"Well, son." He said, turning to shake Mitchell's hand, and then to embrace him. "I love you very much, son. And don't worry about us, we'll be fine."

"We will call you tonight, sweetheart! . . . I love you so much!""

"I love you both very much!" Nodded Mitch as he hugged and kissed his mother, then he stood back to watch as they climbed up and into the mid-sized plane and then waving as his father pulled up the steps and locked the door in place.

The uneasiness returned as the engines were started and warmed up and the flap controls tested, and was still there as he watched his father pilot the aircraft off toward the distant runways. Sighing, he shook the ill feeling off, got back into the car and headed for home.

*   *   *

After getting the okay from the tower, Michael moved the Cessna onto the assigned runway, revved the droning engines to life, and in less than two minutes, they were in the air and lifting high above the airport and immediately banking the aircraft northward as he continued to climb to a cruising altitude of 15,000 feet.

""It looks like we're almost to Santa Fe already." Remarked Nora into the headset.

"How do you know, it's still dark down there?"

"But it is beautiful up here, . . . besides, I can see the cluster of lights way off there." She sighed then as she thought about Mitch, and what he had said about the omen. She knew he was serious about what he told them, and she knew he was scared because of it . . . . But she had no idea of what something like that was all about, had heard of such all her life and had even had people tell her about experiences they had with it, . . . and swore it was true! She had not believed, or disbelieved them, she just had never thought about it in any way other than just a myth.

She was sure of one thing, however, Mitchell believed in it, knew this because he was such an intense young man. She also knew that he would never lie about such a thing, . . . and as she thought about it, she found herself becoming a little afraid. After all, all fear was born from the unknown, something strange, or supernatural, something unexplainable. Maybe that was why it frightened her when he told them about it, . . . and thinking that, she found herself absently studying the many gauges and switches on the instrument panel and all the while, hoping silently that everything would be okay.

"We're going to be okay, honey." Said Michael suddenly, and he knew he had startled her by the way she looked at him.

"I know we will, . . . why did you say that?"

"You were thinking about what Mitch said, . . . and I saw you watching the instrument panel."

"That means you were thinking about it, too!"

"You're right, I was! . . . It was a bit strange, right out of the blue that way."

"Do you believe in such things, . . . could there be anything to it?"

"I don't see how there could be, the plane's engines are running great, oil pressure is perfect, nothing could be better, . . . and we are on coarse, by the way, . . . and I might add, over Santa Fe and turning northwest. You can now see the San Juan Mountains of Colorado off to the right there . . . . Next stop, Durango!"

"Wonderful, how long will it be?"

"Well, we're doing about three hundred nautical miles an hour, which is about three hundred and forty five miles an hour on the ground. We should be there in about three hours, give or take . . . . Hey, that thermos where you can reach it, I'm going to set these controls on automatic and have some coffee."

"Got it right here, give me a moment." She slipped out of her safety harness and headset and leaned out and behind the seat to retrieve thermos and cups, then strapped back in before pouring their coffee. "Don't spill it on yourself, darling."

"Better on me than on these controls, that would make the omen come true." He accepted the cup and nodded toward her side window. "Look at the clouds around those peaks off there, that one mountain has got be as tall as we are high."

"It's beautiful. Some of them look almost red in the sunlight."

"That's because they are, we're still in New Mexico, not much vegetation on them . . . . All that will change in Colorado!"

"I know, it's so wild and beautiful up there."

"Just like you."

"Thank you, darling."

"My pleasure, my sweet!"

*　　　　　*　　　　　*

Mitchell Zant made the drive home in deep thought and with heavy heart, the feeling he had experienced Saturday night had been a fleeting one at most, . . . and had he not been watching his parents drive away at the time, would not have given it a second thought. But he did, and it was very troubling! He had read accounts of people who swore they were warned of danger before it happened. One account was of someone who refused to fly on a certain day because of it and then to hear later that same day, that the plane had crashed killing everyone aboard. Another, that someone had been warned of someone else's danger, and another of a disaster somewhere that was about to happen.

He had also read that anyone and everyone had the ability to foresee the future, if they just knew how to recognize the signs and take advantage of it. Even his American History Professor had used the phrase, "Forewarned, is forearmed" a few times.

And here he was, he thought, with an above average I.Q. and can't decipher a forewarning correctly, . . . or maybe he did? . . . An omen was considered by most, a phenomenon, a means of, or a sign of something to come! Even the dictionary said that. Well, he thought sadly, if he was omniscient, he didn't know it. Besides, it might not have been an omen at all.

Breathing deeply of the already warm, break of day air, he turned the Fairlane Ford into the drive, inserted the key and drove on to the rear of the rambling ranch style house where he parked the car in the garage alongside his mother's Rambler, and his own thirty-four. Getting out, he rested his arms across the top of the car and stared at the little red Ford for a time, still unable to shake the feeling of gloom. Sighing deeply, he moved aside and closed the car's door. Maybe what he needed was to take his pistols to the range and do some shooting, . . . and making up his mind, he walked across the garage and into the house.

The little thirty-four Coupe came to life with a turn of the key and as always, he felt the surge of excitement at the sound of the powerful V-8 engine's exhaust system, . . . and like always, remembered how he and his classmates had worked on the car during shop at school and how after almost a year, they had adapted the 1949 Oldsmobile engine to the smaller car's chassis and power-train. The results had been awesome. The car was a showstopper, the envy of most every young man in school, . . . and a head turner on the streets of Albuquerque. Smiling, he drove around the house and down the long drive, opened the gates and out onto Paradise where he left a few yards of burnt rubber before settling down for the drive to Membreno/ Cortez Gun Club.

Nakito Cortez was watching him from the shade of the long drive-through, overhanging roof in front as Mitch parked the car, and was waiting with a smile on his face as the boy shouldered the strap of his gun case and accessory bag and walked toward him.

"This is a rare Monday morning pleasure, Mitch, . . . getting in some early practice?"

"Morning, Sir!" He grinned. "I thought I would. Had to settle for the black powder, though. Well, either that or the forty-four, Ruger, . . . I like shooting this one better . . . . Anyway, Dad took the keys to the gun cabinet with him." He shook Nakito's hand as he spoke.

"I take it they got off okay?"

"Yes, sir, before daylight . . . . Reno up yet?"

"He's calibrating the targets on the rifle range this morning, I'll tell him you're here." He placed an arm across Mitch's shoulder. "But first, join me for a cup of coffee, I want to talk with you."

"Sure." Curious, he leaned his gear against the wall and followed the Indian inside, and sitting down in front of the large desk at a gesture from Nakito, he then waited while his coffee cup was placed on the desk in front of him and Nakito pulled up a chair beside him.

"Reno told me of what you experienced Saturday night, son, . . . Are you feeling all right about it?"

"Oh, yeah, I guess so, . . . it was probably nothing anyway, Mister Cortez! . . . I'm surprised he even mentioned it."

"Reno tells me everything, Mitch, . . . he also said you were pretty upset over it, . . . did you tell your father about it?"

"This morning." He nodded. "On the way to the airport . . . . I told them I wished they weren't going," He shrugged. "That I was uneasy about it . . . . I told them it scared me."

"Tell me what scared you about it?"

Mitch rubbed his face and grinned sheepishly. "Golly, I don't really know, Mister Cortez, . . . maybe, because they're flying this time? I know Dad's a good pilot and all, but he hasn't flown that plane in a couple of years, maybe that's what scares me, . . . you know, the plane might crash, or something, I don't know . . . . I can't figure it out, and I can't get it off my mind either . . . . I didn't sleep much last night."

"It will pass, son, don't worry . . . . But you did well, you listened! Most don't listen when the spirits warn them." And when Mitch frowned. "Yes, I said spirits, Mitch. I'm an Apache Indian by blood-right, and my ancestors were warriors whose lives were guided by the spirits. The spirits would come to them in a dream sometimes, or sometimes like they came to you. Because a Shaman, or Medicine man was more receptive to the spirits, it was usually him that would interpret the dreams, or visions and in turn use them to guide the people. It was a simple way of life for the Indian."

"Reno told me a little about that." Nodded Mitch. "But who, or what are these spirits?"

Nakito shrugged. "The Apache saw them as the spirits of our ancestors. You can call them Gods, intuition, anything, . . . but they are there, and they do guide us, . . . and sometimes even warn us. Problem is, you, me, nobody can interpret the warnings because they don't know what is true, and what is not, . . . and what's funny is when what you were warned about actually happens, chances are you won't associate it with the warning at all and in fact, most times you won't even remember the warning!"

"Then what do I do about it, Mister Cortez, . . . because I really feel like it was something bad, and it's going to happen to Mom and Dad?"

"I wish I could tell you, Mitch . . . . This won't make you feel any better about it, but all you can do is wait for it to happen because if it's going to, it will. Only then can you know what to do, or if there is anything you can do! . . . And Mitch, knowing you like I do, if something does go wrong you will do what has to be done, . . . and you won't have to do it alone, I hope you know that!"

"Yes, Sir, I do, and thanks."

"It's my pleasure, son." He got up and went across to the speakerphone and informed Reno of his presence, and then came back to sit down.

"You must try and set this aside for now, Mitch. I'm sure that after they call you tonight, you'll know everything is all right and forget about all of this completely. But if they don't call you tonight, you call that hunting lodge and check on them, . . . and if they are not there, you call me!" He got up and gripped Mitch's shoulder firmly. "Now here comes Reno, you two go bust some targets."

*   *   *

The plane's sudden shudder and loss of altitude caused Nora's eyes to pop open in sudden panic, yanking an involuntary gasp of surprise and fear from her as she grabbed the seat's armrest to stare wildly across at Michael's stern profile while he fought to control the plane, . . . and then suddenly it was over, the plane leveled off again and Michael looked at her with a grin on his face.

"We hit a little turbulence, honey, we're okay. You've been through it before."

"Well it scared the life out of me anyway!"

"We'll likely get a little more of it, so hold on, we'll be landing in a few minutes."

"We're there already?" She looked out of the side window at the surrounding mountains. "My Lord, that was quick!"

"Not so quick, you've been asleep for a while. Were you dreaming or something, wind currents never seemed to bother you before?"

"It's been a couple of years, Michael, I just forgot!"

"I guess you did." He laughed. "To tell you the truth, it sort of made my old butt draw up a little, too!"

"Oh look, Michael, is that Durango off there?" Just then the plane dipped again, jerking another gasp from her lips.

"That's Durango! . . . Now hold on, we're descending. It's always a little rough till we get below these cross winds!" He switched on his headset and contacted the airport's tower for instructions, and by the time they were out of the turbulence completely, they were skimming the treetops as Michael cut engine power, lowered the landing gear, set the flaps and glided in for the landing.

By the time they had touched down and the plane had slowed, the tower was giving him instructions to taxi the craft toward the northernmost hangars and when they arrived, they both spotted the waiting station wagon off to one side, and on it the lettering, "Keyah Grande Hunting Lodge".

"Is this service, or what?" He grinned as he stopped the Cessna and killed the engines.

"I think that's Cato!" Remarked Nora as a man left the car and walked toward the plane.

"That's Cato all right, . . . come on honey, unbuckle yourself while I lower the steps." He quickly moved from under the controls and went back to open the side door and pushed it outward, letting the hydraulic system lower the boarding steps. He quickly descended the steps to shake the guide's extended hand.

"It's good to see you again, Cato!" He grinned. "How's our favorite guide?"

"I'm real good, Mister Zant, it's good to see you folks again, too! . . . Of course it's only been six months." He smiled at Nora as she came down to join them and shook her hand. "Very good to see you again, Mrs. Zant, how was your flight?"

"A little bumpy at the end, Cato." Answered Michael for her.

"An understatement, Cato." Replied Nora with a frown, causing all of them to chuckle.

They waited until a mechanic had placed chucks against the plane's wheels before going to unlatch and lower the belly door beneath the fuselage and unloading the gear. Cato pulled the car alongside, and once it was all loaded he closed the rear doors and came back to join them.

"I guess we're ready." Voiced Michael, looking back at the plane. "Is the plane all right where it is, Cato?"

"Not to worry, Mister Zant, I left instructions for the plane to be serviced and waiting for your departure."

"There's something different about you, Cato, . . . are you sure you're still an Indian?" He grinned and closed the door as Nora seated herself then grinned even wider at the Guide's frustrated expression before climbing into the front passenger seat and closing the door.

"Forgive me, Cato." He laughed as the guide got in. "No disrespect, but you seem more, . . . sophisticated than the last time we were here. Your speech is more fluent, smoother, . . . what have you been doing?"

Cato smiled then himself. "You had me worried for a minute, Mister Zant. But thank you. Truth is, I've been attending classes here in Durango during the off-season. But I assure you, I'm still a Ute!" And laughing, he put the car in gear and headed for the airport exit.

On leaving the airport, they were completely surrounded by towering Pine Trees on both sides of the narrow black-top, and were until finally turning East onto State Highway 160 and once again amid the skyscraping forest of Pines as they traveled the twisting, and sometimes treacherous thoroughfare with it's many rattling, wooden bridges, structures that were hardly wide enough for one car, or truck to cross and definitely not at the same time.

"Well, this old road has not changed much!" Commented Michael as Cato stopped to allow another vehicle to cross the narrow bridge ahead of them.

"No sir, it has not! . . . Neither has anything else around here. Cars wreck out on this old road all the time, going way too fast!"

"Tell me about these black bears, Cato, are there really that many of them?"

"I don't know about that, but there are more than there used to be, according to the Forestry Service . . . . And I've seen a few more than usual."

"And that's what inspired this hunt?"

"Not totally, I don't think . . . . There wasn't any reason for you to know this when you were here last, Mister Zant, but over the past two seasons, and maybe longer than that, hunters, and even vacationing campers have periodically been disappearing in the woods, mostly in the northern counties along and bordering the San Juans . . . . Anyway, they were never found! . . . Their campsites and gear were found, but nothing else, not even their hunting rifles. Some even had their wives and kids with them."

"And what do they think, the black bears carried them away?"

"That's what they're saying, yes sir. Bears were seen in the search areas feeding on deer carcasses, and the campsites were ransacked, something that a bear will do anyway! . . . It was the easy conclusion to make! . . . But whatever is going on, it has the people in every small community in the mountains scared to go out of their houses now because of all those man-eating black bears!"

"Sounds like you don't believe that so-called easy conclusion you spoke of?"

"Mister Zant, I've been in these mountains my whole life, and I've never seen a black bear take a bite out of anything that was not already dead! . . . A grizzly, sometimes, but never a black. No sir, there's something else going on in these mountains . . . . If bears were the problem, somebody somewhere would have found human remains out there, and they didn't! . . . It's a baffling situation!"

"Sound's like it, . . . but Cato, I have known you for a good five years, don't you think it's time you called me Mike, all my friends do?"

"It's a habit, Mis, . . . Mike. Keeping things strictly business, you know. I'm lucky if I ever see a client more than once."

"I understand completely, . . . but from here on, my name is Mike!"

"Yes sir, Mike"

"Good! . . . So tell me, . . . have any of the hunters around here disappeared?"

"No sir, not yet, and that's strange in it's self, if it's happening twenty miles away, and the bears are killing folks, it should be happening everywhere in the mountains, . . . and it isn't!"

"What's your theory, . . . and I know you have one?"

"As a matter of fact, I do! . . . I think there's a killer, or killers loose in the mountains, and they are not black bears, or Grizzlies! . . . A grizzly will most always shun any contact with people unless it feels threatened. But a black bear will always run away if it see you."

"Has there been an investigation of any kind into that possibility, . . . the F.B.I., or anyone else?"

"Into my theory, no sir, they won't listen! But the F.B.I., National Guard, State Police, Sheriff's Department, you name it, . . . they've all been here. Trouble is there are parts of the San Juans that are only accessible by air, and some of the wilderness out there is so dense, a man could fall in a hole, or a crevice before he can see it. Most of the search parties called it off once the going got too tough, . . . and a plane can't spot anything from ten thousand feet up, unless it's in an open area, wind currents are treacherous below that! Not even helicopters will try it unless it's a life and death situation . . . . Fly below those winds and you're in the tree tops! . . . No sir, Mike, there's a killer in the San Juan Mountains, and he's where he knows the police won't go, and he's laughing at them!"

"My Lord, Cato, that's awful!" Voiced Nora. "How devastating!"

"Yes Ma'am, it is . . . . Anyway, that's my theory, Mike, and I hope it doesn't scare you off your hunt."

"Not in the least."

"Good, because there's nothing to fear where we'll be hunting. All that activity has been twenty to thirty miles away. We'll get your black bear!"

"If I don't get it first!" Laughed Nora.

Michael cast a furtive glance at Cato and nodded. "She brags a lot!"

Chuckling, he had to stop again at another bridge and while that vehicle approached and crossed, he turned and pulled the cover from atop an ice chest on the seat beside Nora. "I brought along scrambled egg and ham sandwiches, a couple of biscuits and sausage, . . . and hot coffee in the thermos there. You folks help yourselves, . . . looks like it'll be a while, what with this traffic today."

"How thoughtful, Cato, thank you." Smiled Nora. "I am hungry." She gave Michael a sandwich then poured him and Cato a coffee before grabbing a biscuit, sausage for herself.

"Coke and RC Cola in the chest there, Mrs. Zant."

"Thank you, Cato, and please call me Nora?"

"Yes Ma'am, . . . thank you."

"You are very welcome. Oh, is there still phone service at the Lodge, Mitchell will be worried about us if we don't call?"

"Yes, Ma'am, but as always, you'll have to use those in the main lodge." He chuckled. "If you can find one not in use! . . . Never seen the place filled to capacity before, not even during Elk season . . . . I was meaning to ask about the boys though, they're okay, I hope?"

"College entrance exams coming up." Sighed Michael. "Had to miss this one."

CHAPTER THREE

Keyah Grande Lodge was a sprawling, two-storied affair with a circle driveway leading to the front steps and back out again. Large spreading shrubs and flowers decorated the inner circle. The front steps were of brick and cement leading up to a walkway of flat stones and terminated at more of the brick steps leading up to the wrap-around patio entranceway. Hand carved Pine pillars along the front served to anchor the upper veranda some fifteen feet above the lower porch.

Beautiful styled log cabins were nestled just outside the trees bordering the perimeter of the main house, and were used for guest housing. The entire upper floor of the lodge it's self was nothing but guest rooms, numbering thirty in all. Guest rooms also dotted the lower floor of the main house, and behind the Bowman's living quarters, which were behind Ames Bowman's office and that of Carl Spencer, both just off the main lobby on the same side as the large dining room.

Behind the guest cabins, some fifty yards away was the large barn and corrals and next to that the mechanic's shop and vehicle parking garage, serving both for lodge vehicles, and some client parking. There was also a large parking area between the main house and the barn, . . . but this one was not an under-roof affair.

Cato stopped the car at the front steps and immediately, two young men came out to unload, and carry in their luggage, . . . and they were followed by a middle-aged, slightly balding man with a hunting jacket on.

"Mike, Nora, it's a pleasure to see you. How are you?" Smiled Carl Spencer warmly as he greeted them and shook their hands.

"Never better Carl, thank you."

Carl looked at the car then. "But where are the boys?"

"They couldn't come on this one, Carl," He sighed. "So feel free to use their room."

"Won't be a problem there, I'm sure, . . . and your room is ready for you."

"Where are the Bowman's, they're usually here to greet us?"

"Last minute business in Denver, I'm afraid." He shrugged. "You're stuck with me."

"Just how many guests do you have already, Carl, . . . Cato said you were filled to capacity?"

"He's not far from wrong, Mike. We have upwards of thirty couples here already, and there's some that haven't showed yet. It's going to be some hunt, the way it looks."

"A lot of guns to be in the woods at the same time!" Commented Michael.

"Well I think we have that covered, . . . the guides all have a specific area to hunt in. But of course that doesn't always mean a stray bullet won't find someone. The chance they take, I guess."

"A chance we all take." Nodded Michael as he placed a hand on Carl's shoulder. "And I guess we can put up with you on this one. But I was thinking you spent the off-season elsewhere?"

"I was recalled when the state announced this special hunt, . . . and since the business in Denver couldn't be postponed, here I am!"

"And you'll do just fine." Chuckled Michael. "Excuse me for a minute, Carl, you and Nora go on in." He walked back to speak with Cato while Carl escorted Nora into the Lodge.

"What's our agenda, Cato?"

"Everything is set, Mike, yours and Nora's favorite trail horses, pack animal and everything. The area we'll be hunting in is about ten miles north and a little West of here, you've hunted there before with success."

"Sounds good, when do we go?"

"Four A.M. Wednesday, we'll make the campsite Wednesday night and start the hunt Thursday morning . . . . You know how rough the country is out there, so get yourselves plenty of rest."

"Okay, you've got it handled, see you Wednesday morning, if not before."

"Wednesday sounds right, Mike." He grinned. "I've got three groups of dudes to take on trail rides tomorrow . . . . . I'll meet you right over there." He nodded at the trees.

Michael nodded, shook his hand then turned and climbed the steps as Cato drove the car away.

*   *   *

"We love you, too, son, . . . bye." Sighing, he hung up the phone and smiled down at Nora. "He's okay, . . . sounded relieved, two."

"I know he is. He was really worried, Michael!"

"I know, and I hope that was the last of it! . . . If not, it could mean it hasn't happened yet . . . Da-da-da-da, da-da-da-da, . . . Lookout twilight zone!"

"I wish you wouldn't joke about something like that, Michael, it wasn't funny to Mitchell!"

"I am sorry, honey . . . . But I do think we should put it behind us, we'll need clear heads on Thursday." He took her hand and steered her into the large dining room where they were met by a young man in a hunter's outfit and shown to their table.

"Thank you, young man!" Smiled Nora as the host pulled out her chair and seated her.

"You're welcome, Ma'am." He took menu and wine list from under his arm and placed them on the table in front of them. "We have a very good eighty year old Caparzo on the wine list."

"Oh, no thank you. I'll have iced tea please?" Returned Nora.

Michael ordered coffee then studied the crowded room, as did Nora. "See anyone we know?"

"Strangely, no, do you?"

"A man from Kansas, . . . by the window in front there. He usually has his wife along. Simpson, I think. Marcus Simpson."

"That's right, his wife's name is Gladys. Nice people, too . . . . I've never seen any of the others before, and we usually know almost everyone."

"Well I see another one, I recognize." Said Michael. "He's the director of the Senate Ethics Committee. That's Senator Warren Oates . . . . Got a couple of body guards with him, as well."

"Our tax dollars at work." Sighed Nora, looking back at the noisy room. "I wonder why none of the regulars got in on this hunt?"

"Maybe they didn't want a bear rug."

"Michael, do you know that the state is paying a hundred dollar bounty on each bear killed?"

No, . . . I don't recall reading that in Bowman's invitation?"

"Well, that's what Carrie told me when she called on Friday . . . . I think this is going to be more of a slaughter than a hunt!"

"You're right, . . . and we might not have come, if you'd told me."

"Why not, . . . you'd still need a bear rug?"

"These woods are going to be full of people with guns, that's why, and some of them shouldn't even be carrying one! They shoot at anything that moves! . . . Someone is going to be shot, or killed before this is over."

"Lord, I hope not! . . . Do you think any of these people are like that?"

"I doubt it! . . . For one thing, Bowman screens all of his clients. Besides, they won't be allowed to hunt without a guide . . . . I wonder why Cato didn't mention the bounty?"

"Maybe it wasn't relevant, or he didn't think it was . . . . Or he may not have thought of it!" She sighed. "Besides, I'm sure a lot of those people are out there all the time anyway, poachers and the like."

"Not that many . . . . There's thirty or more Game Wardens around the area and I'm sure they watch it pretty close."

"Well, they're not watching it very close, not with people disappearing right under their noses."

"That's a point well taken, honey, . . . and I would sure like to know what's going on with that?" They sat back then as the waiter placed their drinks in front of them.

"May I take your order now, please?"

*   *   *

Except for the decorative lampposts along the wide walkway, and those lining both sides of the circle drive, it would have been pitch black outside at four A.M. in the morning. Michael and Nora, both dressed in their camouflaged hunting apparel, which consisted of a one-piece, water resistant coverall type suit, ammo jacket, knee high, thick leather boots and a soft brimmed rain resistant hat with a drop down insect net, joined the more than twenty other hunters as they crowded through the lodge's double-wide front doors and onto the long, front walkway.

The circular drive was also teeming with guides, restless horses and pack animals, all waiting for the armed and dangerous big game hunters.

Michael took Nora's arm and once down the first set of steps, moved her out of the flow to stop and look for Cato. Seeing the guide waving at them, they continued on down the walk with the others and made their way across the drive to where Cato was waiting with the horses and followed as he led the animals off toward the trees alongside the log cabins.

"I'm flattered, Cato, . . . you remembered my horse again."

"Yes Ma'am, always." He smiled and took her arm, helping her to mount the trail wise little mare then seeing that Michael was already mounted, watched as they adjusted their hunting rifles across their backs before mounting his own horse. He reined the animal around toward one of the many bridal paths and with the help of a flashlight led the way into the darkness.

They were immediately in a dark and unbelievably dense forest of Pine trees and underbrush, and on a narrow path that was so uneven and rocky that they had to closely pay attention to the rider in front of them. Jutting outcroppings of odd-shaped boulders were nestled between, and around the large pine trunks to appear as if they were part of the trees themselves, and Cato made sure the beam from the flashlight touched on every obstacle that might be in their way.

This particular trail, however, was no stranger to them as they had traveled it on numerous occasions on their Elk hunts and knew what to expect. The pathway was fast becoming infested with the jutting stones and on their left side, through the mass of trees were sheer rocky down-slopes, eerie looking in the beam of light, . . . but the worst of it was the insects and in the humid Pine forest, were swarming.

They had not gone a half-mile when they were in and out of their first arroyo and for the next hour, it seemed to be all they were doing, in one gully and out of another, climbing to higher ground and then down again into yet another heavily foliaged canyon-like crevice. Finally, on climbing up another steep wall of dirt and rocks, Cato stopped them on the crest to rest the horses, and to shine the light on them.

"Where are we?" Queried Michael from behind Nora. "I can't identify a thing in this half-light."

"You will pretty soon, we're on the crest of Pine valley, remember?"

"Sure do." Replied Nora. "And it's a long way down, if I remember right!"

"And this trail is narrow." Returned Cato. "I don't have to tell you to stay alert and trust your horses, they've been along here a hundred times! Okay, we can go now." He kept the light switching from the path ahead, to the sides of the crevice wall and a half hour later, and in the first pale light of the coming day he led them off the narrow precipice and back into thick timber where, for the rest of the day they slowly worked their way over the uneven terrain of San Juan National Forest and into the lower areas where it was hotter, and even more humid, having to lower the insect netting over their face and ears to ward off the large mosquitoes.

This was much the case for the rest of the day, only stopping long enough to eat a light lunch, and to relieve themselves and it was late when they finally arrived at the campsite and dismounted tiredly. Cato set about, first unsaddling the horses and watering them, and while Michael and Nora unloaded the food from the pack animal, he rubbed the four animals down and grained them, . . . giving them oats from the stainless steel grain bin before staking them out.

"I'll go close the gate, Cato." Said Michael and headed back toward the trail.

The tall, wire-mesh fence stretched in a semi circle all around the campsite, and was only large enough to for them to prepare food and sleep comfortably, and still have room for the horses.

Cato watched him go and nodded. "In that case, I'll build a fire and start supper."

"And I'll help!" Added Nora.

An hour later they were finishing a meal of fried potatoes, canned beans, skillet-fried ham, pita-bread and hot coffee.

"I didn't think it got this hot here in the summer." Commented Michael as he set his plate aside, . . . those gullies were miserable!"

"Don't worry, Mike, it'll go from one extreme to another after dark . . . . You'll need a blanket tonight!"

"I'll need two!" Added Nora. "I'm cold natured anyway."

"We'll sleep close to the fire," Grinned Cato. "Best to keep it going anyway, keep the prowling beasts away!"

"Speaking of which," Said Michael. "We didn't see a black bear one today. If they were that many out here, you'd think we would have."

"They were there, Mike, . . . at least a couple, I could hear them grunting."

"So did I, but I wasn't sure what they were."

"And all that grunting was from a black bear?" Exclaimed Nora.

"Yes, Ma'am. A Grizzly's grunt is deeper pitched and more drawn out, and usually ends with a growl. We do not want to mess with that gentleman!"

"Well, I'm afraid you'll have a couple of greenhorns to contend with on this one, my friend, . . . it's our first bear hunt!"

"And the last, at best!" Laughed Nora. "One bear rug is plenty."

"Yes it is." Laughed Michael. "I much prefer Elk hunting anyway."

"I saw three of those today." Nodded Nora. "One had a calf. But they ran away when those shots were fired. Where do you think those hunters were, Cato?"

"That's hard to say, . . . sound carries a long way up here . . . . Could be anybody out there. As many hunters as there are this time, we tried to map out the areas accordingly. One hunter's area limit could be a mile from the lodge, another two miles. Ours is another five miles from right here, and all are hopefully far enough apart to keep a stray bullet from finding its way into another area."

"Maybe somebody got their bear already." Said Michael. "What sort of limit is set on them Cato?"

"Ten, I think."

"Per person?" Gasped Nora. "What would he do with ten bears?"

"Skin them and leave them lay, . . . the bounty is paid on the pelts."

"I think that's awful!"

"Yes, Ma'am, so do I. Especially when it's all just a made up emergency!"

"Made up? . . . Oh, you mean those disappearances!"

"Yes, Ma'am, . . . I think it's all a cover up for what's really going on in these mountains . . . . And all because a group of inept lawmen and F.B.I. agents didn't have what it takes to find the truth!"

"You are really convinced of this, aren't you, Cato?"

"Yes, sir, I am, . . . and Mister Bowman, as well as most all the other guides agree with me. But nobody would listen to us! . . . They were all here at the lodge at one time or another, Sheriff, the Guard, F.B.I., all of them! . . . We told all of them what we thought." He shrugged. "They said their facts outweighed ours, and they were going with the facts. It's sickening, is what it is!"

"How many people live up here?"

"Ohhh," He chuckled. "That's almost impossible to say, . . . a hundred families, maybe. Most of them are Indians trying to scratch out a living on a rocky farm . . . . There's a few white families up there, too, and some hermits, mountain men of sorts, and unfriendly! . . . Most of them are dangerous, too, . . . and none of them cater to visitors!"

"Tell me this, . . . if you were in charge of this investigation, and you were convinced that men were to blame for these disappearances, where would you look?"

Cato shook his head and grinned. "God, Mike!" He shook his head. "I think I'd take a few choice men into these mountains and search every farm and out-house on it! Hill folks know everything that goes on up there, . . . because whoever these killers are, kidnappers, or whatever, . . . somewhere there's going be evidence to prove it! . . . I've been thinking a lot about this, Mike, and whatever is going on, whatever the motive, it could very well all be drug related, how, I don't know? . . . But it's been suspected for years that drugs are being grown and sold from somewhere in this part of Colorado, . . . and I believe it could be right here in these mountains."

"You talking Marijuana?"

Cato nodded. "Hill folks grow it right alongside their stills, for their own consumption, they say. There's probably more drug and moonshine money stashed away up there than all the gold in the Denver Mint! . . . They don't spend it, either!"

"Then you think those people were kidnapped and killed, . . . for what, for stumbling onto some Marijuana patch?"

"Hell, . . . I don't know, Mike! . . . But if they did, it's enough to get 'em killed! There's only one true fact about the whole mess, . . . Black Bears are innocent! And what you just said is not out of the question . . . . Hell, I'm almost convinced I'm nuts, Mike, I've been thinking about it so much, . . . I've had so many theories they're all beginning to run together into one big confusion!"

"Surely the F.B.I. has checked out all these places." Voiced Nora

"You'd think." Nodded Cato. "Trouble is, almost none of them are easily accessible on foot, terrain is just too rough! . . . At least to anybody not living there. Some of these hill folks have cars and trucks hidden away, . . . I know because I have found passable roads up there, and they're so well camouflaged that if I was looking for 'em, I wouldn't have found them!"

"Unbelievable!" Gasped Nora.

"I don't think anyone will ever know all that goes on up here! . . . And these disappearances won't stop when this bear hunt is over neither! . . . The authorities will just find another way to explain it away . . . . Whatever's easiest for 'em, I guess!"

"If it does continue, I can see it eventually hurting all the hunting lodges up here, hunters will go elsewhere."

"You're right, Mike, . . . and it may not be that far off."

"I think we should get our bear as soon as possible and go home, Michael."

"I think I second the motion, honey."

"I am sorry for ruining your vacation," Breathed Cato. "But I would prefer you leave than have anything happen to you."

"Thank you, Cato."

"We will find your bear tomorrow, I'm sure of it!"

*   *   *

They were up at daybreak and bedrolls were stowed away, last night's leftovers warmed up and eaten and their coffee drank, . . . that done, they donned ammo-jackets and hunting rifles while Cato put out the fire.

"Are we ready?" Asked Cato, picking up his rifle and checking the loads.

"As we'll ever be." Nodded Michael.

"Then let's go." He led the way to the walk-through gate in the fence and opened it to let them through before wiring it back into place then continued down the worn trail into the deeper underbrush.

"You got a place in mind, Cato?" Queried Michael in a crisp voice.

"That tangle of berry briars about a mile from here, . . . bears love the berries."

They continued to pick their way over the broken, foliage-covered path for nearly two hours before Cato raised his hand to stop them, and they watched as he cocked his head from side to side as if listening for something. Michael and Nora looked at each other and shrugged then began listening also. Not knowing exactly what they were listening for, they listened for any sound that might be heard over the natural sounds of the forest, . . . but even those noises were lacking for some reason, save an Elk's high-pitched bugle-like call from somewhere in the wilderness. Shrugging again, Michael moved past Nora to stand beside Cato.

"What do you hear, that I don't, Cato?"

Cato looked curiously at him for a second. "That's the problem, Mike, I don't hear anything. These woods should be chattering with activity . . . . Something scared the wildlife."

"Like what?"

"Can't tell." He whispered. "Could be a Grizzly, we're getting close to that berry patch. Come on, but move slow, . . . if it is a Grizzly, we do not want to startle the thing." He continued on up the trail leaving Michael and Nora to ready their rifles and follow him.

For several more unsettling minutes they worked their way along the narrow rock strewn animal trail, and all the while were straining worried eyes into the thick tangle of brush, dead limbs and pine trees and were constantly having to duck, dodge or push the sagging limbs away in order to pass, . . . and it was when they entered the clearing where the massive growth of berry vines and briars were that they all stopped again, . . . and each were staring mutely at the bearded man as he got up from the pine stump he was sitting on.

Brandishing his rifle, Cato waited while the large man approached, all three of them staring with distaste at the dirty, sweat stained bib-overalls he was wearing. The man's shoes were scarred at the toes and high-topped, with the pant legs stuffed into the tops and laced up around them.

The man's beady eyes carried no expression, as he looked them up and down, even though he was showing yellowish teeth in a fake smile that was barely visible through his thick growth of stringy beard and shoulder-length hair.

"That'll be close enough, Mister!" Said Cato, slowly raising his rifle, and that gesture caused Nora to turn and allow Michael to embrace her.

"Who are you, and what are you doing here?" Asked Cato sternly, and when the man stopped. "You're on private land here."

The man shrugged as he stopped and he was grinning smugly as he looked Cato up and down.

"Name's Jesse!" He said gruffly. "I'm huntin', . . . same as you are, friend."

"Where's your rifle?"

"What?"

"Where's your gun, . . . you can't hunt without a gun?"

"Oh, yeah." He laughed then. "My gun, . . . it's at th' bottom a some arroya back yonder a ways . . . . Yes'ir, . . . lost it bigger'n hell!"

"Maybe you'd better go on back where you came from, Jesse, this is Keyah Grande land."

"Hey, no problem, guy, you got it!" He laughed again then cocked his head slightly to peer hard at Cato. "You're a Indian, ain't ya?"

"Ute." Nodded Cato.

"That's what I figured." He nodded. "Hey, I'm gonna go now, . . . but first, I got somethin' I want a show you folks." He reached to the pocket of his unwashed, red-flannel shirt and pulled out a grimy, less than white bandana and held his hand out away from his body to let it dangle there.

"What are you doing, man?" Asked Cato. "Just turn around and leave, okay?"

"I just want a ask you folks a question before I go, that's okay, ain't it?"

"Ask your question."

The man grinned again and nodded. "Okay, here it is . . . . What do you think will happen if I accidently was to drop this here handkerchief? . . . Anybody?" When no one answered, he shrugged his broad shoulders.

"Come on now, that's my question. What would happen?"

Cato sighed with disgust. "I guess you'd have to pick it up again! . . . What's your point, man?"

"That's th' wrong answer Indian, . . . but that's okay, nobody ever gets it right!"

"Then tell us the answer, Jesse! . . . What do you think would happen?"

Jesse laughed hoarsely and shrugged his shoulders again. "Hell, man, it's simple! . . . If I was to drop this rag, all three of you would die!"

Cato backed up a step, his dark eyes darting toward the woods with rifle raised.

"Yeah, you better look, Indian!" He growled. "There's two more of us out there. All I got a do is drop this here hanky, and BOOM! . . . You're all dead! . . . Now drop them God damn rifles, all a ya . . . . You don't, you are three dead sons a bitches! Now do it, God damn you!" Jesse's face had become a mask of leering evil as he yelled at them, and the hate in his eyes was unmistakable.

Cato raised his rifle even more, aiming it right at the man's midsection. "I don't believe you, Jesse. Now turn around and get the hell out of here, or I might just shoot you! . . . I won't tolerate that kind of language in front of a Lady!"

Jesse stared hatefully at him for a second then shrugged and looked toward the trees. "Hey, Ethan," He yelled. "Plug his gun arm for me!"

The explosion was ear-shattering in the confines of the clearing, and Cato yelled in sudden overwhelming pain as his right shoulder was splintered, the impact of the high powered bullet spinning him around to pitch him bodily into the tall grass and brush. After the echoes died away, Nora stopped screaming and hid her face against the chest of an ashen-faced Michael.

Jesse walked over to look down at Cato. "Son of a Bitch!" He blurted sarcastically. "That's got a hurt!" He laughed then looked back at them and pointed down at him. "You see that, huh?" He came at them then and grabbed Nora's arm, jerking her out of Michael's grasp and bringing another scream from her frightened lips. He pried the rifle from her hand and slung it over his own shoulder before looking back at Michael. "Drop that fuckin' rifle, Slug, . . . you got two seconds!"

Michael dropped his gun and reached for Nora, but Jesse jerked her against him then put his arm around her shoulders causing her to scream again. She began to struggle violently then, flailing at his grimy face and chest with her small fists and when she did Michael moved quickly to try and grapple with the man, but was met face-on by a burly, meaty fist that felled him like a side of beef.

"Michael!" She screamed, pulling away from Jesse to kneel beside her husband in tears.

By this time two other men of Jesse's ilk came out of the woods to join them, one man stopped while the other came on to collect the other two rifles before standing back again.

"Paw's gonna be fuckin' mad, Jess!"

"Shut up. Ethan." He came on to leer down at them then suddenly bent and jerked Nora to her feet, wrenching a sobbing shriek from her as he pushed her aside to nudge Michael with his foot. "Get up, slug, you ain't hurt . . . . Come on, get up!" He watched Michael struggle to his feet then grinned. "Now, come on, both a you get over there and help th' Indian to his feet, . . . go on, do it!" Still sneering maliciously, he moved back to watch them with hands on his hips

Nora helped Michael steady himself because he could hardly focus as they bent over Cato. The guide's entire arm, side and chest was covered in his blood, the gaping hole in his shoulder forcing her to close her eyes in horror as they struggled to lift him. At first he tried to fight them, but was conscious enough to recognize Nora and began to help them.

Once on his feet and his hand clutching at his shoulder, he reeled shakily on legs that were refusing to hold him and stared at his attackers out of pain-wracked eyes, . . . and his hatred was evident. Still leering, Jesse pushed Michael aside and took Nora's arm again forcing her to move next to Michael, leaving Cato to stand and weave unsteadily as his rubbery legs threatening to buckle again.

Jesse turned his attention To Michael and Nora then, moving in close as he pulled a large, very sharp hunting knife from his belt to slowly wave it in front of their terrified faces, . . . and he was still showing his yellowed teeth in a leering grin.

"What do you want from us, for God's sake?" Urged Michael, holding a Frenzied Nora closer to him. "You want money, I'll get you all you want, man, . . . just leave us alone, let us get Cato to a Doctor?"

"I don't need money, Slug, . . . I got what I fuckin' want! . . . I got you!" He laughed viciously then, still turning the knife over and over in his ham-like fist in front of their faces.

"I don't understand, man, why us, . . . you don't even know us?"

"Wh, . . . Why do you wa, . . . want us?" Cried Nora. "We didn't do anything to you?"

"Why do I want you? . . . Now that's a good question!" He snickered and looked at one of the men with him. "You takin' notes, Benji, we got a remember that one?" He looked back at them and reached up to scratch his shaggy chin. "What did Paw say before we left, . . . oh, yeah. Go get me two replacements! . . . Yeah, that's what you are, replacements!"

"Replacements?" Repeated Michael in a shocked voice. "For what, man, . . . this is 1956, you can't do this sort of thing! . . . Not and hope to get away with it!"

Jesse moved his face down close to Michaels, his breath causing Michael to wince. "I already did get away with it, Slug, . . . now didn't I? . . . And as far as what for, . . . you'll just have to wait and see!"

"Well what about Cato, . . . he's our Guide, man, he needs a Doctor?"

"Who, . . . this fuckin' Indian? . . . Shit, . . . he don't need no Doctor!" His knife-wielding hand suddenly arced sideways, instantly spraying them both with blood and wrenching a gurgling scream from Cato as his throat was slashed, . . . and then he fell limply back into the bloody grass to jerk spasmodically a time or two and died.

Jesse quickly back-handed Nora's open mouth to stop her screams, and as she stumbled back into Michael he took a step toward them to hold the bloody knife in front of her.

"Now, you listen to me, you Cunt! . . . I don't like screamin' women! . . . To me, ain't none a you Cunts good for nothin' but fuckin' when I'm horny, . . . and when I ain't, I'd just soon slit their fuckin' throats as look at 'em! . . . We got us a couple miles a walkin' to do now, . . . and I don't want no trouble out a you, understand? . . . We'll be home by mornin', so I'm gonna say this just once! . . . You cry, you talk, you scream, you even fart, anywhere along th' way, . . . we're just gonna stop right there on th' spot, and I'm gonna take this razor sharp knife right here and cut them fancy duds off' a you right down to your naked ass, . . . and you know what then, Cunt? . . . Huh?" He put his face right down close to hers.

"All three of us old boys are gonna fuck your brains out, and when we're done, I'm jest gonna slit yer fuckin' throat and leave ya lay! . . . Now, . . . if you understand all that I just said, jest nod yer fuckin' head!" And when she frantically nodded, he stepped back and leered at her evilly. "I thought you would, you fuckin' Cunt!"

It was all Michael could do not to reach for the man again, and listening to him abuse Nora right in front of him made his ears flutter inside with dread. But he was smart enough to know that the man could beat him to death, and just might kill them both if he did. He also believed that as long as they could stay alive, they could find a way out of this. He also knew that the man meant what he said to Nora. He had to make sure she stayed quiet and didn't upset him, because if that man attempted to do what he threatened, he would jump him! No man was going to violate Nora that way, . . . he would rather they both be dead!

"Okay!" Growled Jesse, and nodded at them both. "Now we got th' ground rules all set, and we got a mutual understandin' goin', . . . I want you both to foller old Ethan there real quiet like, he knows th' way. And don't you ferget now, . . . I'm right behind you." He laughed loudly. "I like seein' a woman's ass wiggle when she walks!"

"Move 'em out, Ethan, and keep yer eyes open, woods'r full a fuckin' hunters!"

Gun laid across his shoulder and his hand gripping the stock in readiness, the baggy clothed, heavily bearded Ethan moved off through the vines and brush with Michael and Nora behind him. Jesse and the other man shouldered the three backpacks them and Cato had carried and moved in behind them, . . . and for the next eight hours, they were led westward through some of the roughest terrain imaginable and with no rest stops, or water-breaks. They were having to constantly fight the heavy foliage, pricking briars, dead limbs and slapping Pine branches as they made their own trail through much of the tangled forest. The killers took them through areas that appeared impassable to the naked eye, . . . and it was that way until they were nine hours away from the death scene to finally stop and rest, and by this time they were both desperate with the need to relieve themselves.

Jesse called out for Ethan to stop and when they did, he walked up beside Michael and Nora. "Sit down on th' ground here and rest, we ain't got too far to go!"

Holding back the pain of not stopping to relieve them-selves, Michael spoke to Jesse as he came by. "Can you tell us where we're going?" He flinched slightly as Jesse sneered at him. "Come on, man, . . . who are we going to tell?"

"You ain't gonna tell nobody, Slug!" He grinned then pointed northward. "We're goin' about twenty miles'r so, right up in them mountains off yonder! . . . Now shut up, Slug." He saw Michael squirming then and grinned. "You better take a piss, too, looks like! Better get to it! . . . Both a ya." Laughing, both him and the other man relieved themselves right in front of them before going on to sit down with Ethan.

Michael turned his back to them and did the same. "Don't you have to go, honey, come on."

"I can't, Michael, not with them watching!"

He finished and bent down to help her up. "You've got no choice, honey, unless you do it in your clothes now come on, you don't want to do that! . . . Come on, honey, I know it's humiliating, but it's necessary." When she nodded, he urged her in behind the trunk of a large Pine where she worked her arms and upper body out of the coveralls enough to hunker down out of sight.

"Okay, Slug." Said Jesse as Nora finished dressing. "Get on in behind Ethan there, and keep your mouth shut!"

Nodding, he urged Nora in front of him again and followed the man back into the trees. They had been hearing gunfire off and on all day, and some had sounded a little too close as a few wild bullets could be heard whining their way through the trees, and hearing the dull thump as a trunk was struck, yet they kept moving through the unforgiving wilderness before finally coming to the crest of a deep, heavily foliaged and rocky-floored arroyo, . . . and that's when they saw the large, very tall truck.

Michael was not surprised to see the truck at all, nor that it was a fully camouflaged Army Surplus vehicle. What did surprise him was that it was sitting some fifty feet down in the bottom of a canyon with no way out, that he could see.

It was already growing dark as they worked their way down the shifting sides of the slope, having to use the large rocks for leverage on the way into the depression but they made it and were pushed forward to the rear of the canvas-topped truck. Ethan continued on to the front and climbed into the cab.

"Okay, Slug." Said Jesse. "You and your Cunt get on up in there."

Sighing heavily, Michael lifted Nora bodily and sat her on the tall edge of the truck's bed and as she got to her feet to sit on one of the metal benches, he climbed up and in beside her to once again hold her against him while Jesse climbed in. The third man went on to climb into the cab with Ethan.

Jesse took Cato's rifle from his shoulder and laid it on the opposite bench then squatted in front of them to let down one of the folding doors beneath the bench and retrieved a couple of long, white plastic slip-ties.

"Okay, Slug, you and th' Cunt hold out your arms, put 'em side by side. No, your right, her left." When they did, he bound their arms together at the wrists. "Now your feet." He did the same there, binding them at the ankles, he then used a third strap to anchor the ankle tie to an iron ring on the floor of the bed then grunting, backed away to sit on the bench across from them where he grabbed the ends of two lengths of rope and tied them around his upper body.

"Sorry, Slug, guess you'll just have to hold on to something'. It's gonna be a bumpy ride, too, so hold on tight!" He looked toward the open-ended cab then. "Let's go, Ethan!" He looked back at Michael then and grinned. "Grab holt a one a them ribs there, Slug, both a ya, . . . go ahead, you got another arm!"

CHAPTER FOUR

The explosions were loud as Mitchell fired the black-powder, 44 caliber replica handgun and as the smoke cleared, both him and Reno removed their earplugs to look at the numbers registered on the monitor.

"Not bad for thirty yards, brother!" Laughed Reno. "Three ninety-fives, a ninety-six and two ninety-nines, almost dead center, man!"

"I wish I could do that well at fifty."

"Hey, you're in the upper nineties here, upper eighties at fifty yards is excellent! . . . You won't find many that can top that, not with a gun like that! . . . A man wouldn't have a chance with you at that distance."

"Yeah, well I hope I never have to prove it!"

"Amen."

"I love shooting this thing, though, the way the power surges up my arm. It's incredible!"

"Want to pop a few with my Smith?"

"Awww, I think I'm done, Reno, . . . let's get something to eat."

They gathered their guns and equipment and headed for the gun club's diner.

"Mister Zee call last night?" Asked Reno as they walked.

"Dad said they wouldn't call me again before tonight, . . . unless they have his bear rug already . . . . He'll have to brag a little!"

"No doubt." They entered the diner and sat down, each placing their gear on the floor beside them.

"I'll say one thing, Reno . . . . If either of them sees one, it's a goner!"

"I know that's right, they're both great shots!"

"And what will you two handsome gentlemen have?" Smiled Lisa Cortez as she came to the table. "You here to eat or drink?"

"A ham and egg sandwich and a coke would suit me fine, Mrs. Cortez."

"And you, my favorite son?"

"Grilled cheese, mom, . . . and a root beer!"

"Coming right up!" She smiled at them and made her way back to the kitchen, speaking to other diners on the way.

"What's our plans for tonight, Mitch, . . . back to the Reservation?"

"I don't know, . . . last night was a little dragged out to suit me, what about you?"

"Well, it was fine till they started smoking that loco weed! . . . I'm sort of glad we left when we did! . . . Okay, that new John Wayne flick is at the Realto tonight, a sneak preview. What do you think?"

"Eleven thirty?"

Yeah, but brother, the previews looked real good, . . . and guess what's showing first?"

"Come on, Reno, you know I don't read the paper."

"Well, . . . it happens to your favorite, and mine?"

"Shane?"

"You got it, old Bud . . . . We can load up on popcorn and drinks, watch Shane and the Searchers and afterward, cruise up to the Pig-stand!"

"Sounds okay, we'll do it. What time is the first movie?"

"Shane's showing all day, the last time at nine I think. We can make that one."

"That'll work, if Mom calls, it'll be before seven."

"Good, we'll use my wheels tonight, be over about six."

"Here you go, boys," Smiled Lisa and placed their food down. "Enjoy."

"Thanks mom."

"Have you had any more of those chills, or omens?" Queried Reno as he ate.

Mitch glanced at him as he swallowed his food. "It's eerie, man." He said taking a sip from the coke. "I don't know what it was, but I started feeling a little gloomy at the festival before we left, . . . sort of a dark, anxious feeling. I didn't think too much about it because mom and dad called Wednesday night, so I know they're okay! . . . But for some reason, I can't stop thinking about it! It's almost like I know something isn't right, and I can't fix it! . . . Or maybe something has happened, and I can't find out what it is? . . . And here's the big one . . . . Something is going to happen, but it hasn't yet! I don't know, man, . . . it's like a giant maze that I can't find my way out of, it's weird!"

"You said a mouth full there!"

"But given that! . . . Last night's gloom wasn't as bad as that was Saturday."

"And what if they don't call tonight, Mitch?"

"Mom and dad?" He shrugged. "I'm not going to get real worried about it if they don't. I'll give then till tomorrow night to call . . . . After that, I'll start calling!"

* * *

The old, four-wheel-drive Army surplus truck was like riding a rollercoaster as it bounced and groaned its way across the rocky, very uneven San Juan National Wilderness, almost tipping over at times as it clawed its way over huge boulders and fallen timber. At times the truck's nose seemed to be pointed straight up and then, straight down as it crawled down one steep embankment and up another, tossing them around so violently at times that they would lose their hold on the ribbed cage and fall to the floor, and each time they would cry out in pain as the plastic ties cut into their ankles causing them to hastily right themselves on the bench to ease the pain. Then only to repeat itself, and this went on for hours until sometime around the middle of the night, the truck suddenly leveled off and began to move even faster across the broken terrain.

They had to be on a road of some kind, thought Michael, he could hear the sagging branches of trees bumping and slapping at the covered sides of the bed, and the sounds of brush and tall weeds scraping and scratching at the undercarriage. But then it was over and once again they were being pummeled as the truck sped on through the night. Having to hold to the steel ribs on either side of them as Ethan steered over the unlevel landscape. They learned quickly when to hold on and when to relax by the sounds of the engine's whine, and the meshing of gears as the vehicle slowed to crawl up one steep precipice and down another one, leaving both of them to tumble about like rag dolls as they silently prayed for their very lives.

Neither him, nor Nora had ever been this close to a life-threatening situation before, and neither had the slightest idea of how to deal with it. Nora was scared out of her mind and he could feel her body violently trembling as she clung to him, and he could do nothing but hold her close and pray.

He was not a brawler by any means, had never struck another man in anger, nor had he been struck by one until now. He never had to fight before this happened, his intellect had always paved the way for him, that was his success! But at this very moment he hated himself for his obvious inability to protect his own wife in the face of danger. He was always too busy becoming rich and famous, when he should have taken the time to learn self-defense. He knew he was not a coward, but he was not overly brave either, . . . and bravery was not going to help them now anyway! . . . Even if he had known martial arts, Jesse would probably still have beaten him! He stared at the dark hulk of Jesse sitting across from them. The man was vicious, cruel and mean, he thought, . . . just the opposite of himself.

They righted themselves on the seat again after the truck had crawled its way over another batch of huge rocks and groaning, he stared hatefully at Jesse's dark shape again and was startled when the killer spoke.

"You'd like to kill me, wouldn't ya, Slug?" He asked loudly, his voice bringing a slight gasp from Nora. "Well it ain't gonna happen!" He laughed then as they were pitched off the bench again. The truck seemed to almost tilt over as they went over the rocks., and then they were in trees again, and on level ground.

Another road, thought Michael as he helped Nora back to the bench. He could hear the raking of branches again as the truck increased its speed, . . . and that's when Jesse leaned forward again.

"I'm gonna tell ya somethin' now, Slug, and ya best remember it! . . . You and your Cunt are gonna be here fer a long time. Do what yer told, when yer told and you'll be okay! You don't, I'll strip you bare-assed and use th' whip on ya, . . . try and run off, I'll kill ya! . . . Now, we'll be there come daylight, and th' best thing you can do is hop to when you're told . . . . Now, I'm gonna tell ya one more thing, and I want your Cunt to pay close attention! They ain't but a couple a things I like better than fuckin', . . . one of 'em is using my black-snake whip on a bare ass, th other is killin'! . . . Both make me cream my britches ever time!" He leaned back against the high sideboard and chuckled just as the big truck slowed again to nose over another steep embankment.

The dread was even stronger now, and as they were thrown backward again to climb up another steep incline he had the sinking thought that if they were not found soon, they might die up here. There was one thing that he reluctantly had to admit as truth. Jesse would not allow them to leave the place they were going to, because both of them had seen their faces! . . . That thought chilled him as he wondered where they were going, and exactly why they had been abducted? Were they to be put to work, sold into slavery, tortured and killed in some sick game, . . . what? . . . The latter sounded the best bet, the man had killed Cato quick enough!

But then again, he had called them replacements, that could mean they were replacing two other people, but why? . . . That brought the game scenario back to his thoughts. He could picture a Roman type arena with people fighting for their lives in front of a crowd. Maybe they tried to escape and Jesse killed them for their efforts? The whole thing would be ironic if their lives were not being threatened. What price a bear rug?

They were in the midst of large boulders again and having to fight to remain seated, enduring two hours of this before they once again were pitched forward as the vehicle descended another steep, rocky slope, and at the bottom it slowed to a stop. That's when they heard the vicious snarling and barking of a huge dog, and some voices before they began to move again, and Michael knew they were on a road and in trees once more. It was then that Jesse leaned forward again, startling them both.

"We're almost there, Slug, and yer gonna meet th' old man, . . . and so you'll know, . . . he's meaner than I am! . . . He's gonna have some duds for ya. Now he might throw 'em on th' ground, he might have 'em on th' porch, but either way, you're gonna take them fancy duds off on th' spot and put yer new ones on! . . . He ain't gonna ask ya to, or tell ya to, . . . just do it! . . . You don't I'm gonna whip ya! . . . And I hope ya don't!" He leaned back and laughed again, leaving them to dread their arrival to wherever they were going, and to listen to the drum of constant limb slaps on the heavy tarp.

It was daylight when Ethan steered the heavy truck up to the crest of the forested slope and onto the bare grounds of the compound. Jesse had untied himself before they got there and now had come across to their side and was pulling down on a rope to roll the sides of the canvas cover up. He tied it off then did the same on his side of the truck allowing them to view the vast area of canopy-covered acreage.

The Tightly woven camouflaged mesh covered everything, even the barns, and there were two open-sided ones, plus a covered, smaller shed and another enclosed one with a door. The sagging, weathered planking on the structures seemed about ready to collapse, as did the large dilapidated old house along the backside of the compound. From the ground, looking up, thick greens, yellows and brown representations of foliage, tree branches and bare sand had been woven tightly into the mesh and on seeing it, Michael's heart sank even further.

Search planes would not see anything but a never-ending forest, and bare ground when looking down at it. The only way in or out of this hell hole, he determined, was the way they had come in, . . . or, . . . he pushed the latter from his mind as he continued to survey the deep shadows beneath the canopy and could just make out the hundreds of thin, tall sapling poles that were holding up the giant cover. But what caught his attention the most was the tall plants growing there, acres of them. He instinctively knew what they were and therefore knew why they were here. He saw the large cast-iron pot then, and the two toga-clad women, one was starting a fire beneath the pot while the other fed the flames with dry wood to start it, . . . and both of them looked as if they were about to cry when they saw them.

Jesse leaned toward them again and pointed at a tall, almost obscure post at the edge of the compound, and the chains dangling from it. "Know what that is, Slug?" He chuckled. "That there's my play-purty, my whippin' post! . . . When I use it, I bring everbody out to watch, keep that in mind, both a ya . . . . You're just in time fer breakfast, too, looks like, how's that fer timin'?"

"Now listen to me, Slug, a bit of damn good advice . . . . Two meals a day is served here, and they are cooked in that there pot. You don't eat at meal time, you wait till th' next. Come Saturd'y after breakfast, you throw yer clothes out to be washed, they'll be washed in that same pot! . . . Ya got a be clean, ya know, Pap says cleanliness is next to Godliness!" He laughed at that. "Okay, . . . when ya change yer clothes, you go eat, then you go to work like everbody else, and Slug, learn yer jobs fast, and do 'em right, I don't take to laziness!" He looked at Nora then. "How about you, Cunt, you been listenin' to me?" And when she nodded, he laughed again and pulled his knife just as the truck stopped then leaned over to cut the ties from their feet and hands. "Come on now, get out! . . . Remember what I said about yer duds, you don't hop to, old Pap'll get mad, and if he gets mad, I'll get to whip yer nekid asses on that post out there! . . . Only rule here is to do your jobs, no talkin' to nobody while you work, no cryin', and no screamin, . . . except while I'm whippin' yer ass, that's the only exception . . . . Now move out!"

Michael climbed down to the hard-packed and worn-smooth ground then helped Nora down as Jesse climbed down beside them.

"Go on, Slug, . . . stand in front a th' porch." He pushed Michael forward as he spoke, and he urged Nora in front of him to move to within a few steps of the old house's front porch-steps to stop when Jesse told them to. Three or four minutes passed before the front door creaked open and a large, almost fat old man walked out and across the porch where he stopped to glare down at them, his long, shaggy beard almost hiding his mouth and eyes completely.

The man stared at them for a long couple of minutes, his wrinkled arms resting inside the bib of his baggy overalls. Finally he looked at Jesse.

"You're a piss-poor excuse for a son a mine, you know that? . . . Any no good son of a bitch can foller orders, exceptin' you! . . . We lost two fuckin' men, you Jackass, not a man and his bitch! I sent you after two God damn men! . . . Couldn't ye find any?" He looked at Ethan and his brother then, who by now were standing in front of the truck.

"And you two, why do ya think I sent you with 'im? . . . Go on, get out a here, park th fuckin' truck, ya God damn Heatherns!" He looked back at Jesse then.

"Well, . . . couldn't ya find two men?"

"I did, Pap, . . . but I kilt th' other one!" Said Jesse as he stared at the ground.

"You kilt 'im? . . . Why in th holy fuck would you do that, God Damn it? . . . I told you not to fuckin' kill nobody!"

"He was a fuckin' Indian, Pap, that's why, . . . a God damn Ute!"

Old man Baxter stared at him for a minute before shaking his grizzly head. "You're a stupid son of a bitch sometimes, Jess . . . . Okay, put 'em both to work at th cave, them trucks got a be unloaded and loaded by tonight."

"Th cave? . . . Pap, we need 'em out here, we're two men short!"

"Maybe you'll get two men next time I send ya out! . . . Now get to it, ya hear me?"

"Yeah, yeah, I hear ya, Pap!"

"Leave them duds on th porch, they won't need 'em!" He glared at Michael and Nora then abruptly turned and went back inside. "Dumb son of a bitch!"

"Okay, Slug!" He growled angrily. "You and th Cunt get out'en them duds, all of 'em, boots and all, fold 'em up neatly and put 'em up there on th porch." He laughed when he saw the wide-eyed hesitation on their faces. "If I got a tie your bare asses to that post out yonder, you'll be sorry as hell, . . . now do it, Slug, both a ya, no talk and no cryin', Cunt, just strip!"

They slowly did as they were told, first by sitting down to remove boots and socks, and by now they saw the twenty or so other men and women being escorted out of the two barracks by rough looking guards with machine pistols hung around their necks by nylon straps and held ready to fire should they have to.

Another toga-clad woman tiredly pushed an old wheelbarrow to the now boiling pot with a large bucket of tin plates and spoons. A few of the girls, and one or two of the boys could not be much out of puberty, and all of them were dressed in the same baggy green outfits as those stirring the pot, . . . but all of them walked with their heads down, taking their plates from the cart and holding them while one of the two women poured a ladle-full of the steaming concoction in their plates before filing back past the wheelbarrow to take a spoon and continue back almost to the barracks before sitting down on the ground to eat.

A few short minutes later, Michael and Nora Zant were standing red-faced and humiliatingly stark naked in front of the rambling old house.

"Now that's not bad, Cunt!" Nodded Jesse. "Not bad a'toll." He looked at Michael then. "But you could use a little help in th crotch area there, Slug! . . . Where was you when peckers was handed out, huh . . . Behind th door?" He chuckled then and looked back toward the pot.

"You want a eat, you got a few minutes?"

"Like this, man?" Blurted Michael, looking down at himself. "At least let my wife cover herself."

"Ain't nobody gonna pay you no mind over there," He chuckled. "Cept maybe ol' Rafe'ell, . . . maybe Tonio, . . . they're horny bastards! But they'll be lookin' at th Cunt there, not you, Slug! . . . So what'll it be, ya hungry'r not?"

"We'll pass." Said Michael.

"Suit yerself, Slug, next meal's jest before dark, course you can dress fer that one. Okay go put yer duds on th porch and wait till th rest get through eatin'. You got a take a piss, let it fly, you won't get to once ya go to work."

"Right here?"

"Right here." Laughed Jesse, turning back to watch the others.

They reluctantly relieved themselves, then picked up their clothes and did as they were instructed, . . . and then waited and watched until everyone finished eating and returned their utensils to the wheelbarrow. Jesse held them there until the armed guard, five men and seven women filed past them then walked ahead of him past the old house as they followed the other workers.

They were going past another old building when Jesse stopped them. "Wait right here fer a minute, Slug, . . . be right back." He walked the dozen or so yards to speak with two other guards standing in the structure's entranceway and while he was there, Michael and Nora could see the large heat-lamps just inside, and by the amount of light escaping the open doors, there had to be several of them in use.

"My God, Michael!" Asked Nora speaking for the first time in many hours. "What's going to happen to us, . . . it's so cold?"

"Darling, I don't know, . . . what I do know is that we have to be strong now, we do not have a choice!"

"Surely the Bowman's will look for us, . . . somebody has to find us, Michael!" She began to silently cry then. "They have to!"

"You need to stop that, honey, . . . I'm sure Jesse meant what he said!"

"I can't, Michael . . . . I've never been so humiliated, I feel so defiled! . . . We're going to die here, I just know it! We'll never see Mitchell again, what will he do?"

"Mitchell is our son, Darling, he'll be okay. He knows we love him and that's all that counts."

"What is this place?" She sniffed, still trying to cover her lower extremities with her hands. "God, it's so cold!"

"They're drug dealers, honey. That field back there is planted in Marijuana, look, here comes the workers with armloads of it right now. This barn is where they dry the plants."

"Dear God!"

"Honey, I want you to listen to me before Jesse comes back . . . . It's important! They will probably separate us, . . . we may not see each other much. I can handle that as long as I know you're okay. You have to stay strong, do what you're told at all times . . . . Don't look any of the guards in the face, they could take it as an invitation." He sighed then. "I don't think they really need one, . . . just don't draw attention to yourself. As long as we're alive, there's a chance we'll get out of this, so promise me, right now, here he comes! . . . Promise me!"

"I promise, Darling, I love you so much."

"I love you, honey, always have."

"Okay, Slug," Yawned Jesse as he came back to look them over. "Jest follow that path there, I'm right behind ya!"

They continued on down the worn path in the wake of the others and as they came to the large cave in the bluff, they saw the three other covered camouflaged surplus trucks, one behind the other about thirty yards from the opening, and both were on an old wagon road. Two naked men were already unloading large bales of something that looked heavy, and were taking them into the large lighted tunnel, . . . and as they approached the entrance, Jesse stopped them again and called to the guard that was watching the men carry their loads.

"Got another Slug for ya, Pete." He said as the man approached. "Put 'im to work!" Pete nodded and Jesse pushed Michael toward him and they both walked toward the vehicles. Grunting, Jesse looked down at Nora's worried face as she watched Michael leave.

"Okay, Cunt." He grinned then reached down to cup her slim buttock in his meaty hand, causing her to emit a startled gasp and pull away quickly. "Get on in there." He pointed with his finger and pushed her toward the cave's lighted opening.

As they entered the cave, he stopped her again and walked toward another guard sitting on an old forklift along the cave's inner wall.

'What is this place?' She wondered, suddenly shivering violently as she stared in awe at the long table, and the naked women on stools lining both sides of it. They were all wearing white masks over their nose and mouths, and with some sort of goggles covering their eyes. A white scarf was tied tightly around their heads, their hair stuffed up inside of it. Each had a small scales in front of her with what appeared to be a bowl on one side, and a weight on the other, . . . and all of them were silently dipping white powder from a stainless steel oblong tub in the middle of the table with a small tin cup and depositing it in the bowl on the scales. Once the scales were perfectly balanced, the woman would open a plastic bag and pour the bowl's contents in it then sealed the bag with a heating iron before passing it to another woman behind them, who in turn would place it on another long table behind her.

Nora saw the guard nod at Jesse and climb off the forklift, and as Jesse started back she saw the guard take the bags, weigh them again and place them on a pallet atop the other bags.

Jesse motioned for her, then waited until she came in behind the other women before stopping her again to wait while the woman behind them moved a stool in place at the table and placed another scale there.

Jesse took Nora's arm and pushed her toward the vacant stool. "Sit down here Cunt." And when she did, he laid his heavy hand on her slender naked shoulder and leaned down close to the young woman beside her, reached down to tweak the nipple on her breast and laugh.

"Listen up here, Little Bitch!" And when she stopped working. "Got a new Bitch here, her name is Cunt! . . . You have permission to talk to her. Show her what to do and how to do it. Tell her what will happen if she don't do it right! . . . If she fucks up because you didn't teach her right, I'm gonna fuck you tonight, understand me, girl?" And when she nodded.

"Right up yer skinny little ass, by th way!" He laughed and walked away, leaving Nora barely able to hold back her terrified tears. Her entire body was trembling violently, both from fear and the freezing early morning cold, and her hands shaking so she could hardly hold the dipping cup.

"You don't do it, they'll do bad things to you." Whispered the girl. "And to me! . . . So please, don't cry, we have to work, okay?"

Nora smiled weakly at her and nodded as she put down the cup and pushed her long black hair up in a bundle and wraped her head in the large cotton scarf . . . . And donning mask and goggles, she took the cup and dipped it into the white powder.

"I'm Nora." She said, glancing at the girl. "What is this stuff?"

"It's dope, . . . Heroin, now don't talk, just work. They're watching us!"

*   *   *

"Good movie, don't you think, Mitch? . . . The best yet!"

"Yeah it was, . . . very intense, with a good story behind it! I give it an A plus!" laughed Mitch. "I liked Hondo a lot, but I think this one was top notch."

"Better than Shane?" They each hesitated for a few seconds, then in unison. "NAAAA! . . . Pig Stand, here we come, . . . right, Mitch?"

"Sure, I guess, . . . I could use a burger and fries."

"I'm thinking the same thing." Laughed Reno as they got in the car. "Might even have a shake."

Mitch could not get over his parents not calling last night, had argued with himself remembering that his dad had said they would be out for three days and if that was true, they wouldn't be calling until today sometime. So why was that icy feeling still in his gut? . . . The thought that they would call today somehow didn't ease his mind any, nor that feeling of urgency in his stomach. There was something not right about the whole thing, going hunting in July was out of the normal routine of things, the decision to go on a bear hunt out of season was all wrong in his mind. They should not have gone, he thought, they should have waited for bear season! . . . And why the decision to fly? . . . None of it added up to a norm in his mind. But then again, he thought, he'd thought it a perfect idea before he found out about the early entrance exams . . . . Maybe that's what brought on the whole thing, he was disappointed, upset that him and Reno wasn't going with them? . . . He sighed as he stared out the side window, thinking he had made this same argument a hundred times already, . . . and it still didn't help!

But that couldn't be it, he thought as he remembered last Saturday's icy feeling, and he shivered all over again just thinking about it. The dark feeling he'd had after the initial chill was something akin to a cold, black cloud settling down on top of him, . . . and no matter how brief that feeling had been at the time, it was enough to scare him! Something was wrong, he was sure of it, . . . and his mind was a total blank, void of any ideas of what he would, or should do if something had happened to them. His was an I.Q. of a hundred and seventy and until now, had been enough to make any decision he had wanted to make, the right ones, usually. But somehow, he knew that I.Q. had nothing to do with this, . . . he was lacking what an L.Q. couldn't give him, . . . Maturity, the experience to handle emergencies, . . . and he didn't know what to do!

"Wasn't very many at the movie tonight, was there?" Voiced Reno as he drove, jerking Mitch out of his semi-trance.

"What?"

"The Movie, . . . not very many there."

"No, there wasn't, but I sort of like it like that, . . . nobody throwing popcorn, wads of bubble gum."

"Yeah, childish things like that." He looked across at Mitch then. "They'll call today, brother, stop thinking about it! . . . There's one thing we both know, Mister and Mrs. Zee can take care of themselves."

"Hey, I know that! . . . But what if they couldn't, Reno, . . . what if it was out of their control? . . . Somehow things are just not adding up."

"Like what?"

"Well, like that omen, if that's what it was, . . . and the fact that it's still with me, and the fact that they haven't called me since Wednesday night. I know the plane didn't crash, so it must be something else! . . . It's really got my gut tied in knots, brother."

"I'm sorry, Mitch." He sighed. "I'm worried, too. But all we can do is wait, somebody will contact you today, . . . if not Mister and Mrs. Zee, then someone else. We'll know what to do when they do call, . . . now, don't that make sense? . . . Besides, they haven't been out three days yet."

"Yes, I know." He laughed. "You know something else, man, . . . you have something I'm lacking a lot of, . . . common sense! . . . You're right! . . . They'll call today for sure."

"Now that's the brother I know." Laughed Reno. "Hey, not many cars here tonight either, what's going on?" He steered the 1954 Bellaire into the Pig Stand's semi-empty parking lot and pulled in under the awning.

"Mitch, . . . would you look at that? . . . You ever see anything so sexy?" They both watched the shapely form of the girl's mini-skirted torso as she roller-skated toward them. "Makes my tongue hard, buddy!"

"My tongue is not what's hard, Reno."

"Hello, handsome?" She smiled, leaning down to peer into the car's window. "Both of you, . . . hello, Mitchell?"

"Hi, Jenny."

"Can I take your order right quick, we close at two?"

"What's going on tonight, Jen?" Asked Reno. "The place is usually packed this time of night."

"You don't know? . . . Everyone's at those old softball tournaments, must be a dozen of them going on!"

"Happens every year!" Nodded Reno.

Mitch leaned over to see her smiling face. "Cheeseburger, coke and fries for me, darlin'." He drawled.

"My word," She smiled. "You do say the sweetest things, Mitchell . . . . What about you, sir, . . . the same?"

"Vanilla shake with mine, sweetness, . . . and you, sexy."

She placed a hand on his arm, leaned in and kissed him on the cheek. "All that may be a bit too much for you, have you thought of that?"

"I love it when you talk dirty, Jen." Grinned Reno.

"I'll bet you do!" She giggled. "Be back in a jiff, boys." She turned and skated away." I think I just creamed in my pants, Mitch."

"You think?? . . . I still think you should latch onto that!"

"Oh, yeah, what about you?"

"One night with me would ruin her for you, Buddy . . . . The only reason I'm not doing her right now is because you're my best friend, . . . remember that!"

"Good God, talk about dreaming, . . . I have heard it all now! . . . Truth is, she prefers a man she can conquer, . . . like me! Intellects like you would hold her back . . . . She knows all this, my man. Yes sir, I have got her number!" He smiled and looked across at Mitch then, seeing him staring out of his window again.

"You back in the gutter again, brother? . . . I thought we were past that?"

"Sorry, Reno, . . . you just don't know how powerful that feeling is, man. It crowds its way back into my mind, whatever I'm thinking, and I can't shake it!"

"Seriously, Mitch, . . . I'm sure they're okay. They'll be calling you today and bragging on how Mrs. Zee was the one that bagged the bear!"

"God, I hope so, buddy . . . . I just can't shake the feeling that they're not able to call me."

"If anything was wrong, Mister Bowman would have called by now, him or Carl Spencer. You know that, don't you?"

"Unless they don't know yet, . . . dad said they would be out for three days, and the hunt didn't start until Thursday."

"Then there you have it, today is day three! . . . They may have decided to stay out even longer, too, the hunt is for a week."

"I know you're right, Reno, I guess I'm becoming paranoid . . . . But damn it, that feeling just won't go away! . . . What if it is real and something bad has happened, what do I do about it, . . . I'm not Phillip Marlow?"///

"Yeah, but you're not in the movies neither. Something else is writing this script for us, brother, and all we can do is wait for the last act . . . . Now come on, man, it's Friday night, enjoy yourself . . . . And the question is not, what you will do? . . . It's what will we do, and we will do whatever it takes! . . . That's why I told Mom and dad I was staying at your place tonight . . . . Because truth is, buddy, your omen has rubbed off on me. I want to be there when they call today."

"Thanks, Reno."

"Not necessary, Mitch, . . . that's the way it is!"

*   *   *

Mitchell opened his bleary eyes, somewhat groggy from staying up poolside until four A.M., and yawning mightily swung his legs off the bed and got to his feet then grinning, took his pillow and threw it across the room at Reno's face.

"Hey!" Yelled Reno and threw it back at him. "That's no way to treat somebody you made sleep on the day sofa . . . . Besides, I was almost in Jenny's pants, you ruined it all!"

"What can I say, maybe I saved you the disappointment of a last second turn-down . . . . Now get up, old friend, it's noon, . . . rise and shine!"

"Then why do I feel so bad?"

"You stayed up all night, . . . I'm going to have some milk and cereal, what about you?"

"Right behind you." He yawned. "But I need a shower first!"

"Right on, you can use mine, I'll use mom and dad's." He grabbed fresh clothing and went off down the hall.

A half-hour later and fully dressed, they were pouring milk over a bowl of cocoa-puffs and sitting down at the table to eat when the front gate buzzer sounded, causing Mitch to look at Reno and shrug.

"Who can that be, . . . it's Saturday?" He got up and walked through the spacious living room to press the intercom button beside the front door.

"Who is it, please?"

"It's Sean Webster, Mitchell, I need to talk with you."

"Sure, Sean, come on in!" Feeling the icy chill grip his heart again, he worriedly mashed the button to open the entry gates before turning to find Reno standing behind him. "My, God, Reno!" He muttered, and then sighing reached to open the heavy door.

"I guess you were right, Mitch." Breathed Reno as he followed his friend out onto the wide porch where they watched the white BMW Sedan come up the twisting driveway, . . . and seeing them on the porch, Sean Webster turned off the drive into the circle driveway and came to a stop. Both of them were nervously anticipating what they would hear from the Vice President of Zant Industries, . . . and as he walked up the steps to the porch, could tell by the worried look on his face that it was not good.

"Hello, Mitchell." He said in his usual mild mannered voice and shook his hand. "Reno," He shook his hand as well then looked back at Mitch.

"Mitchell, . . . by any chance has a Mister Carl Spencer been in touch with you, maybe last night, or this morning?"

"I haven't heard from anyone since Wednesday night, Sean, . . . has something happened to mom and dad, . . . are they hurt?"

"No, no, . . . I don't think so, . . . well, I don't know, Mitchell, . . . But in all truth, I fear the worst! . . . This Carl Spencer called Zant Industries early this morning and since no one was there, he talked with Security. He told them that he had been trying to reach you at home, both last night, and this morning . . . . Security called me at home this morning, and when I couldn't reach you by phone I came right over. Security also said this Carl Spencer works for the Keyah Grande Hunting Lodge! . . . And well, I know just about everyone at the Lodge, but I've never heard of any Carl Spencer, do you know him?"

"Yes sir," Nodded Mitch hoarsely as tears began running down his cheeks. He felt Reno's hand grip his shoulder and blinked rapidly. "Uh, . . . Carl is the assistant Manager at Keyah Grande, Sean." He cleared his throat of the lump that was suddenly restricting his breathing, and swallowed a time or two. "I'm sorry, Sean, please, . . . come on in and sit down. He held the door for Sean to enter then him and Reno led the way back into the kitchen.

"Sit down Sean." And when the Vice President was seated. "Did Carl say anything else, . . . about why he called, . . . anything?"

Sean shook his head. "All the guard told me was that it was urgent he speak with you!"

Nodding, and with a glance at Reno, he looked toward the phone on the breakfast bar before getting up to go sit on one of the cushioned stools there. He used a tissue from the open box to wipe at his eyes then blew his nose before opening his mother's index of phone numbers. With a deep breath, he looked up at Reno and Sean then slowly dialed the long distance operator and gave her the number.

CHAPTER FIVE

Young Reno's hand never left Mitch's shoulder during the gut-wrenching conversation with Carl Spencer, a conversation that Mitch was barely able to have because his heart was breaking, as was his voice while he questioned the Assistant Manager.

"Yes sir," He choked. "I will, . . . I appreciate your concern, Carl, thank you." Tears were streaming down his cheeks as he hung up the phone, and it was the same with Reno, even though he had not heard what Spencer had said, and they reached for the tissue box together, . . . and all Sean could do was stand and gape at them both in shock, not knowing what had been said.

Mitchell blew his nose and left the stool to go stare out through the large, glass patio doors at the pool area, leaving Reno and Sean Webster with nothing to do but to stand and watch him because as yet, no one but Mitch knew what had happened . . . . But Reno thought he knew, and it was breaking his half-Apache heart.

Both of them silently waited and watched Mitchell's shaking shoulders, . . . and they knew he was crying, and yet they waited there in silence the several long minutes it took for the sixteen year old man to compose himself. When he finally did, he straightened his shoulders, wiped his eyes and blew his nose again before turning around to face them.

"Mom and Dad are missing, Reno," He shrugged then. "They were supposed to check in last night and they didn't, Cato didn't radio in at all yesterday."

"That don't mean anything, Mitch!" Said Reno. "Maybe they decided to stay longer?"

Mitch shook his head. "Cato would have told someone, he had a walky-talky with him, Reno, all the guides do, you know that . . . . Cato was supposed to check in at noon every day and when he didn't on Friday, Carl tried to call him." He turned away again to stare out through the window.

"What happened, Mitch?" Urged Reno, almost overtaken with grief again.

"Carl said the last time he heard from them was at noon on Thursday. Anyway, . . . When Cato didn't answer his radio Friday," He turned to face them again. "Carl sent another guide out to look for them . . . . Cato's dead, Reno, . . . he was shot, and his throat was cut."

My dear God, son!" Gasped Sean. "Wh, . . . what about Michael, a, . . . and your mother, are they . . . .""

"They weren't there, Sean, they didn't find them! . . . All they found was Cato, his radio, and evidence of several others being there."

Reno stood mutely by for a minute as Mitchell spoke, and when he finished he swallowed the lump in his throat and then nodded when his eyes met Mitchells'. "I'll be back in an hour, buddy!"

"Wait!" Said Mitch, stopping his friend at the patio doors. "What'll you tell your folks?"

"That's easy, we accepted the Laguna's invitation for their trail ride."

"Now wait a minute boys," Insisted Sean. "What are you planning here?"

"We're going to Colorado, Mister Webster." Choked Reno.

Sean looked at them both. "I'm sure they are doing everything possible to find them, boys . . . . What can you hope to accomplish by being there?"

"Search parties are still out, Sean." Sniffed Mitch. "They have been out since late yesterday, calling in every hour on the hour . . . . Carl said the National Guard lost the trail five miles from the campsite. Said they have expanded the search outward, but so far have not found where they went!"

"I will say it again, Mitchell, . . . what can you hope to do?"

"Find my mother and father, Sean!"

"Look boys, I've known you both for a long time, I know how resilient you both are, you're both excellent hunters, I know that! . . . But you are sixteen years old, . . . how can you hope to find them when experienced people can't?"

Mitch smiled slightly and put a hand on Reno's shoulder. "They didn't have the incentive I do, . . . and they didn't have a tracker like Reno, Sean. One way or another, I will find mom and dad!"

Sean stared at them both with an open mouth for a minute, then suddenly closed it and smiled. "It's crazy, boys, but I think I believe you. What can I do to help?"

"Are you serious, Sean?"

"Damn right I am, Mitchell, your mom and dad mean the world to me! . . . I'll even go with you."

"No, no." Said Mitch quickly. "Dad depends on you to run Zant, and so do I, besides, you have a family yourself. So thanks Sean, but no thanks."

"Well I have to do something!"

"You can loan me one of those company vans, . . . can't get much gear in my Coupe?"

"I can do a lot better than that! . . . I'll have you flown there in the Company plane, we keep a licensed, certified pilot on stand-by at all times, co-pilot as well."

"That would be great, Sean, thank you very much!"

"And Mister Webster," Broke in Reno. "I'm about to lie big time to my parents, . . . and you'll have to do the same if they ask you, and that means you don't know anything."

"I'll do what I have to, son, don't worry . . . . May God go with you boys." He shook their hands and hugged them. "I'll go arrange for the plane right now, I'll be waiting at the airport when you get there . . . . You can hide your car inside the hangar." He hurried back through the house and left.

"Be back in an hour, Mitch." He said again.

Mitchell grabbed his arm in a grip of friendship.

"Don't say it, brother," Said Reno. "They're my folks, too!" He pulled away and left through the patio doors, leaving Mitch alone to finally release his frustration and grief.

*   *   *

Michael had counted twelve guards in the compound, able to do so as they all pulled on their green togas and then walked back up the long path toward the cooking pot at the marijuana field. Everyone appeared exhausted as they were pushed and shoved up the pathway and especially him, having not eaten or slept since they were abducted, . . . and he was afraid to even think of what Nora was going through until he felt someone's hand touching his and looked down into her haggard eyes. The men and women with them all walked docilely and with bowed heads, their eyes on the ground as if afraid to look at anything around them. Those workers from the marijuana field, and those that did the weaving and repair on the camouflaged canopy were already in line and taking their tin plates from the wheelbarrow as they converged.

He had the opportunity then to grip Nora's hand reassuringly before they were ushered into line, and as they took their plates from the bucket they all could see the naked man, his arms stretched upward and his wrists chained to the top of the whipping post, leaving him barely able to touch the ground with his tiptoes. The man was cursing Jesse and crying openly as he tried to ease the pressure on his body. When everyone had their plates and spoon, they filed past the cast-iron pot for their ladle of stew and were ordered to stand aside and wait.

Michael maneuvered Nora in front of him and once they were served, a guard directed all of them to sit on the ground in a semi-circle around the whipping post to eat. He managed to sit beside Nora, as many of the others did and reluctantly, yet hungrily ate the tasteless plate of stew, finding only enough meat in it to keep up their strength, and not much else in the way of sustenance!

The man at the post was exhausted, but was still cursing Jesse for everything he could think of, and both their hearts went out to him and at the same time wondered what he might have done to deserve a whipping like that. But Michael knew that it probably did not take much for Jesse to whip somebody. They cleaned their plates, but if not for the fact they hadn't eaten in so long, could not have done it . . . . But if they were ever going to get away from this place, they would need their strength, . . . all of it!

"Okay now!" Came the boisterous voice everyone recognized, . . . and everyone of them were staring down at their own laps as he walked shirtless in front of them to stop behind the naked, middle-aged victim of the whip.

"Don't look at yer God damn laps when I'm talkin'!" He raged. "I want ever Bitch and Slug of ya to look at this piece a shit up here!"

"Fuck you, Jesse, you Bastard, you raped my wife!" Yelled the man. "You sorry piece of shit, I'll kill you, you don't leave my wife alone!" He started to cry again then, and as he grew silent. "You sorry, son of a bitch!"

"You all been here before and seen this!" He chuckled. "Most a ya been where he is, ain't ya, . . . huh? . . . Yeah, you know what happens when you don't show respect, . . . same thing as when you don't give me a solid days work! . . . And for fuckin' sure, you don't cuss th' boss man!" He uncoiled the long lash from around his neck and laid all twenty feet of it along the ground behind him.

"I want ya to watch ever minute a this, I see anybody look away you'll get th' same thing!" He backed away several steps, relayed the whip along the ground again and delivered the first blow to the man's bare back, wrenching an agonizing scream from deep within his lungs, and leaving him sobbing brokenly until the next blow landed.

Michael watched in terrified silence, listening to Nora's sharp intake of breath every time the lash cut into the man's back, and he counted seven lashes before the man stopped screaming and went limp, never feeling the last three. He felt relief for him when it was finally over and watched the guards unshackle his wrists, letting him fall to the ground unconscious before grabbing an arm each and dragging him across the compound to the second barracks.

Jesse watched him being taken away then glared at them all for a minute before grinning evilly. "Anybody got anything to say, any of ya want a take his place, huh? . . . You will, you don't give a full day's work!" He looked toward the barracks then. "That Slug broke my rules, he opened his mouth without permission! . . . And you all better God damn remember what them rules are . . . Silence, that's my rule, a full day's work! . . . that's my rule! Do what your told, that's my rule! . . . You don't, you get a whippin'! . . . And that goes for you young'uns, too! Yeah, I been watchin' you. You don't work, I'll be whippin yer Pap and Ma'am's nekid ass!" He laughed again then.

"Well don't jest sit there like fuckin' Slugs, put yer God damn plates up and go to yer barracks!"

They got up and filed past the wheelbarrow depositing plates and spoons, and as the burly guards walked with them, were all ushered to their respective barracks. The one called Pete walked with those from the cave to stand at the door as they filed in, showing Michael to a vacant cot in front as he passed, and allowing Nora and the rest to find their own. He told everyone to sit on their beds and then went to each of them, squatting to place and lock a steel shackle around their left ankles before coming back to sit on his own cot in the open side of the building facing the compound.

Michael had cast a sidelong glance toward the old house as they were walking and saw Jesse, Ethan, and the other one walking up the steps with four young women in tow, and then the shaggy old man as he took the arm of one and yanked her into the house. He had not mistaken the groans and sobbing of the defeated husbands, or fathers, whom-ever they were as they walked.

He was still sitting on his cot watching the compound grounds as the whole area grew dark in the coming night, and wondered how this sort of thing could be happening in America? . . . Could he have been so engrossed in himself that he was out of touch with the real world? . . . He obviously was! He turned then to strain his eyes back into the dark barracks to try and pick out Nora's bunk, but could not and sighing, turned back to watch as Pete got up to walk out a ways and talk with one of the guards in the compound. He laid down and pulled his aching legs onto the bunk, then lay listening to the exhausted groans of the other slaves as they tried to fall asleep.

These poor souls, and now him and Nora were in a hell that no one would ever believe existed, or could exist in such modern times. Yet here they were in forced slavery, at the mercy of a group of sadistic madmen, forced to work all day and chained up like animals at night. All lights were out at night except for the heat lamps in the drying shed, and the doors were closed on that. That way, he knew that no aircraft would be able to detect anything of a curious nature beneath the expanse of camouflage.

Being a scientist himself, Michael Zant's nature was to analyze and experiment with things of an unknown nature, . . . and this place certainly filled the bill! He was constantly observing his surroundings, the activities and habits of the guards on duty at night. He knew that each of the barracks were of nothing more than old, weathered and sagging lumber, making him believe that the place had been a working farm at one time. That, or maybe gold had once been discovered here, and it had been a community for the miners. That would explain the large cave. But the thing that interested him the most was the fact that dried lumber would burn very quickly and if it came down to it, he would find a way to set the whole place on fire. The authorities would surely see that! . . . If they were even interested in looking for them anymore?

What he couldn't understand was how an uncouth, unlikely clan of monsters like Jesse, Ethan and that old slob of a man could give birth to a drug oriented slave camp of this magnitude? Not one of them possessed an I.Q. of more than twenty! They were vicious animals, all of them, and most likely in place to oversee what was obviously only a small part of a much, much larger drug operation! Not Jesse, Ethan, the other brother, Benji, or the guards could have come up with the idea of a giant camouflaged canopy of such proportion, . . . or know that to an airplane it would give the appearance of a living forest of trees. That idea, and knowledge had to have come from much wiser and experienced people.

His opinion was that the old ogre of a father and his boys were, or had been unsuccessful hillbilly farmers when approached by these drug dealers and since, had let the thrill of brutality and the authority over people, go to their heads! Whatever it was, he thought, they were certainly doing the job, . . . and that brought up another question. Who came up with the idea of kidnapping hapless holiday campers and hunters and enslaving them by instilling in them such agonizing fear and helplessness? . . . Jesse and his bunch would have been too afraid of the law to do that on their own, . . . unless they had been convinced that the law would be taken care of?

At any rate, they were doing it, and using the threat of a whipping post and bullwhip as the incentive for hard work and compliance, and using the whip in front of everyone to demonstrate their cruelty was smart! He also knew that should all this not be discovered and soon, they would all die here. Whether it be from Illness, or other means, Jesse and his clan of drug dealers would not allow them to go free, . . . they couldn't! Should this place be discovered and one of the slaves should talk, . . . it would mean certain conviction and death for them all.

He knew most of this to be true. He also knew that if he didn't find a way to get him and Nora away, or if someone didn't happen to find them and soon, . . . they would die here along with everyone else. It could be weeks, months, or years away, but it would surely happen.

He folded his arms beneath his head to pear into the freezing darkness as his thoughts turned to Nora, on her own bunk somewhere in the rear of the barracks. Their first day here had been totally exhausting, and she had looked so drawn and helpless. He was worried about her, but knew she was a strong woman. But he also knew that something like this could do many things to a person's mind, . . . and obviously already has to some of the women here. He could see deep signs of depression in a few of them, resulting in some form of domestication akin to that of a household pet, anxious to obey their masters. He couldn't allow that to happen to Nora and somehow, he would not!

He heard Pete coming back to sit on his cot and turned over on his, and Pete must have heard him utter an aching groan as he did, because his voice startled him.

"What's wrong, man, can't sleep? . . . You need to try, ya know!"

"My mind is too active, but I'll try, . . . thanks." He whispered in a low voice.

He was about to fall asleep when he heard the sound of trucks leaving the cave area and knew they were the same ones he, and the other two men had worked to unload, and then to reload with the Heroin and bales of dried Marijuana. He listened to their departure and briefly wondered where they were going? It would not be all that far, he thought, unless they had a place to hide the trucks during the day. But in reality, he almost knew there had to be a remote airfield somewhere nearby where the trucks could be off-loaded then reloaded from an airplane. The drugs had been loaded onto the same trucks they had unloaded!

This thought made him wonder if these departing trucks might be a means of escape? But it probably had already been tried, or thought about, and besides, the drivers of the trucks were armed with machine guns. Even if it were possible, most everyone here had a spouse with them, or a son or daughter, . . . and he couldn't leave them at the mercy of Jesse . . . . With these thoughts on his mind he fell asleep again.

He had only slept a few hours when the sound of trucks woke him again, only this time they were incoming, and he just was not looking forward to another day of unloading those heavy bales of Opium Poppy . . . . And with that depressing thought, he was somewhat dejected as his thoughts turned to his son, and silently thanked God that he had not come with them. By now he was sure that Mitchell had been told of their failure to contact the lodge, and it was something he had forced himself not to think about until now. But he knows, he thought, and then wondered what he might try and do? What could a sixteen year old young man do, he would be devastated, lost, and wouldn't know what to do! He also knew that Mitchell was far more mature in his intellect than most his age, . . . and the same could be said for Reno, . . . and that alone led him to believe that he did not actually know what they might do?

He would hope Mitchell would take the company over once he was convinced they were dead. But there was also an agonizing thought in the back of his mind, . . . Mitchell just might try to find them himself, he had the initiative and both him, and Reno were excellent marksmen and hunters.

If Cato had been right, and everything pointed to it, Jesse and his brothers would have the upper hand with anyone caught hunting them. They would be ambushed just as they had been. If they weren't killed by trying to fight back, they would only wind up here, . . . or dead! He remembered what the guide had told him then, . . . that the search parties would give up when the going got tough! . . . With that troubled thought, he drifted off to sleep again.

*   *   *

Reno returned within the hour and hurried into the house just as Mitch was zipping up his large travel satchel.

"That was quick!" Nodded Mitch as he entered. "Any trouble at home?"

"No." He sighed. "If you can imagine how hard it was to lie to them? . . . I've never done that before, Mitch, . . . and I never want to do it again!"

"I'm sorry, buddy, . . . you can still back out, you know."

"No way in hell, Mitch! We're in this together, . . . do or die!"

"Agreed! . . . What did you bring?"

"My Smith/Wesson Mag., Remington seven hundred, and all the ammo I could sneak out in my bag. I also brought my long-bow, dad's quiver and thirty steel-tipped arrows! . . . What about you?"

"Me, you brought everything we'll need!" He grinned. "Well, I couldn't open dad's gun cabinet, and I didn't want to break the lock. But I've got my Marlin thirty-thirty, Ruger single-six, my black powder forty-four pistol and holster, a shoulder holster for the Ruger, my hunting knife, clothes and what ammo I had . . . . And if that ain't enough, we're in trouble, old friend!"

"We might be anyway." Sighed Reno. "I guess we're ready."

"Except for money," Sighed Mitch. "And the bank is closed today, . . . I think I may have fifty dollars."

"Sixty." Nodded Reno. "Maybe we can write a check somewhere."

"Maybe, I've got mom's check book . . . . Grab my rifle, buddy." He shouldered the heavy satchel and together they left through the front door to deposit their gear into Reno's Bellaire. Locking the house, they drove out of the circle drive then down the twisting driveway and out through the gates, each of them with their own dark thoughts and fears for the days ahead.

*   *   *

Reno steered the car into the airport and followed the black-top around the large main terminal to at last pull up in front of Zant Industries Aircraft hangar where a mechanic was waiting in the wide open, sliding doorway and was motioning them inside. Reno parked his car along one side of the vast building's inner wall and as they got out, Sean Webster exited the office, accompanied by the Corporation's Pilot and Co-Pilot and all walked toward the car to meet them.

Both Mitch and Reno shook hands with Sean, and then the pilots.

"Do you boys have everything you need?"

"Yes sir." Sighed Mitch. "We're a little short on cash, we have a hundred bucks between us, and mom's check book."

Sean reached into an inside coat pocket and produced a card. "I have something better." He said, giving it to Mitch. "That's a credit card, son, issued and backed by the Government. Use it same as cash, it's honored everywhere, Underwritten by the World Bank and is bearer legal!"

"Here is also a Zant Industries I.D. card with your name on it, plus a letter of authorization signed by me, . . . and I think that's all you'll need."

"Thank you, Sean."

"Don't mention it, boys. You need anything else you call me. Now let's get your stuff loaded." With the help of both pilots, they carried their gear toward the plane and as they neared, they both stopped to look it over.

"Is this a new one, Sean?"

"Yes it is, son, it's a prototype, ordered by the Air force and presented to Zant Industries. They flew it in to us the day your parents left for Colorado." He stood back and looked at it too. "That is the Beech Craft E-fifty, Twin Bonanza, co-named Business-Twin! . . . These planes are not scheduled to go on the open market until next year."

"Proto-type? . . . Is it safe?"

"Don't worry." He laughed. "It's been put through every test there is. Both Bob, and Morgan there have logged over a hundred hours in this very plane before they flew it in, . . . they are certified to fly it!"

"Sure is pretty . . . . You like it, Reno?" He grinned as he asked the question.

"I don't like flying!" Said Reno as he continued on toward the plane.

"He's afraid of heights." He said as he walked behind him with Sean.

Once their gear was stowed, the pilots entered the plane, and in a few seconds the large Twin Engines roared into action.

"You boys take care of yourselves up there, you hear me? . . . Anything happens to you your folks will hunt me down like a dog! . . . Keep your wits about you!"

"We will, Sean."

"A car will be waiting for you at Durango, I made all the arrangements. Don't worry about a thing here, just do what you have to do! . . . Bring them home, son, and God Bless you both!"

Nodding, they climbed the steps into the plane's cabin, and the co-pilot pulled the steps up and locked the door into place. Two minutes later they were belted in, and the new Beech Craft taxied out of the hangar and continued on toward the airport's many runways in front of the tower.

The plane was not all that large in the cabin area, but would seat eight passengers quite comfortably, four on either side. Each seat had its own window with a pull down shade of which, Reno had taken advantage of early on. The aisle was comfortably wide enough to allow a hostess to serve special guests. The seats were just as plush, having retracting armrests, reclining seat backs, and enough legroom for a tall man to cross his legs. Behind the seating, a small lavatory with a locking door was on one side and on the other, a bar with a small, under the counter Frigidaire beneath it.

Oxygen masks were hidden inside a small compartment above their heads should a sudden drop in cabin pressure occur. Air ducts were also embedded, along with a light over each seat to provide a reading lamp and cool air if needed. On the backs of each seat was a pocket to store reading materials, and a fold-down tray to eat on. Ashtrays were embedded into the armrests with a flip-up cover on them and of course, nylon seat belts. The plane was or seemed to Mitch, equipped with all the modern technologies available and a lot of them, if not all of them of his father's own design and construction.

All the comforts of home, thought Mitch as he stared out of the window, feeling the plane as it lifted off the runway and the solid clunk as the wheels were retracted, . . . and then they were airborne. The steady, even drone of the engines as they lifted them thousands of feet per minute above the city of Albuquerque, and then to bank sharply toward the North and their eventual destination climbing to an altitude of seventeen thousand feet as it came out of the turn.

He watched the tall buildings as they grew smaller and tried to find his home by searching to the west of town, but could not. He looked across the aisle at Reno and smiled when he saw his friend's hands gripping the armrests. Their eyes met briefly, and Mitch picked up the headset, gesturing for Reno to do the same, and put them on.

"You okay, buddy?"

"I'm still swallowing my stomach back down, but I'm okay, how about you?"

"My gut's still tied in knots, man, . . . what we're about to do scares me to death! . . . Not knowing if mom and dad are okay is almost too much to handle."

"It's called anticipation, brother." Said Reno. "I have it, too. We'll be okay, man . . . . How long till be get there anyway?"

"About three hours to Durango, another two to the lodge, thereabout. We should be there between seven and nine o'clock today."

"I hate flying, Mitch, but I got to say it beats driving for two days."

"We start hunting tomorrow morning, Reno and old buddy, . . . I sure hope your tracking skills are in order?"

"You're not alone . . . . If they're still in those mountains we'll find them, Mitch, you can count on that! . . . What worries me is what we'll do when we do find them, . . . we don't even know if they're, . . ."

"Still alive? . . . You can say it, Reno, . . . because I'm thinking it! But they are alive, brother, dad will see to that!"

"God, I hope so, Mitch! . . . Think you'll be able to kill a man?"

Mitch thought about that for a minute. "They've got mom and dad, Reno, yeah, I think I can! What about you?"

"Let's hope we don't have to. Maybe between us, we can come up with a plan? . . . Some way around that!"

"Maybe . . . . But first things first, . . . we have to find them! There's some pretty wild country in them mountains and we've never been more than fifteen miles from the lodge. We don't know what to expect!"

"I know, Mitch . . . . Just promise me one thing, brother, and I'll do the same! . . . If it should come down to it, and we have to kill somebody to save our own lives, . . . don't hesitate, man! . . . We freeze up at the wrong time we are dead!"

"I promise, Reno."

"So do I, Mitch! . . . What do you think, brother, . . . could they have been taken for ransom?"

"Kidnapped? . . . I don't know, . . . as far as I know, no one but us and the lodge knew they were going to be there! . . . But it is a logical question . . . . I do know dad would be worth a lot of money to them, if they knew who he was."

"That's what I'm thinking, too! . . . If that is the case, do you think someone at the lodge could be in on it?"

"God, Reno, I don't know, man! . . . Right now, I don't feel so damn smart anymore! My head's been so screwed up all day I can't even think straight."

"I know the feeling!" Reno was quiet for a few minutes then. "We're nothing but a pair of punk kids, Mitch, . . . we don't know a damn thing about the real world! We don't have a clue about what goes on outside our own space, and I'll tell you something else! . . . Whoever has Mister and Mrs. Zee are not punk kids, and we had better be something more than what we are when we catch them!"

"We will be, Reno." He sighed. "I hope!"

"The way I see things right now, . . . we might have a week, maybe two to grow up in. School is far behind us now, so is the shooting range, the Pig Stand, mom and dad, everything! . . . We're not kids anymore, all that is behind us now. From this moment on, old buddy, we are soldiers going to war, . . . we are the searchers and I for one, do not plan on dying out there! . . . We do what we came here to do, and we kill if we have to, no second thoughts before, or after . . . . Agreed?"

Nodding, Mitch reached across the aisle and high-fived Reno. "Agreed! . . . Tell you what, . . . you just keep reminding me of that, and I'll come up with a working plan when we find them, Deal?"

"You got it, brother . . . . Now I'm hungry, think that fridge back there has anything to eat in it?"

"One way to find out!"

*   *   *

Michael opened matted eyes at the shrill sounds from a police whistle and grunting from his aching muscles sat upright on the cot before turning to place his feet on the cold ground and as he did, winced from the pain in his cut and bruised feet. As he cleared the dregs of sleep from his eyes, by using the heels of his hands to rub them, he remembered his thoughts from last night, and the truck departures and arrivals and this morning, none of it made a lot of sense.

Yawning he sat and waited for Pete to don his heavy boots, then sat while he got up and came around to stoop and unlock his shackle iron.

"Stand up and be still till I get back." He said groggily then moved to the next bunk. As each iron was removed that person was told to stand and wait to be walked out. Once he was done, he walked them all forward to move out in single file past a water pail on a table just outside the barracks and allowed one dipper of water each before moving to another table and ordered to remove their gowns and put on clean ones.

Afterwards they were allowed to go back through the barracks and out the back to a ditch that had been dug for the purpose of relieving themselves. A roll of paper towels was on the back wall and each would take a liberal amount before doing their business and when finished would wash their hands in a pail of water there before coming back to stand in the barrack's entrance.

Michael stood aside long enough to wait for Nora before following the others, and gripped her hand reassuringly before letting her move in front of him. Once both barracks were empty, and all the workers were back in front, they were ordered out into the compound to deposit their soiled gowns in the wheelbarrow, get plates and spoons and line up for the morning meal of warmed over, yesterday's stew. While they were waiting their turn, Michael saw the four women run crying from the house to the barracks where they quickly changed their soiled clothing and then went back inside, he assumed to the man-made latrine ditch.

Him and Nora were just moving to get their ladle of stew when he saw the four run out to deposit their clothing and get their plates, noticing that all four were still silently crying and holding their midsections as if in pain. They were all ordered to sit on the ground again to eat, and the hard soil was freezing cold through the thin garments and all were shivering from the cold as they ate, their breaths creating a thick mist of fog as they breathed and when they were done, Jesse came out of the house in the same old worn overalls, but now he had a heavy coat on as he walked in front of them.

"I want two extra men on net repair today, birds tore holes in it yesterday. That means th' rest a you Slugs'll have to double up in th' field, and I don't want no slackers, ya hear?" He nodded at the guards then and went back to the house.

By full light those working in the cave were ushered in that direction by Pete as he walked along beside them and once at the entrance, they removed their gowns and folded them before going inside to don masks, head-wraps and goggles.

Michael joined the two other men and began unloading the trucks that had arrived early that morning, lugging the heavy bags of Opium Poppy into the cave past the table where Nora was working and on to the lab at the rear of the old mine shaft where three men were already in the process of cooking and drying the deadly drug.

Pete would walk with them each time, and Michael figured it was to insure they did not drop or lose any of the seeds from the bags. But as they were carrying the last three bales from the first truck into the cave, he was startled when Pete spoke to him in a low voice.

"What's your name, man?" He queried. "No, don't look up, just keep moving, . . . who are you?"

"Will it make a difference?" Asked Michael nervously, expecting a trick of some sort.

"Nope, . . . but you're different than the other men here, . . . you're smarter, always observing things, I can see your eyes moving . . . . I just want a tell you it won't do you any good, man, . . . there ain't no way out!" They walked on into the cave in silence, and after the first two men filed past on their way back, he placed his bag on the stack and chanced a look at Pete's haggard face.

"Michael," He said, looking away again. "My name is Michael . . . . Is this going to get me the whipping post now?" He started slowly back toward the trucks then.

"My name's Pete, Mike." He said as he came back up beside him. "And no, it won't get you a whippin' . . . . I don't cotton to anything that goes on here, it makes me sick!"

"Leave then! . . . What's keeping you?"

"They'd track me down, same as you, Mike, then Jesse would kill me, same as you!"

"Jesse's a man, Pete, . . . not much of one, but you have a gun, same as him, . . . and I would suggest that he can die, same as you!"

"I have thought about that, a lot . . . . But I can't!"

"Then I'm as sorry for you, as I am for all of us, Pete." The second truck was in place by the time he got back, and there was no further conversation between them the remainder of the day. But he filed it away in his mind as a possible means to get Nora out of there should the opportunity present itself.

*   *   *

The crosswinds were in full stride as they made the descent into the Durango airport, the plane was skimming the treetops by the time they were out of the turbulence. The Pilot cut power on the new plane and lowered the flaps before lowering and locking the wheels in place and a minute or so later, the sounds of friction as the tires settled on the runway and the plane began to taxi.

"You okay, Buddy?" Asked Mitch, looking across at him and seeing him nod, he smiled and removed the headset to look out through the window as they circled the large terminal, . . . and five minutes later the Beech Craft rolled to a stop beside a fuel tanker that was waiting for them. The Captain came into the cabin and lowered the boarding ramp as they unbuckled their seatbelts and together, walked down the steps to the blacktop.

The first thing Mitch saw was his father's Cessna backed tail-first against the hangar, and a lump formed in his throat at the sight of it.

"Don't look at it, brother." Said Reno, turning him away as both pilots came down the steps to open the luggage compartment. One of the hangar attendants drove out through the wide doors in a new Nomad Wagon and parked alongside the plane then hurried to help the pilots off-load their gear.

"We got a nice ride, at least." Nodded Reno. "I'll drive, Mitch."

"I thought you would."

Once the car was loaded, the Captain and co-pilot came to shake their hands. "Sean told us what happened, Mitch, our thoughts go with both of you on this!"

"Thanks, Bob." Nodded Mitch. "You flying right back?"

"As soon as we refuel." He nodded.

"Tell Sean we'll be in touch, . . . I just don't know when."

"I will do that, . . . Good bye, boys."

Mitch nodded and walked around the car and with another devastating look at the Cessna, got into the passenger seat and closed the door, . . . let's go, Reno!"

"Which way, . . . We've never been here before?"

"Just drive, I guess, we're bound to see an exit sign, . . . just head for Durango. We should come across State one-sixty somewhere . . . . That'll take us to the lodge."

"I remember that old road, and I don't like it!" Returned Reno. "Too many twists and turns and if I remember right, . . . one lane bridges!"

"Want me to drive?"

"I'm good, don't worry!" Reno grinned and stared out at the forest of tall Pines then shook his head. "Here we go!' He said, turning onto the oil-topped road. "Durango ten miles, . . . says so right there."

"I can't see ten feet into those trees." Commented Mitch. "And you know what? . . . This is tame compared to where we're going. Are you going to have any problem following a trail?"

"I worry some about that! . . . I've never had to track people before, . . . but I remember everything dad taught me about it. I've tracked Elk up here, buddy, and it can't be all that different! . . . Don't worry, if they left a trail, I'll find it, . . . if it don't rain!"

"If it don't rain?"

"Oh, yeah, rain will wash away all traces of a trail, everything!"

"Now I am worried!"

"Me, too." Sighed Reno. "It's rained on us every time we've been up here."

"But that was in September and October."

"That's all we've got going for us, . . . we've never been here in the summer."

"God, Reno, . . . I didn't realize this before, . . . I know we talked about it but, . . . here we are, sixteen year old kids, . . . fresh from High School! We have studied and learned everything about just about everything. We have aced every test on the subjects! . . . And now, . . . I am fast realizing the fact, that I do not know much of anything about much of anything! It's a vicious, cruel son of a bitch, Reno! . . . We are about to attempt something that was never in any of those books we read. Things that until now only happened in the movies, . . . things we watched from a comfortable seat over popcorn while we experienced the thrill of adventure! . . . We don't know a damn thing, old buddy!"

"I was wondering if you were listening to me on the plane, . . . I made that conclusion, already? . . . Hell, just think of this as a crash-course, and we're cramming for the final test!"

"Reno Cortez, you are a brave man!"

"Yeah, well when we get to college, I expect you to let every pretty girl on campus know that!"

"Leave it to me."

"Thanks . . . . And Mitch, if it is bravery you see, it's the Apache in me! I just think that if something has to be done and there's no easy way to do it, a man has no choice but to just do it! . . . We don't have a choice here, old buddy, because if those search parties haven't already found Mister and Mrs. Zee, we'll have to, . . . and that is a factual reality! . . . Who knows, maybe they'll be back at the lodge when we get there?"

"I pray you're right! . . . There it is, Reno, State one-sixty!"

*　　　　　*　　　　　*

"Yes sir, Mister Webster, I will have him call as soon as they arrive. Yes sir, we're doing everything we can to find them . . . . I will, sir, right away. Good bye."

Carl Spencer hung up the phone with a frown on his face, thinking he did not need young Zant and Cortez in the way, . . . not right now! He did, however, understand their fear and concern over the Zant's disappearance, . . . and he knew that he would have come himself, had it been his parents!

'Oh, well' he thought, then went back to the dining room and the sit-down strategy conference with F.B.I. Special Agent, Ron Howard, and National Guard's General Rinehart. He stood for a moment to watch, and listen as the two men looked over the map of the areas in question, and had the sudden feeling they were about to give up the search, . . . again!

"What are you saying, Mister Howard?" Asked Carl as he sat back down.

Special Agent Howard turned his narrowed, authoritative eyes on him and shrugged. "What I'm saying, Mister Spencer, is that the search party has lost the trail . . . . General Rinehart's Lieutenant radioed in saying they followed the ruts of that vehicle for a half mile before losing the trail, . . . they could find no ruts, no marks on the rocks, no broken twigs, nothing that would tell of its passing!"

"And this call came in, when?" Asked Carl suspiciously.

"My aide brought me the message while you were on the phone." Said Rinehart unapologetically. "And I have ordered the squad to return to the lodge, Mister Spencer, at least for the night, . . . they can't track in the dark anyway."

"In other words, you're a stone's throw away from calling off the search!"

"That's not what I said, sir!"

"Need I remind you both that there have been disappearances going on in the San Juans for over two years now, . . . and you have called off the search each time after a day or two? . . . These are human beings, General, United States Citizens, your Government's tax payers! . . . And that makes them your responsibility!"

"Mister Spencer, we have already determined cause for those earlier disappearances. The Governor has authorized the black bear hunt, and that takes it out of our hands completely!"

"Oh, how well I know that! . . . And what about this one? . . . Do you have any idea what Michael Zant means to the Government, if not, shouldn't you find out? . . . And Gentlemen, a black bear did not shoot my guide, nor did a black bear cut his throat! Cato was murdered, Gentlemen, and need I remind you again that Michael and Nora Zant are highly respected Government contractors, and they have been kidnapped by these same murderers? . . . That, gentlemen is what you'll find out so go ahead, call Washington, ask Mister Hoover if he wants you to call off the search?"

"Mister Spencer, get a grip on yourself, sir, or I swear I'll have you removed."

"Well pardon me Sir, Special Agent Howard! . . . But those troops have only been out there for one day, not even twenty miles in! . . . These mountains and forest areas are a hundred miles long, and the Zants are out there somewhere, gentlemen, . . . and my guide's killers have them!"

"Mister Spencer, please! . . . Lieutenant Rodgers has informed me that the area of that vehicle's disappearance is, for the most part, impassable . . . . a rabbit couldn't go in there!"

"A truck did, General! . . . Your Lieutenant Rodgers just doesn't want to scuff his pant legs, . . . or he is he just following orders, . . . is that what he's doing?

"Mister Spencer, that is just about enough of that kind of an outburst! Remember who you're talking to, Sir!"

"How can I forget, I've been hearing this same thing from you for two years, . . . and please, let me apologize for allowing a kidnapping and murder keep you gentlemen from your golf games, I know how important they are! . . . . Okay, . . . if you won't try to find them, let me send my guides to do it, they grew up in these mountains?"

"My orders stand on that subject, sir!" Returned Agent, Howard. "We can not have a mob of vigilantes, hell bent on revenge loose out there, . . . and I expect you to comply with that order! . . . And now, I'm going to add to that order Mister Spencer, because I think I know what you are about to do . . . . If you do not comply with my orders, I will close the doors on the Keyah Grande Hunting Lodge, . . . and I do not believe Mister Bowman will appreciate that! . . . Am I understood, sir?"

"Oh, yeah, I understand that you do not want to find these people! . . . For what reason, I don't know. However, I will relate this to Mister Bowman . . . And if you don't mind my saying so, . . . and with all undue respect! . . . You, sir, are a pompous, uncaring son of a bitch! And again, I will inform Zant Industries of this, and Mister Bowman. They will take it from there, I am sure!"

"Now, gentlemen, please." Interrupted Rinehart. "I did not say I was calling off the search completely, Mister Spencer . . . . As a matter of fact, I intend to speed it up a bit. I'm ordering the County Sheriff to keep men in the area while he puts his helicopters under my command for the next few days. If they spot anything from the air, his men can converge on the area. Also, there are several crop dusters in the area and I intend to enlist their help as well. If we can find that vehicle then maybe we'll find the Zants."

"Well, at least that's something, thank you General! . . . Now, if you'll excuse me, I'll let Mister Howard resume his plans for the weekend!" He scraped his chair back, glared angrily at Special Agent Howard as he got to his feet, then left the room.

"Don't you think you were a bit hard on him, Ronnie?"

"Eugene, we both know, they'll never find those people, it's a wilderness out there. Besides, we're saving the taxpayers a shit-pot full of money by calling it off! Spencer was right, though, I do have a wedding to go to this weekend, and meetings to attend Monday, Tuesday and Wednesday, . . . and as it is, it'll take two days to write all this up! But you do what you want with, . . . that thing with the helicopters, . . . I'm leaving in the morning."

Carl was at his desk when he saw both of them going to their rooms and looked at his watch. 'Nine-thirty' He thought, thinking it was about time for his newest unwanted arrivals to show up and sighing heavily, he got up and walked across the large reception room and pushed through the glass doors.

CHAPTER SIX

He was standing on the lower section of the expansive front veranda when the Nomad entered the large circular drive to finally come to a stop and still, he waited until Mitch and Reno got out before going down the steps to greet them.

"It's good to see you, Mitchell." He said reaching to shake his hand. "And you as well, Reno." He shook his hand before turning back to Mitch. "It's good to see you both, but I wish it were under happier circumstances."

"Have they found them yet, Carl?"

"No, son, they have not! . . . National Guard troops have been out all day looking for them." He looked at the car then. "Please, lock the car and come on in, I'll have someone bring in your luggage and park the car." He took both their arms and urged them up the steps.

"The dining room closes at nine on Saturday night, but I kept it open because I knew you'd be hungry, . . . I can fill you in while you eat."

"How did you know we were coming?" Asked Reno as they walked along the brick walkway.

"Sean Webster called to see if you had arrived yet? . . . He'd like you to call him at home, Mitchell."

"I will, thanks, Carl." They allowed Carl to show them through the glass doors and then followed him into the large, exquisite dining room where a very pretty black girl came from the kitchen to wait on them. She waited until they were seated, then took their orders and left.

"Mitchell, never in a hundred years could you know how sorry I am this happened! Nothing like this has ever happened here before, and we certainly had no reason to expect it."

"Where did it happen?"

Carl sighed heavily. "Jimmi found Cato at a place he calls Bear Trap Berry Patch."

"We know the place!" Nodded Reno. "When did you go look for them?"

He sighed again. "Cato, . . . well, . . . as you know, it's mandatory that all guides call in on their radios every four hours, . . . it gives us some idea where they are, and if things are all right! . . . But you know all that, . . . Cato carried one, and we expected him to call in at four P.M. on Thursday, and at noon on Friday and when he didn't, we tried calling him, . . . but I couldn't raise him, . . . I gave him another hour to be sure before calling Jimmi," He shrugged then. "I gave Jimmi the sector they should have been hunting in, . . . and him and the hunter he was with set out to look for them." Carl stopped for a moment, having to look away as he swallowed the tightness in his throat away.

"Jimmi made a gurney out of branches and together, they managed to carry Cato back to the campsite. They brought him back here with the horses . . . . Nothing was taken from him, either, not even his radio, . . . except of course, his rifle, . . . and his life, . . . and your mother and father! . . . There must have been a scuffle as well." He reached into his pocket and brought out the wallet.

"Jimmi found your father's wallet." He gave it to Mitch and watched him go through it. "Nothing was taken that I could tell."

"No, it's all here . . . . But whatever took place out there, dad didn't lose it, he left it for you to find . . . . He's telling us they're still alive, he also didn't want them to know who he was . . . Did Jimmi find any tracks, . . . anything?"

"He said that by all indications, there were three large men there, besides Cato and your folks."

"How did he know that?"

"Said he could tell by how deep the prints were. He also said that all five of them left a fairly good trail going North, . . . but he didn't follow it. He brought Cato home instead." He sighed heavily again.

"There's not much you can do here, Mitchell, but wait. General Rinehart is putting helicopters in the air tomorrow morning, some crop-dusting planes as well. There's not much else I can say that will ease your minds on this, boys, . . . or mine for that matter, I'm sorry."

"What about the National Guard, did they find anything?"

"They followed the trail to a place called Rattlesnake Gorge and said they found tracks of a large vehicle at the bottom of it, but couldn't find any going in, or coming out, . . . and none around the top of the Gorge. There was nothing to indicate that the vehicle drove down over the rocks, or drove out over them, no rubber marks on the rocks, nothing . . . . That's all I know at this point, except that like always, when the going got a little too tough, they quit looking! . . . The guardsmen are on their way back in as we speak." He sighed then.

"I guess I shouldn't be speaking of our Government this way, boys, but the men in charge, . . . out here anyway, are the most incompetent people I have ever seen, F.B.I. included! . . . We have had people disappearing in these mountains off and on for two years, now, . . . and these men were called in each time to find them! They quit then, too! . . . Blamed it on the black bears. That's why we're having the hunt, by the way . . . . Here comes your food, you boys eat while I get someone to bring in your luggage, . . . I'll need the keys."

Reno gave him the keys and watched him leave as the food was placed in front of them and began eating, doing so in silence because each of them were deep in their own troubled thoughts, . . . and were until they were finished and Carl returned.

"That's all taken care of!" He sighed and sat down again. "I had your gear put in your parent's room Mitchell. How was your meal?"

"Great food, Carl, like always."

"Thank you, . . . now you boys will not pay for anything while you're here, and I will keep you informed of the search progress as it is reported to me."

"Carl," Began Mitch. "From what you are telling us, this whole search party thing is nothing but a joke! . . . Makes me think they just don't want to find my folks."

"My thoughts exactly, son, but I think I detected something else, what is it?"

"He means they're not going to look for them al all, Carl." Said Reno. "You just got through saying they quit!"

"The ground search, yes. But there will be an air search tomorrow to find that vehicle. I feel pretty sure they will, too!"

"Really, Carl?" Asked Mitch. "Do you really believe that?"

Carl looked at them both and sighed, then slowly shook his head. "No, . . . it will be the same as it's always been, I'm sorry to say! . . . Boys, there have been upwards of thirty people disappear up here in the last two years, . . . and they were never found. None of them on Keyah Grande land, thank God! . . . They were all further North, and every time the country got a little too rough for them, the search was called off, and they conveniently blamed the black bears for it!" He dropped his head then.

"Your mother and father are the first to disappear on Keyah Grande, Mitchell, and there's nothing I can say to make that fact any easier for you!"

Mitch swallowed the sudden lump in his throat and nodded. "Carl, . . . is Jimmi still here?"

"They all are." He nodded. "The F.B.I. made me call off the hunt, so I called everyone back in. Most of the hunters have already left, in a hurry, too once they heard what happened! . . . Why, do you need to talk with Jimmi?"

"Yes sir, and I'd like to borrow him for a few days, if it's okay?"

"What for, son?" He cocked his head and peered at him curiously. "What are you about to do?"

"We're going to find my mom and dad!"

"You can't be serious, Mitchell, . . . good Lord, son, it's dangerous out there, . . . you're just, . . ."

"Kids?" Asked Reno. "You're right, Carl, we are kids, . . . but at this point we're the ones that's dangerous!"

"Like you said, Carl, no one else is even seriously going to look for them." Added Mitch. "But we are serious, and we'll never quit, . . . and I pity the man that tries to stop us!"

"Mitchell, son, I can't let you do this! . . . The F.B.I. is here, right down the hall! So is General Rinehart, wh, . . ."

"You can't stop us, Carl, and neither can they! . . . But it would help a lot if Jimmi could go with us, next to Cato he's the best guide at Keyah Grande."

"Are you boys sure you know what you're doing, . . . do you really have any idea the kind of men you're going after? These men are killers, Mitchell, murderers of the worst kind!"

"And they have my mother and father, Carl, . . . and someone has to find them!"

"And they had better look out for us!" Grinned Reno tightly. "Because we're coming!"

Carl peered at them for a moment then shook his head. "You boys almost make me believe you can find them!" He sighed then and shook his head. "But the reality is this, you are sixteen years old, . . . and even if you were twenty, you wouldn't have the experience to succeed! . . . Men like that will eat you alive! . . . I'm sorry, boys, but compared to them, you two are babies."

"We know that, sir, . . . but we are going, with or without your help!" Said Mitch flatly. "Now what about Jimmi?"

"There's nothing I would like better, Mitchell." He sighed. "Fact is, He would already be out there if he could! . . . Believe me, . . . he would jump at the chance."

"But?" Asked Reno.

"But I can't allow it, . . . Special Agent Howard has said he would put Keyah Grande out of business if I did not keep my people out of the mountains until this is officially over . . . . Mister Bowman is in Denver, . . .

and I certainly won't be responsible for his losing his life-long dream . . . . I am sorry, Mitchell."

"Don't be, Carl, we understand." He looked at Reno and saw him shrug. "Okay, will it be okay if Jimmi shows us a few points of interest on a map?"

"That would be my privilege, and his, I'm sure . . . . I'll call him in, and I'll get an aerial map. Be right back!" He pushed his chair back and left.

"Well, brother," Sighed Reno. "We have taken the first step."

"It's the next one I'm worried about!"

Carl and Jimmi were back in less than ten minutes and the smile, and concern on the guide's face showed his relief at seeing them, . . . and he quickened his step to greet them.

"Mitch, Reno, it's good to see you . . . . I am so sorry this happened."

"We're sorry, too, Jimmi." They shook his hand as Carl spread the map out on the table. "Did Carl tell you what we need, Jimmi?"

"Yeah he did, . . . and if Keyah Grande weren't my home, I'd quit my job and go with you! . . . But I can't do that to Mister Bowman."

"Understood completely, . . . but it'll help if you'll mark some areas of interest on the map for us?"

"I can certainly do that!" He took a black marker and bent over the map to mark a spot with a circle. "Right here is where they supposedly lost the trail."

"Rattlesnake Gorge?"

"That's right! . . . Now I don't know if they did, or didn't lose the trail, but I do know that a truck, car, or whatever that vehicle was, it didn't fly in, or out of that Gorge. It drove out! . . . That Gorge is too deep and narrow for a helicopter, . . . and as wide as they said the tire tracks were, it wasn't a helicopter anyway! . . . That vehicle drove in, and then out of that Gorge on it's own, and by God, it left tracks to follow!"

"Is there any place, any cabins or farms where they could be, . . . maybe someone who might have heard, or seen anything?"

"There's a few old cabins in the areas North of there." He sighed and began marking them on the map. "But I have to tell you, these people ain't going to talk to you about anything, they're mountain folk, and most of them are kin, . . . some of them are my kin. But all of them could shoot you, . . . they don't like strangers."

"There's even more of them further north, a couple of dozen that I can think of, . . . and several of them might be capable of something like this, especially if they know who your father is. All of them are very hard to get to without knowing where a road, or a trail is . . . and I don't! . . . There are roads up there though, probably a lot of them. I know because a lot of the folks up there have vehicles." He circled one of the cabins, barely a speck on the map. "See the house, . . . and that black spot beside it? . . . That's either a car, or a truck . . . . Up here is a blue one. This map can show houses on the mountain, even rocks, canyons and timber, . . . but the camera can't see the roads." He laid the marker down on the map and stood back.

"It would take a dozen good men a solid month to check out every house and cabin in those mountains, Mitch, and then they wouldn't find them! . . . If you want my opinion, . . . find those tracks the truck left and follow them, you'll find your folks at the end of them . . . . The farther you go into them mountains, the wilder it gets, remember that! . . . Remember this, too, . . . any and all of the people living up there will kill you, because most are moonshiners, making shine is all they know, . . . and they will protect their business, so be careful! . . . I don't know much about that far northern area," He drew a circle around it. "That's Sunlight Peak . . . . Between there and here is where you'll find them!" He laid the pen down again.

"If it was me, Like I said, . . . I'd find them tracks that all-terrain vehicle left and stick with 'em. You find that truck you'll find your folks! Now a warning! . . . The mountains are full of Timber Rattlers, mean ones, . . . there's Grizzly Bears, Black Bears, wolves and Pumas, and any of them can kill you, and will if they feel threatened. Stay sharp and keep your ears and eyes open, . . . every one of these animals, even the snake will give you some kind of a warning if you get too close!" He straightened up then and looked at them

"Cato was my best friend, has been since we were five years old, . . . and the men that murdered him are sadistic, sick animals, and they won't give you any warning at all. If they see you, they'll kill you, . . . unless you kill them first! . . . They will not barter, Mitch, don't forget that."

"Neither will we, Jimmi!" Returned Reno. "Thanks for the help, man."

"My pleasure, Reno." He sighed then and stared up at the ceiling for a moment "I'm ashamed that I'm letting you do this alone, when I should be the one avenging Cato, . . . I am sorry."

"We wish you were going with us, Jimmi, but thanks anyway . . . . We'll be heading out in the morning."

"If you are," Broke in Carl. "Do it before daylight. I wouldn't want the F.B.I. to see you leaving. That National Guard unit will be coming back sometime tonight as well, and they're staying in the cabins outside there . . . . Now you boys better get some rest, it may be the last you'll get for a while."

Nodding, Mitch shook Jimmi's hand again. "Cato was our friend, too, . . . thanks, Jimmi."

"I know that." Said the guide. "I'll have horses saddled, outfitted and waiting for you in the morning. I'll be out front!"

"We'll be there." Nodded Mitch. "Good night, . . . Mind showing us to our room, Carl?"

*   *   *

Carl called their room at three A.M. getting them groggily out of bed, but after a shower, they were wide awake and putting on their hunting clothes, . . . the brown and green pants and shirts not giving them the excitement they were used to. They were worriedly silent as they stuffed pant legs into thick leather, high-topped boots and laced them up then breathing deeply, they stood and grimly buckled their holstered side-arms in place around their waist, . . . Reno with his Smith and Wesson, 44 caliber Magnum and Mitch with his 44 Navy Colt, then both donned a brown ammo vest with several zippered pockets, all containing ammunition for both rifle and side arm. A knife scabbard had been sewn inside the vest's left inside lapel and in these, they inserted sharp hunting knives before turning to view themselves in the long mirror alongside the dressing table.

"We look like a two man raiding party!" Sighed Mitch and reached the other holstered pistol from his bag, only this one he put on like a shirt and adjusted the shoulder holster under his left arm, . . . pulled the Ruger, single-six 44 and checked the loads before returning it.

"We are a raiding party!" Nodded Reno. "Or will be when we find Mister and Mrs. Zee! He bent and retrieved the long bow, sliding it over his head and right arm to rest on his back, then the full quiver of arrows over his head and right arm to dangle almost to his side. "We're sure carrying a lot of weight, Mitch, . . . and we still got our rifles."

"We'll tie them on our horses! . . . We'll get used to the weight." He sighed then. "Only problem I see is the heat, we'll need to take plenty of water."

Reno nodded and pulled on his cap, as did Mitch. "We got everything? . . . Chap-stick, iodine, gauze and tape?"

"In my side pockets."

"Okay, I've got matches and, whatever? . . . We're ready, I guess."

"God help us!" Muttered Mitch.

"Amen!" Said Reno and they left the room, stood for a minute in the dimly-lit hallway then made their way past the dining room, across the main lobby and through the glass doors, . . . and once outside, stopped to quickly search the darkness.

"I don't see, Jimmi, do you?" They saw the fleeting, on and off beam of light then and both hurried across the wide veranda, down the steps and toward a lone log cabin at the edge of the trees where Jimmi waited with the horses.

"Right on time!" Whispered the guide. "That National Guard troop got back an hour ago and went to bed. Okay, men, . . . these are the best trail horses we got, the saddles are light weight, and there's two canteens of water on each horse, also a hundred feet of nylon rope. You got bedrolls and blankets rolled and tied behind the cantle and supplies on top of that . . . . You eat sparingly, they can last you a week, maybe more! . . . After that you'll need to hunt, . . . but be careful, you don't know where they are . . . . They could be anywhere, and a gunshot in these mountains can be heard a long ways off.

"There's a gun-boot beneath the stirrups for your rifles." He turned the flashlight on. "Right there, slide them in! . . . Now, I've already told you about the dangers out there with animals and snakes, so you best remember it! You get snake bit, quickly cut an X over the cut and tie a tourniquet above it, it'll slow the venom flow, then find a shade and lie down while the other one goes for help. You might prevent that altogether by always carrying a short stick with you, maybe a forked one, beat the grass on both sides and in front of you as you walk. You see one, use the stick to drive it away, or pick it up and toss it away. You don't see it, the horse will, so pay attention."

"These horses are pretty sure footed, both are used to climbing, but even they can slip and fall. You come to a place that's too steep, or rocky, get down and lead them, they'll climb with you if you hold the reins. If you have to leave them, or they get away, don't worry, they'll eventually come home . . . . And boys, once these search parties are gone, I'm coming after you!"

"We'll be looking for you . . . . Because frankly, you told us a hell of a lot to have to remember!"

"I know, but Reno here has generations of warrior blood in him, those instincts will come alive when he needs them, . . . Just listen to him."

"I always do. Thanks, Jimmi."

"Good . . . . There's a Government Walky-talky radio in your bedroll, that was Carl's idea, . . . I don't know the complete range of the thing, but we all carry one. The base station is in Carl's office, the aerial is on the roof. We monitor it on four, point nine, one, one megahertz, code name, Echo . . . . Do you remember the way to the campsite?"

"I think so, yes." Said Reno. "I know where the Berry patch is, too!"

"Then it's all yours, and you might need this, Reno."

Reno mounted then reached down, felt for and took the flashlight. "Thanks."

"Yes," Replied Mitch. "Thanks a lot, Jimmi." He mounted and reined his horse in behind the dark shape of Reno and followed him down the dark trail.

*   *   *

"Can I ask you something, Pete?"

"I guess so, Mike, but keep th' voice down." He took a quick look to see if they were being watched. "What's on your mind?"

They passed the returning two men before he answered. "How long have you been here?" He went on to deposit his load on the stack and started back.

"I was a driver on one of th' first loads of this Opium Poppy brought in, . . . that was when this part of the operation got started."

"How long ago was that?"

"Over two years ago."

"Then why did you stay, if you don't like it?" At that moment, one of the men was returning with another load of seed, and then the second man and Pete stopped while he went on to shoulder his own load before falling in beside him again.

"Like I said, . . . I had no choice! . . . It was join 'em, or be shot."

"Why, for God sakes, . . . how did you get mixed up in this anyway?"

"I was on th' streets in Denver and they needed a driver, I was broke and they made an offer! . . . Five hundred dollars for one trip . . . . I was out of work! . . . When I got here, they said I had seen too much and that's when they gave me th' option." They stopped talking as the two men walked past and he stopped there to wait while Michael deposited his load again.

"I was the second truck in a convoy of four, one had equipment on it, two had Opium Poppy, and one had twenty young girls in th' back, I guessed stolen from Denver just like I was . . . . Some are still at that table there with your wife, some were moved to work on that damn camouflage, . . . and a few, I didn't see again! . . . Them still here ain't young anymore, neither, been raped and abused too much!"

Michael shouldered his bundle and came back. "Were Jesse and the rest already here?"

"Yeah, Moonshiners, . . . lazy bastards jumped at th' deal! . . . And th' kind a men they were was just what th' Cartel was lookin' for!"

"Cartel, . . . are you talking about a drug Cartel, an organization?"

"Bingo! . . . A Colombian Drug Cartel! . . . Them drivers back there are straight out of Bogata, don't speak a word of English!"

"Good God! . . . And the Marijuana?"

Pete waited again while Michael deposited his load. "The Cartel's idea. They told the Baxters they could have all th' profits from it for th' use of the cave and property . . . . Gave 'em th' plants, showed 'em how to make that crop cover, and how to harvest and dry th' drugs, . . . even told 'em how to get th' help they needed."

"What happens to these people when they're through with them, Pete? . . . What if they get sick, or hurt and can't work?"

"Jesse kills 'em, . . . Bastard likes it! . . . There's a killin' field out there in th' woods somewhere, . . . and you can bet he didn't bury 'em! Now we better end this conversation, Mike, nothin' I said will do you any good anyway."

Michael continued on to shoulder another bale, and on his return. "One more question, Pete, . . . do you mind?"

"Okay, . . . just one."

"What's that constant droning I hear at night, is that a generator?"

"Yeah, it's in th' trees in back a Baxter's old house, and it's a big one . . . . I think that sound is what drove th' old man crazy!"

"Crazy? . . . He didn't seem all that crazy the other day."

"When he runs out a medication, you'll know it! . . . Old Bastard ran out a th' house a couple a weeks ago with a gun in his hand yellin' Revenuers! . . . Shot two men while they carried Marijuana across th' compound, and he did it before Jesse could tackle 'im."

"This place is right out of a horror film, Pete."

"No, Mike, . . . this place is hell! . . . Nobody will ever leave here alive, th' guards will see to that, . . . they're all Colombians, too!"

"And you're the only outsider?"

Bingo again, and I'm lucky they didn't kill me! . . . No more questions now, Mike."

"Thanks, Pete." He placed the bale on the pallet and started back as the other two men came back with the last two bundles from that truck, and he moved aside while the truck was being moved, . . . and with head still bowed managed to make eye contact with Nora as she dipped the heroin onto the scales. He knew she was doing her best, but for how much longer, he was afraid to guess. He had no reason to think that Pete was lying to him about any of it, but he did know that if he didn't find a way out of here, he would be right about their dying here! What was a Colombian Drug Cartel doing by setting up a drug operation here in America, In Colorado of all places? . . . Any why haven't they been discovered? . . . But by looking at that canopy, he knew the answer! From the air it would appear like nothing was here at all, and the high winds would prevent any plane from flying low enough to identify the camouflage as anything other than mountain.

With everyone guarded day and night, sabotaging the canopy was out of the question, too! . . . They were having to repair it every day anyway, and he figured that was because the large birds were playing havoc with it. He also knew there was a radio room in the Baxter's house somewhere, his observance allowed him to spot the antennae as it was being raised late yesterday, but to get to it a man would have to first pick the lock on his ankle iron, find a way past the barracks guard and then cross the entire open area of the compound without being seen! . . . And then, . . . he would have to forget the entire plan, because it was suicide!

This whole abduction was about drugs, he thought sadly. Cato had been right, and even told the F.B.I.. So why didn't they believe him? . . . Was there some sort of pay-off going on, . . . one would wonder? . . . Maybe something that would convince the Colorado Agency to turn a blind eye and deaf ears on this area of the mountains? . . . He sighed and looked back as the second truck was backed into place, and was waiting with the other two men as the sliding door was raised and began unloading.

His thoughts were confusing as he worked. He could not ever remember reading that drugs of this kind were becoming such a problem in the country, Marijuana, yes. That particular substance had been around for centuries, but Heroin? . . . Had he been that naive all his life? . . . Maybe so, he had been so involved with his own future to think of anything else. Hard drugs had been a world apart from his.

Sighing loudly, he deposited the bag of poppy and started back, glancing up at Pete in passing. Pete could be their only chance of escape, . . . if there was any chance at all. But as afraid of this bunch of killers as he was, that could be impossible as well. He would just have to wait and see.

*   *   *

It was late in the day when they finally made the familiar campsite, and Reno dismounted to open the wire-mesh gate before leading his horse inside and allowing Mitch to ride in.

Mitch dismounted to stand and look drearily around the small enclosure. "Mom and Dad were right here four nights ago, Reno."

"Set it aside, old buddy." Said Reno coming to place a hand on his shoulder. "We can't afford to be distracted! . . . Now come on, let's beat the grass in here, make sure no snakes are sleeping around . . . . Female or not, I don't want to sleep with one of them things!"

"Yeah," He sighed. "You're right about that!" They each began walking the inside perimeter of the fence to finally meet each other in the middle.

"No guests for dinner tonight." Grinned Reno as they went to unsaddle the horses. They removed saddles, supplies, everything and deposited them around the remnants of Cato's fire, . . . and by dark were sitting around the small fire and eating refried beans out of small plastic bags with a spoon.

"We've got meat in one of these bags, too!" Said Mitch. "Already cooked."

"We'd best save it, brother." Said Reno. "We each have seven of these bags left, if we want it to last we'll have to eat one at a time, one a day! . . . We can always eat wild berries, onions and such when we find them . . . . We are not going to have time to do any hunting, Mitch, . . . We'll have to keep moving, agreed?"

"You know it!" Mitch finished his beans, placed the empty bag on the fire and wiped his spoon clean with a cotton rag from his food sack then watched Reno do the same before reaching to unbuckle the gun belt and laying the weapon aside. He shrugged out of the shoulder rig and lay it down and then pulled the Colt to check the nipple caps before putting it away again.

"Must have been rough using one of those in the old days." Commented Reno as he watched him. "Takes too long to reload."

"Well, . . . most probably carried two guns, maybe three." Nodded Mitch as he put it away. "I know one thing, . . . when a man got shot with one, he was a goner, . . . makes a hole big as a quarter in front, one the size of a half dollar in back! . . . Like it's gonna do when I find whoever took mom and dad!"

"And you wouldn't hesitate?"

"Reno, I don't think so, . . . as mad, scared and hurt as I am right now, I think I'd empty it on him!"

"Jimmi said there was three men, you gonna leave me the other two?"

"I have my Ruger." He grinned. "If you miss, I'll use it, don't worry, I won't let anything happen to you, brother!" They heard the grunting then, and that was followed by a low, throaty growl that caused the two horses to snort and move around restlessly.

"That has got to be a bear!" Whispered Reno anxiously. "Big, too, . . . could be a Grizzly!"

"I hope it's not hungry!"

"Whatever it is, it's leaving I think." They could hear the animal's retreat through the trees and brush and both sighed a gush of relief.

"We've had bears come close before," Said Mitch as he watched the trees. "But being with mom, dad and Cato made it all the more exciting! . . . It's all different now."

"We'll be okay, Buddy." Assured Reno. "He was just curious, I think . . . . Hear those wolves?" And when Mitch nodded. "He did, too, probably why he left."

"Just so he left." Sighed Mitch as he looked around the small enclosure. "You know what? It took all day to get here, . . . and it can't be more than ten miles from the lodge? At this rate it could take a week, even two if we can't go any faster than this!"

Reno took out the map and spread it between them. "From the looks of it, we've got another six, or seven miles before we get to Rattlesnake Gorge, . . . and that's before we even start the hunt! . . . It could take all day tomorrow to get there, too . . . . Old buddy, looking at this thing, the going is going to be a lot slower, too! . . . Jimmi's right, we're going to have to find the trail that truck left and follow it. And if that trail was going to be easy to find, one would think the soldiers would have seen something!"

"At least the one in charge, don't forget, Reno, most of those Guardsmen are no older than us! . . . Probably wouldn't know a trail if they saw one."

"That's true, . . . but Carl could be right also, and the man in charge just decided to stop looking! . . . Or was ordered to."

"Don't that seem a little strange to you, Reno? . . . The F.B.I. is famous for finding kidnap victims. Why would they call off a search like this?"

"Maybe someone paid that Special Agent Howard to call it off? . . . It's been known to happen. Anyway, you've got Mister Zee's wallet, they don't know who they've got, . . . unless they knew to start with? . . . And that takes us right back to a payoff theory."

"Maybe it's not a kidnapping at all," Said Mitch. "Maybe it is drug related, . . . maybe they stumbled onto something they shouldn't have, and were just abducted because of it?"

"Come on, Mitch, abducted and kidnapped is the same thing. But if it's true, why kill Cato and not Mister and Mrs. Zee? . . . Only reason I can think of is ransom money . . . . They wouldn't need Cato if that's the case, . . . and it sure doesn't explain why the National Guard stopped looking? Carl said this has been going on for two years, and every time they stopped looking after a day or two, what's wrong with that picture?"

"Payoff!" Nodded Mitch. "And it can't be for ransom, not that many people of stature goes hunting up here, . . . I wouldn't think so, anyway . . . . I don't know, you're probably right about the whole thing, Reno. The only thing I do believe, is that the black bears had nothing at all to do with it! . . . And that leaves us with the original question, why were they taken, and Cato was not?"

"Well that's a question I think the F.B.I. should answer, they're the Government? . . . It would be easy for one of them to get the information on

Mister Zee, and they would know he designs and builds aviation equipment for the Air Force, top secret at that! . . . Maybe they think he'll sell their secrets or something."

"Wow, Reno," He shook his head incredulously. "That would be a whole different ball of wax, old friend, . . . you're talking Espionage and Conspiracy here! That could involve a lot of Government bigwigs, . . . maybe even Zant Industries! . . . No, Reno, I don't think we should go there with this! . . . The F.B.I. in Colorado could be involved, and probably are, but I'd rather think you and Jimmi are right about that other thing . . . . It's probably drug related. I don't really think it was a kidnapping for ransom, you remember last year at school, that Kelley Richards character? . . . When they busted him, he had ten grams of Heroin on him in his backpack. That is some kind of hard-core, nasty stuff, old son, and it's catching on! . . . I've never heard of that stuff being on campus before that."

"Let's hope you're right." Sighed Reno. "But none of it explains the abductions . . . . What are they doing with all these people?"

"When we find mom and dad, we'll know, brother." Yawned Mitch. "But right now, I think we'd better get some sleep, I'm already dead tired."

"I think we'll keep the fire going all night, too!" Reno got up as he spoke and when Mitch followed suit, they both went to water and grain the animals. Mitch opened the lid on the large, metal storage container, left there for that purpose, and scooped oats into the feedbags while Reno watered them.

*   *   *

Neither of them remembered the terrain along the worn trail as being that broken, or treacherous and had to walk the animals for most of the morning, The trees were so thick and infested with briars, rocks and dead branches that they were constantly being gouged or scratched by the thistles, . . . and to top it off, the horses were experiencing the same discomfort and they were having to constantly calm them into submission. The rocky ground would suddenly drop off into narrow cracks, some wide enough to force them to jump across the openings.

Flies and Mosquitoes were the worst for them as they appeared as a cloud of pests swarming around them every step of the way, and the heat in the dense forest was stifling, . . . but still they followed the well-used trail deeper into the broken hills.

By late afternoon, two o'clock by their watches, they were nearing the berry patch when Reno suddenly stopped to squat in the trampled grass of the large clearing.

"What is it?" Queried Mitch, leading his horse in beside him. "What did you find?"

"Cato's blood!" Sighed Reno as he looked up at him. "He was killed right here, Mitch, look at all the blood, it's everywhere!" He stood and walked out into the clearing a ways to squat again, and as Mitch stopped beside him.

"Jimmi was right, . . . this print is a good inch and a half deep. This man was a big one, . . . and he chewed tobacco, there's where he spat." Sighing, he stood and was peering at the trail ahead when they both had to quickly grab the reins of both squealing horses to keep them from breaking away in a panic, . . . and that's when they saw the large black bear. The animal was standing on two legs on the berry patch's opposite side and was watching them intently as they quieted the animals.

"What do we do?" Whispered Mitch somewhat urgently.

"Nothing we can do! . . . Hold on to your horse and let's get out of here!" Holding the horse's reins tightly they slowly walked the nervous animals on past the berry patch, . . . and once the bear huffed a couple of times and dropped out of sight, they both mounted the skittish ponies and continued on into the tall grass along the obvious trail left by Mitch's parents and their captors.

The trail was easy to follow in the tall reed-like grass and rocks as the tall weeds and many varieties of leafy undergrowth was laid flat and trampled. But it was not long before they once again were forced to dismount and walk. The rocks were fast becoming larger and the land so uneven as they gradually climbed higher, that they at times had to tug hard on the reins to convince the animals to follow them. The trail itself was becoming harder to follow in the shale and boulders, but they knew where they were going, . . . and by five o'clock in the P.M. they were finally standing on the upper ridge and looking down into the very rocky floor of Rattlesnake Gorge

"Well," Sighed Reno. "This is the Gorge!" He began scanning the deep slope for a way down, and seeing a possibility some twenty feet from them led his mount through the brush and grass and stood for moment looking down the soft dirt of the decline before looking at Mitch.

"Here's where everybody went down at, so watch yourself, brother, don't let the horse run you over, . . . stay to one side of it on the way down!" With that, he stepped off onto the loose dirt and began working his way down the very steep wall of the canyon.

Once on the bottom they both could clearly see the deep ruts left by the truck, one very wide set coming across the floor of the Gorge to run almost the full length of it, and another set going back the same way, and that's where they led the horses to stop and look up the treacherously steep and boulder-covered slope stretching high above them.

"It's got to be fifty yards to the top of this thing, Mitch." He commented. "And it's trying to get dark on us! . . . Okay, right here is where the great National Guard searchers said they lost the trail, . . . and this is where the hunt begins."

"What are we looking for?"

"Anything and everything! . . . First, the truck isn't here, so it had to climb out somewhere. We look for disturbed rocks, broken sticks, black marks on the rocks, whatever looks suspicious."

"From here it looks impossible!"

"It does, don't it? . . . It would take some kind of special truck, that's for sure! . . . Come on, it's almost dark, let's look around, . . . and watch for snakes, there's a reason they named this place, . . . WOW! He yelled. "And here it is!" He bent and grabbed a piece of slender, dead branch from between the rocks and began poking at the grass beside them then suddenly lifted the stick, five foot snake and all to toss the reptile farther up into the large rocks.

"Grab you a stick, brother, and keep looking or we may be spending the night here!"

"Oh, hell no!" Voiced Mitch as he grabbed himself a stick and began searching for sign.

The shadows were deep and dark gray in the arroyo when Reno finally shouted, bringing Mitch and the horses at a trot.

"They went up right here!" Breathed Reno, once again looking up the steep incline. "It was right against the wall here, that's why they didn't find it . . . . That took some kind of a truck to do that!" He looked back at Mitch then.

"See the rubber mark on that rock?" He pointed down closer to the ground, then up at the rock above that one. "Another smear there, and over here the other tire left one. I've never heard of a truck that could do this . . . . Somebody put some engineering into something like that, each axle is working independently, from the looks of it, able to pivot at least a 45 degree angle up or down on either side, front axles, too, looks like . . . . And with all four wheels pulling, . . . no wonder they got out. That thing crawled out of here like a giant spider with eight legs!"

"What now, it's getting dark?"

"We go up right here!" Reno took his horse's reins and began climbing slowly into the rocks, using the dead stick to poke and beat at the tall tufts of grass and poking beneath the giant boulders as he went. Luckily they encountered no more of the deadly asps and it was almost an hour, and full dark as they used the flashlight to finally climb out of the Gorge, only to find themselves faced with even more large boulders and broken terrain. The tall boulders stood out eerily in the beam of light against the surrounding darkness, made even more scary by the towering Pines that grew thick on both sides of them.

"Well, brother?" Sighed Mitch, able only to see Reno's outline beside his horse against the reflected light on the rocks. "Why is it still climbing over the rocks that way?"

"Not to leave a trail on the ground, I guess, . . . and it's working!"

"How far can we track it in the dark? . . . We could be here half the night climbing these things . . . . It's got to get off of them at some point, don't you think?"

"Yeah, you're right." He breathed. "He could rock-crawl that thing a mile away before turning back. Okay, Mitch, let's find us some clear ground. I don't like making camp in these rocks, we're a little too close to that Gorge right here!"

"You got that right!" They used the light to locate a decent spot of clear ground, took time to check the area for snakes and then made a small fire before getting their bedrolls and food.

"Leave the horses saddled, Mitch, they'll be okay for one night, we can water them with the canteen from our caps, . . . and they can eat the grass."

CHAPTER SEVEN

Night birds had kept him from falling to sleep at first, and afterward had been only a troubled one and now, . . . the sounds of revving, lugging engines and grinding gear boxes woke Michael again. He lay listening as not two, but three of the large trucks pulled into the cave area behind the barracks, Only this time one of them continued on past the cave and up the worn pathway to the compound in front of the barracks before it stopped.

Curiosity was strong in him, but he lay still and by rolling onto his side he could see the truck and the men as they got out and moved behind it. He could just hear the voices of Jesse, and what he took to be those of his brothers as they talked to another man who spoke to them in broken English, . . . and by the sounds of that man's voice, he was a foreigner himself and translating for someone speaking in the Columbian dialect. As hard as he tried, the Spanish he had learned in college eluded him somewhat because he was unable to make out more than few words now and them, . . . but he couldn't hear well enough to be sure.

The truck was started again and backed up closer to the front of the house and the engine was killed again. He looked out at the dawning of another day and knew the trucks had just made it before daylight this time, as the deep shrouded gray of day beneath the canopy gave the dawning a ghostly effect. He could see Pete, already up and watching the men at the truck, then saw him move forward as someone approached, . . . that's when he recognized Jesse's coarse voice.

"I want three men to unload this truck, Pete, . . . right now!"

Nodding, Pete came inside to Michael's bunk where he squatted to unlock the ankle iron. "You awake, Mike?"

"Yes, I hear him."

"Wait here, . . . Keep your head down and don't look at nobody when you go out there." He hurried off to unshackle the other two un-loaders and when they came back, Michael followed them across the wide expanse of canopy-covered compound toward the Baxter's old house, and the truck backed up to the porch.

Michael could make out all the men at the truck and besides Jesse, Ethan and the other brother, saw two other men. One of them, he took to be the driver and translator because the other one was well-dressed in a dark suit and light-colored shirt with lace on the collar, . . . he was a dark man with well-groomed hair and a dark mustache that wrapped around both side of his mouth to join with a pointed goatee. The cigar in his mouth said this man was a Cartel bigwig!

The two men with Michael went on to immediately shoulder a large sack of what appeared to be potatoes and each carried one into the house accompanied by Ethan and the other brother, Benji . . . . Michael waited his turn, shouldered his bag and followed suit. Going up the steps he crossed the creaking porch in front of Ethan and entered the musty house while his eyes took in everything along the way.

None of the inner rooms had doors, and it was just light enough to see the furnishings inside each of them. Because of the large sack across his shoulder, he was only able to see the rooms on his left and the first one was large. He could see several chairs, a leaning, but large buffet and cabinet, an old sofa and not much else. The next room is what made his pulse quicken because he had been right, it was a radio room! A table against the outer wall housed the large equipment. He couldn't see any more than that in passing, . . . but it was enough. With Benji looking on, he deposited his load in the large pantry and hurried back through the house, catching a glimpse of the sleeping old man in his bed in the last room on the other side.

He quickly accepted the sack of flour, placing it on his left shoulder this time and hurried up the steps again, this time scanning the first room on his right, seeing what he thought to be a couple of bales of paper on the floor beneath a window, . . . the only other piece of furniture being a mussed up old bed. The next room had two slept-in beds one on each side. He hurried on to leave the flour and come back.

It took the three of them a half hour to unload the supplies and on his last trip, Michael was given a large, tightly bound bale that was similar to those he had seen in the room, . . . and as he crossed the porch Ethan went inside with him and directed him into the first room where he placed that bale on the floor with the others. That's when he saw the corner of a one hundred dollar bill protruding from one of the torn bales. As he stood up, he also saw three more of the bales against the far wall.

"Okay, Slug." Growled Ethan. "Back to your barracks!"

He heard the police whistle as he hurried back outside where Pete and the other two were waiting, and they walked back to the barracks where Pete told them to wait while he unshackled the others. Standing to one side, he waited as they filed out then moved in beside Nora to once again squeeze her hand reassuringly as they all lined up to drink their morning water before going back through to the latrine ditch.

Counting the one he carried in, he had counted six of the large, hay-size bales of what he now knew contained money, . . . and if they were all filled with one hundred dollar bills, there had to be several million, if not a hundred million dollars in that room and from the looks of things, if it belonged to the Baxters, they were not spending any of it! . . . They never left the compound, . . . except to steal their slave laborers, he thought, or maybe to murder someone! But he thought he knew the answer, . . . they couldn't afford to! He also suspected these drug dealers knew they couldn't spend it and that being true, . . . also believed the Baxters may be destined to meet the same fate as the workers when the Cartel decided to shut down their operation, . . . and they surely would! . . . He smiled at the thought of that as he imagined what it would be like to watch it.

Back from the latrine, he waited for Nora again and moved in behind her as they all lined up at the wheelbarrow for plates and spoons.

""I dreamed about Mitchell last night!" Whispered Nora as she bent to take her plate and spoon and straightened up, startling him from his thoughts, . . . and as he reached to get his own plate he frowned as he looked out a corner of his eye at her.

"He talked to me." She had a smile on her face as she went on to accept her ladle of stew.

He was confused by what she said and wondered if she was all right? They had not spoken to each other since they arrived, except for an occasional, I love you, but she had seemed fine. He watched her get her food then got his own and followed her to sit on the ground beside her and eat.

"I'm okay, Michael." She whispered as he sat down. "It was only a dream, I know that, . . . but he spoke to me." She began eating then, . . . as did he.

"He said he was coming for us, Michael, . . . his voice was strong, and loud!"

He nodded and they both continued to eat. But the suddenness of what she had said was starting to worry him. He knew that the mind was not something to take lightly, it was too frail! . . . What if hers was not as strongly sound as he thought? . . . Because he knew there was only a thin balance between sane and insanity, . . . but then again, she could have been breathing in too much of the drug she was weighing. But the mask should take care of all that, . . . shouldn't it? . . . What if it didn't?

""It's okay, darling." She whispered. "I'm okay, and I'm not on those drugs either!" She saw him frown then. "It's not hard to figure out what you were thinking, Michael . . . . I'm okay!"

He cleared his throat, and from the corner of his eyes checked to see if a guard was watching. ""You had me worried, honey." He whispered. "I need you to be okay."

"I am okay, Darling . . . . But I still believe Mitchell is here somewhere and he's coming to find us."

*   *   *

It took them another hour to find where the truck had left the rock roadway and took to the ground, the ruts were fairly deep at that point, . . . and they followed them for a ways before finding where it had began its upward ascent. Reno stopped his horse in the rocks to peer up the tree covered slope seeing the sliding ruts, thrown dirt and debris left by the spinning wheels, . . . and the wide slide marks where it would slip back down before digging in again.

"That's some truck!" Breathed Mitch, also looking up.

"We'll have to lead the horses up on foot." Reno turned then to look over the rim of the drop-off beside them. "If one of these horses were to slip, or fall over backward while we're climbing, it's going to have a long fall . . . . That has to a hundred feet down!"

"Maybe there's a better way up." Said Mitch, looking toward the trees. "Maybe over there."

"Too steep, Mitch, you can tell by looking . . . . We'll have to go up here."

"No use debating it then." He dismounted as he spoke, and with the already skittish animal in tow he started up the steep incline.

After another nervous look over the canyon's crest, Reno dismounted and followed him, both having to dig in and crawl over the loose dirt at times until they could regain enough of a footing to tug their horse's reins and urge them to climb, . . . while at the same time holding those reins tightly against the shifting dirt to keep the animal's head low, because doing this prevented the horse from trying to rear as it wildly pawed the earth for its own footing. After pausing a half dozen times to rest, he was finally tugging the squealing, wild-eyed mount onto a slanting, but more level crest of the hillside where Mitch had stopped to breathlessly wait for him

Regaining some of their composure, they stood to look up the tracks the vehicle had left, following them all the way up the rock-field and into the trees above them, . . . and with a look at each other continued the much easier climb.

Large rocks still infested the hillside as well and literally hundreds of dead, fallen timber and brush along the eroding landscape as they continued to lead their frightened mounts higher up the incline until finally, after what seemed like a very long time they were urging the wild-eyed animals up to the tree-line where Mitch sat down on one of the smaller rocks to rest. Reno tugged his squealing horse the last few feet and sat down on one of the other rocks, and both them and their mounts were breathing hard from the exertion, . . . the animals with white rivulets of caked sweat on their necks and withers, and them with their sweat-soaked clothing.

"That was a little scary, Mitch." Breathed Reno as he looked back down the hill. "And I could wring water out of my clothes, brother . . . . Damn it's hot!" He released the hook at the bottom of his ammo vest and pulled it off. "Should have left this thing on the saddle, like you did." He grunted to his feet, patted the horse on its neck and hung the vest on the saddle horn before turning back to look along the slanted, rock strewn crest.

"Tracks are still going North, too, right along the edge of the trees, . . . and from here it sure looks rough!"

"How far do you think we've come today so far?"

"Not far." He looked at his watch. "It's one o'clock. We might have come a half mile, maybe three quarters, . . . but I doubt it! . . . We walked the whole way, . . . up hill! . . . We're quite a bit higher than we were this morning."

"What are you thinking?"

Reno unbuttoned his shirt and held it open. "See how wet we are? . . . It could get below freezing tonight, brother! . . . We're going to need to make camp somewhere before it gets dark, and we'll need to get a fire going, . . . I sure don't want to get sick up here, not now! . . . Besides, we need to check ourselves for ticks anyhow, they carry the plague, ya know."

"Let's go then," Grinned Mitch. "I'm ready if you are . . . . Do we ride now, or walk?"

"We walk for a while, the horses have to cool down."

"I'll follow you, man." Sighed Mitch, getting off the rock, . . . and as Reno led his horse in the truck's wide ruts along the slanting grade, urged his own horse in behind him and followed.

The next few hours found them in even worse terrain and even though they were riding now, they did not dare push the animals too hard, and kept them at a steady walking pace across the rock littered landscape, and it was covered with dead and rotting timber that had obviously been uprooted by the ongoing erosion of the mountain side. Broken Pine trunks and shattered branches lay where the large trees had fallen, their impacts on the rocks scattering smaller limbs for hundreds of yards down, and along the slopes, . . . and causing them to follow in the all-terrain vehicle's tracks carefully because should they, or their horses be gouged by a protruding branch, blowflies would have a field day. And an infected horse could put them afoot permanently.

However, the truck they were following did not seem to have a problem with the broken terrain at all as the ruts never seemed to waver more than a few feet from its direct line of travel, climbing over the dead timber as if it were not even there, . . . and only swerving to miss some large, lone boulder in its path, deeming it unnecessary to climb over.

The rest of the afternoon went slowly as they were in and out of broken ravines, following the vehicle's ruts sometimes a hundred feet down one chasm's wall before climbing up the opposite embankment, . . . and most of the time on foot. The biggest problem, however, was still the afternoon heat and even though they could see the tops of towering trees swaying in a hard wind above them, there was hardly any at all where they were and because of that, they were forced to be even more cautious, . . . and sharing the water with their horses was fast depleting the contents of the four large canteens. The steamy heat was taking its toll on them as both were near exhaustion as they climbed to the crest of yet another deep arroyo and stopped to rest.

They were high above the massive forest of Pines in the valleys below them, yet not high enough to enjoy the trade-winds. However an occasional gust would find its way down through the tangle of trees, as it was doing now, . . . and both removed their sweat soaked caps to enjoy it.

Reno raised his sleeve to check his watch. "It's almost five o'clock, Mitch, how you making it, brother?"

"I don't remember ever being so tired." He sighed. "Legs feel like rubber." He nodded toward the trees below them. "Guess Carl was right, I see a helicopter down there."

"They're not looking for anything, Mitch, . . . likely some moonshine still. They're Looking in the wrong places anyway! . . . What's that make, eight or ten times today? . . . Probably the same one!" He looked up then at the mountain's crest above them. "I did see a couple of small planes up there today, . . . but they'll be lucky to spot anything that high up, especially that truck!"

"Yeah, . . . By now that truck is already where it was going." Sighed Mitch. "And hid in the trees somewhere out of sight." He looked then to gaze at the deep ruts and followed them with his eyes up the incline to the timber above them, . . . and suddenly became overwhelmed.

"God, Reno, where did they take them?" Tears filled his eyes as he mentally pictured what might be happening to them and released an uncontrollable sob, . . . suddenly becoming so weak-kneed that he sank to his knees on the rocky dirt, . . . and in almost that same instant, the horse reared with a shrieking squeal and jerked Mitch backward, . . . and if not for its reins being looped around his wrist and hand, would have broken away. Mitch yelled as he fell backward, finding himself flat on his back and hurting from the rocks bruising his back, . . . and he was unaware that at the very moment he was thrown backward, the large Timber Rattler had struck at him, striking nothing but air as it missed its target, the snake's momentum carrying its long, thick length up out of the rocks and onto the dirt where it quickly coiled to strike again.

Reno had started toward Mitch when he went to his knees and just saw the monstrous snake as it struck and missed, . . . and just as it coiled again used the stick he was still carrying and began beating the reptile with it until it broke in half. The snake continued to coil and recoil as it still tried to strike at Mitch, who was hanging on to the horse's reins for dear life when Reno finally found an opening and placed his foot on the snake's wide head, . . . and as the reptile coiled its length around his leg, took his hunting knife and severed the head from its body.

Breathing hard he went to help Mitch to his feet and they both watched in awe the writhing, thrashing length of death for several long minutes, both wide-eyed with fear at the close encounter and both gasping for breath! The horse was still squealing as it tried to pull away, and almost jerked Mitch backward again when Reno grabbed its reins and bridal to calm it enough for Mitch to unwrap the reins from his wrist and rub his arm briskly. He was still numb from shock as he stared at the enormous snake.

"Are you okay, brother?" Breathed Reno, still trying to calm the frightened animal.

"Hell no, I'm not okay!" He sobbed. "I almost died!" He wiped at his eyes with his fingers and took the horse's reins again to wrap them around his wrist. "Reno, don't you ever let me hear you say I'm smarter than you, ever again!" . . . Thank you for saving my life, man!"

"It was your horse that saved your life, buddy, not me! . . . Well I guess I did, too, it was still after your hide, . . . anyway, don't embarrass me, Mitch, you'd have done the same for me!"

Mitch nodded then managed a small grin. "I didn't think an Indian could be embarrassed?"

"I'm half Indian." He grinned then went forward to stoop and pick up the snake up by its tail, having to use both hands to hold it up, . . . and there was still a good portion laying along the ground.

"Only snake I've ever seen this size was a Python at the zoo, . . . it's got to be seven or eight feet long! . . . Twenty six rattles."

"Throw the damn thing over the cliff!"

"Looks like Jimmi was wrong about one thing." Remarked Reno as he lowered his arms. "This one never gave us any warning! . . . If I hadn't been watching you, I'd never have seen it! Looks like we were both lucky today, . . . but your horse is the only hero here!"

"Well I'm thanking both of you, now get rid of that thing."

Nodding, Reno started to drag the snake toward the deep drop-off when they were both startled again by the shrill voice of someone yelling at them from the trees above them.

"Heyyyy!" Came the almost squeaky voice again "Stop!"

They looked up to see the skinny old man in what was once a pair of faded Levis, but had long since worn thin at the knees and all but lost their color completely. They looked at each other and shrugged then looked back at him.

"What do you want?" Yelled Reno.

"I want that damn snake, don't throw it away, it's good eatin'"

Reno dropped the snake's tail with its heavy bouquet of rattles, and both watched the brown skinned, and very lean old man make his way down through the weeds, grass and rocks toward them, beating the grass and poking at the rocks with every little jumping step until at last he was standing in front of them and rubbing his hands together.

"That's some good vittles right there, youngsters!" He grinned, looking them up and down as he walked in between them, his pale eyes quick and alert as he looked from them back to the snake. "Yes'ir, heard th' ruckus from camp up there, missed most of it though." He looked them up and down again.

"You boys ain't out a puberty yet, are ye, . . . what'cha doin' up here anyway, this is hard country?" And when they didn't answer him, he shrugged and bent to grab the snake and lay it out lengthwise on the ground between them, . . . then nodded and stood back to look at it first, and then at Mitch.

"You near'bout met your maker today, son." He said nodding at him. "That old Mother's son carried enough venom to kill fifty like you two, . . . Granddaddy is what he is, twenty odd pounds a good eatin'!" He studied them some more then. "Well, cat got yer tongues, what'cha doin' up here?"

"We are following these ruts!" Reno waved his arm down at the tire tracks. "Who are you?"

The old man peered real hard at Reno then and nodded. "You're an Indian, ain't'cha?"

"Half Apache." He nodded.

"Well it shows!" He held out his small weathered hand. "Nice to meet'cha, . . . name's Tucker, Alvin Tucker."

Reno winced in pain from the man's strong grip. "Reno Cortez, Mister Tucker. Meet my friend, Mitchell Zant."

He gripped Mitch's hand and looked him in the face. "Good to meet you, too, boy, . . . you got sadness in ya, son." He turned back to look at the snake then.

"You boys can call me Pot-luck, most people do that knows me, . . . got me a camp up yonder in th' trees a ways, . . . and I'll make you two a deal! You help me tote this hunk a meat back up to camp you got a invite to supper, . . . yer gonna need to dry out them duds anyway, freeze ye to death tonight, ye don't! . . . Now come on, be dark in a few minutes."

Reno looked at Mitch and both shrugged then looped their horse's reins around their arms again and between the three of them, spent the next fifteen minutes scaling the slope's brush and rocks with a thirty-pound rattlesnake in their arms.

*   *   *

Mister and Mrs. Bowman got out of their Buick and both were smiling at sight of Carl and two of the guides coming toward them. They were a handsome couple neither one resembling their middle aged status, but rather appearing like what they actually were, successful, happily married business owners in an occupation they both loved.

This area of the Keyah Grande, so called by the Pueblo Indians has always teemed with wildlife. Elk, Deer, bear and wild Turkeys roamed the meadows and forests, as well as the vast array of canyons and Mesas of the San Juan Mountains. The lodge itself was not a great distance from the infamous Chimney Rock and was a popular retreat for most everyone in the four state area, . . . including United States Senators and other Government officials from time to time. But this was a time of trouble for the Bowman's, and it was evident on their faces as they were welcomed home.

"Welcome back, Ames," Greeted Carl as he shook his boss's hand. "I'm glad you're here, sir." He immediately took Mrs. Bowman's hand and kissed it. "Welcome home Catherine."

"Thank you, Carl."

"Is there any news yet about the Zants?" Asked Bowman as he took his wife's arm and walked with Carl up the steps.

"Not a word, Ames, . . . and they've called off the search again, . . . the National Guard pulled out a half hour ago."

"After two days search? . . . Good God, what's wrong with them Sons of bitches, don't they know who Michael Zant is?"

"Evidently it makes no difference, . . . because I asked them the same thing! . . . Rinehart said there was no trail to follow and without one, there was no hope of finding them. He did say he had ordered local law enforcement to continue the search, . . . they have helicopters and crop-dusters in the air now, . . . supposedly!"

"What good will that do, the sons of bitches know a plane can't fly low enough up there to see anything?

"Oh, no, . . . They said the truck they used would be easy to spot from the air, so that's what they're looking for!"

"No good Bastards are full of shit!" He spat. "What about the F.B.I., they still here?"

"Special Agent Howard left Sunday morning, his four men, too. He did say he would check on the progress, and that if we needed him, he would return."

"Ass hole! . . . If we need him, . . . his own wife don't need him! . . . Special Agent, my ass!"

"Ames." Soothed Catherine Bowman softly as she squeezed his arm. "Remember your blood pressure, dear."

"Yes, dear, I will, thank you . . . . You go on ahead now and get ready for dinner, I want to talk more with Carl. Go on now, I'm all right!" He sighed as she followed the guides and their luggage on through the glass doors and across the main lobby. "He is still an ass hole!" He growled as they went into the lobby and ushered Carl on into the large dining room to sit down.

After Carl had filled him in on what had transpired while he was away, even to his lengthy argument with Rinehart and Howard, Carl looked at him and sighed heavily. "I have something else to tell you now, Ames, and you won't like it any better."

Bowman frowned at him then raised his hand, quickly bringing the young waitress to their table. "Bring us some coffee dear, please?" And when she had left. "Let's have it, Carl."

"Young Mitchell Zant is here, Reno Cortez as well."

"In the lodge, right now?"

Carl shook his head. "In the San Juans."

"What the hell for? . . . No, don't tell me! . . . They're looking for Mike and Nora! . . . Why didn't you stop them?"

"I tried!" He gestured helplessly with his hands. "They said no one could stop them, and I believed them, . . . so would you if you had seen their faces."

"Dear God!" He sighed. "I'm going to be responsible for the destruction of not only Michael Zant's entire family, but the only son of the Cortez family."

"Oh no, sir, you can't be blamed for that!"

"Maybe not, Carl." He sighed. "But I sent the invitation. It's devastating, Carl." He accepted his coffee from the girl and sipped at it.

"What about Cato, you notify his family?"

"Yes sir, . . . his father and brother came for his body Saturday."

"When is the funeral?"

"Two o'clock tomorrow . . . . I have the information."

Bowman sipped more of his coffee and sighing, looked around the empty dining room for a minute. "Place is like a morgue!" He said, turning back around.

"Are all the guests gone, too?"

Carl nodded. "F.B.I. said to call in all the guides and hunters and that's what I did, . . . the last of them left this morning . . . . How was your trip, by the way?"

"Hell, . . . we waited two days for a meeting, Carl, finally got word that it was set for this morning at ten A.M., five days from the original appointment date! . . . Ahhh, hell with them! . . . Anyway, your call took the wind from my sails, we left for home shortly after . . . . How long have those boys been gone, Carl?"

"Before daylight, Sunday morning . . . . Ames, Jimmi has been chomping at the bits to go after them, but so far I've managed to hold him back! . . . Agent Howard said that until he said so, no hunter or guide was to go into them mountains. He said if they did, he would close you down! . . . He said there was to be no activity of any kind until he officially closed the investigation."

"Oh, he did, did he? . . . Well you tell Jimmi to pick his men and go find them, Carl, . . . and tell him I said to find those boys. At the very least, they're going to need some help! . . . Tell Jimmi, I said to bring everybody home!"

*   *   *

Pot-luck Tucker's camp consisted of a fairly large and time-worn tent that was anchored by ropes between two large Pine Trees at the top, . . . and the bottom of the old tent was held down by wooden stakes driven into the ground every few inches all around it. Bedding and cooking paraphernalia lay strewn on the inside and in front was a cooking fire with three iron rods placed teepee style across the top and wired together at the tips, . . . and served to support the cast-iron pot hanging over the fire. Hewn blocks of Pine were placed at different spots around the fire pit.

An axe, a hatchet and a carving knife were stuck in the top of one of the stumps, . . . and one skillet, a tin bowl and a large wooden ladle dangled from one of the taut tent ropes. Everything else that happened to be on the ground consisted of a fresh water bucket, a wooden keg, a homemade dredge for washing gold, a metal splash pan for stream panning, a short-handled spade, pick and a pry-bar. All else was for comfort's sake, such as it was.

Mitch and Reno took it all in at a glance as they carried the reptile into camp and lay it down, then they both stood aside while the old man tied a length of rope to the tail, threw the other end over a pine branch and hauled the snake off the ground.

"You boys sit." He chuckled. "I don't gut this thing now, it'll ruin. Go ahead, stump or ground, suit yourself!"

They tied the horses to another low branch in reach of the tall grass then seated themselves on the hard blocks to watch him. Pot-luck had the rattler skinned, cleaned, and the meat chopped up in the cast-iron pot in under ten minutes, . . . leaving the foot and a half wide, seven foot long snake skin hanging there to dry. Without a word, he poured water in the pot to cover the meat, and then put more wood on the fire. Reaching a tin can from a sack behind him, he added salt, and other seasoning before covering the pot with a lid.

"Got a boil it first." He nodded, looking up at them. "Then I'll roll it in flour that's been salt and peppered and fry it up, . . . tastes just like chicken, it does." He came on to sit down beside them on the ground and crossed his legs before looking back at the monster snakeskin. "See 'at skin there, there's folks would give me fifty dollars for that, and I got a couple dozen of 'em! . . . None that big though . . . . I been huntin' that old Granddaddy snake for weeks, set traps fer it and ever'thin'. Get up in th' mornin' and he done ate th' rabbit and left th' trap empty!" He looked back at them then. "You boys was lucky." He nodded. "Okay now, what brung you boys up in this wilderness chasin' tire tracks?"

"Tell him, Mitch, . . . maybe he saw something."

"They kidnapped my mother and father." He shrugged then. "They were hunting bear at Keyah Grande hunting lodge . . . . These men murdered their guide and took them hostage!"

"Search party couldn't find the trail and quit looking!" Added Reno. "We didn't!"

"Good God almighty, boys!" Muttered the old man as he reached his pipe from a pocket and packed it from a sack of tobacco. "I seen your truck, I did." He took a burning twig from the fire and lit his pipe. "Wee hours a th' mornin', it was, motor noise woke me up so I went to look! . . . Th' thing come up that hill just a growlin', it did, crawlin' over 'em rocks and timber like a big-assed Tarantula spider, it was! . . . Yeah, I seen it! . . . Looked like a ghost, weren't a light one on it!"

"What morning was that?"

"Oh hell, time and date don't mean much up here, son, . . . let's see now, today, yester'dy, three days ago, no, four nights ago, it was now . . . . A big tall son of a bitch, it was, too, and all spotted lookin! . . . Couldn't tell that much about it in moonlight."

"That has to be them, Mitch, four nights ago was Thursday night!"

"Where would they be going, Pot-luck?" Queried Mitch. "We know they're going North, but what's out there? . . . Can you think of some place?"

"They's cabins all over them mountains, son, . . . one in that valley where you was gonna throw that snake, . . . all got trucks, too, . . . but nothin' like what I seen, no, sir! . . . Nothin' them shiners got will do what that thing done."

"Then there has to be some roads up here somewhere, . . . except we haven't seen any of them?"

"Nope, nary a one this high up, . . . they're all down below yonder . . . . Some on th' other side a th' mountain behind us there . . . . You won't find 'em though, that's cause most a these folks up here are moonshiners, they hide th' roads, yes sir. You find a road up here, it'll be cause you ain't lookin' fer it! . . . Be in th' trees so them helicopters and planes can't spot 'em!"

"How about North, any that way?"

"Well, I seem to recall one or two, used to be was a moonshiner lived way back in there somewhere, course that was a few years ago. Had three sons, he did, . . . and I seem to recall a sickly woman at one time. Anyways, I know that cause they used to bring shine down to th' store in Cimmarona and sell it! . . . Might not be up there any more, though, ain't heard tell of 'em in a long while now."

"Where is this place?" Asked Reno.

"Oh my, it would be a good twenty mile across yonder . . . . Just pick out th' tallest peak ya see and head fer it!"

"Twenty more miles in this mess?" Sighed Mitch dejectedly. "Mom and dad could be dead before we find them, . . . or out of the mountains somewhere completely?"

"Don't think like that, brother, or we might not find them . . . . remember the pledge we made, okay? . . . Those tracks out there are going to lead us right to them, I promise!"

"I know you're right, Reno . . . . Don't worry, I'll never quit!"

"damn tootin' he ain't!" Cackled Put-luck. "I ain't never quit neither! . . . Heyyy, you young'uns best get out a them wet duds, clean down to yer drawers, go on, they's blankets in there to cover with! . . . Go on, get it done now, hang 'em on th' ropes there, be dry by mornin'." He got up and lifted the lid from the pot as they undressed, grabbed the ladle from its wire hook and stirred the meat.

"You a moonshiner, too, Pot-luck?" Chattered Mitch as he hung up his clothes.

"Me, oh hell no! . . . I wouldn't fool with that shit! . . . I'm a prospector, . . . that's my rig and tools over there."

"Gold?" Asked Reno, also hanging his clothes up to dry out.

"Ain't nothin' better! . . . Been doin' it nigh on fer fifteen years now."

"If you don't mind my asking, . . . have you found any?"

"Is a rattlesnake poison? . . . Have I found any?" He got up and rummaged around in his belongings then tossed them two blankets.

"I didn't mean to offend you, Pot-luck," Said Reno as he caught the blanket and wrapped it around him. "It's just that looking at all this you know, the way you live and all, I thought, . . ."

"I know what ye thought, son . . . . Why am I livin' like this, stead a down there in some town? . . . Well I could be, ya know, might some day, too!" He placed hands on hips then and nodded. "Okay, you young'uns seem like honest people to me, come over here." He went to his knees in the tent and moved the bedding aside enough to pick up a cover of branches that had been tied tightly together with heavy twine, and sitting it aside revealed a three by three by two hole in the ground and grinning, reached in with both hands and lifted out a heavy deerskin bag, tied at the top with a string of rawhide.

"You ever see a gold nugget, either one a ya?" And when they said no, he untied the string, reached in and brought out a handful of the precious metal. "Jest look at that, . . . have I found any gold, hah! . . . Go on, touch it, hold it, . . . that's pure gold, it is, . . . and I got four more bags just like this 'un in that hole there . . . . And just between you boys and me, this ain't th' only cache I got neither!"

"It is pretty." Nodded Mitch. "Heavy, too . . . . Worth about four hundred dollars an ounce on today's market."

"You're holding more than an ounce in your hand." Nodded Reno.'

"More like four or five." He said giving it back to Pot-luck. "But isn't that a bad place to hide it?"

"Oh, I'll move it before long." He retied the bag and returned it to the hole.

"Okay now, . . . one a ya grab that tin bowl out there, and one a ya get that skillet, I'll bring th' flour." After everything was prepared, he put a small slab of deer fat into the skillet, placed a piece of wire mesh on the fire and put the skillet on it. He dipped flour into the tin bowl, then a generous portion of salt and pepper and mixed it together, . . . next he lifted the lid from the boiling pot and with the ladle dipped the snake meat out and dropped it into the flour and rolled it around.

"You boys see them big leafed weeds off yonder in th' trees? . . . Ye can barely see 'em there. Them's wild turnips, wild onions there, too, go pull up some." He began placing the meat in the skillet while they picked their barefooted way across to the wild vegetables and pulled them, and a half hour later they were all sitting on the ground on blankets and eating rattlesnake and raw vegetables.

"Hey, not bad!" Laughed Reno as he chewed. "It does taste a little like chicken."

"Told ye, . . . rattlesnake's good eatin', . . . and this old timer was due fer th' skillet, too. No tellin' how big he would a got, you hadn't killed 'im?"

"We sure do want to thank you, Pot-luck." Said Mitch.

"Nonsense, . . . Yer th' first people I talked to in a while, . . . get's pretty lonesome up here at times . . . . Now eat up, got plenty more here!"

*   *   *

Pot-luck had the fire going before waking them up, and while they dressed and buckled on their weapons, he was frying up more of the rattlesnake meat for breakfast

"You youngsters got yourselves a hard row to hoe in them mountains yonder." He said as they finished. "And findin' your folks ain't gonna be easy! . . . But if ye do, here's somethin' to think about. Men like them fuckers are nasty mean, as soon shoot ye as look at ye! . . . Now, if'en your folks are still alive, they'll be locked up somewhere, likely be guarded, too . . . . Now hear what I'm sayin' here, . . . there's gonna be more than just them guards guardin' 'em, . . . gonna be a lookout guard somewhere else to warn 'em you're a comin', . . . remember that! . . . I learned all that in W.W. two, . . . I was a sniper! . . . Nearly got me kilt a time'r two learnin' that."

They sat down as he dipped meat onto their plates, and accepted them in silence.

"Where do you think a lookout would be?" Asked Mitch as he chewed. "How will we know him?"

"You'll know 'im, be armed to th' teeth, he will! . . . Be somewhere along th' way, before ye get there . . . . Maybe a cabin, maybe a tent, ye never know, . . . but he'll be there!" He looked at the two of them in the fire's light then.

"You boys bring a coat'r somethin', it get's colder'n hell at night where yer headed?"

"We'll manage, Pot-luck, thanks for everything."

"Awww, that's my pleasure, son, I hope all th' luck in th' world fer you boys . . . . Oh, I filled yer canteens with fresh water, . . . put a few a them turnips in yer vittles sack, too, . . . makes fer good eatin' while yer ridin'. Now eat up, times a wastin'!"

"I was wondering," Said Mitch again. "Do you walk everywhere you go?"

"I mostly do, but Naaa, . . . I got me th' sweetest lil Spanish Mule ye ever did see! . . . Got 'er own little shed down by th' crik, plenty a hay and veg'tables to eat."

"Well I know this will sound dumb, Mister Pot-luck," Said Reno. "But what is a Spanish Mule?"

"Cross between a horse and a Jackass, 'bout all I can tell ya . . . . Most I ever seen was about half th' size of a full growed mule, and better lookin'! . . . Looks more like a horse than a mule does, better lines, ye know. Only ones I ever seen was when I was a youngster, till now, that is . . . . Used to be some rich folks come by th' house, had a pair a matchin' Spanish Mules pullin' th' carriage . . . . Always thought them mules was th' prettiest things! . . . Anyway, my gal thinks she's a race horse, I think."

Accordin' to th' Moonshiner I got 'er from, near 'bout all of 'em are th' same color and size . . . . And My Charlott is one of 'em! Friendliest, most hard workin' mule I ever seen. She don't balk, bite or try to lay down on ye like reg'lar mules, no sir, . . . I treat 'er right, too!"

Reno looked at Mitch and shrugged before sighing and looking up at the brilliant, and very cold star-studded sky. "I feel like I just went to sleep a few minutes ago." He yawned. "And you're right, it's freezing!"

"Told ye!" He chuckled, eating a mouthful of meat. "Been thinkin' on that truck yer trackin'." He said as he chewed. "It don't look nothin' like trucks I seen up here, . . . looks more like a Army truck to me, 'ceptin' it's been worked on! . . . Thing's a lot taller, got wider axles, wider tires, . . . and them axles, . . . never seen axles bend like 'at before. But it's a Army truck, prob'ly Army Surplus, got camouflage an' ever'thing like Army." He pointed his spoon at them and shook it.

"Yer lookin' fer a high-dollar Army truck!"

CHAPTER EIGHT

They were made to watch another session at the whipping post during last night's meal, and that was what Michael was thinking about as they sat on the ground having their morning warmed over breakfast. He was now of the opinion that a man did not have to do much of anything wrong to be punished, in fact, he wondered if the subjects were not just randomly chosen and flogged, . . . and that making everyone else watch it was just a ploy designed to keep the rest in line, . . . and it seemed to be working! He came to this conclusion when he noticed there were hardly any cuts or blood from the victim's wounds, except when Jesse would become overly excited. He was sure the pain was just as extremely agonizing to the man being whipped and their backs must hurt like hell for days after, but they were always able to return to work the next day, . . . their injuries were not crippling!

"I love you, Michael." Whispered Nora as she suddenly broke his chain of thought.

He spooned stew into his mouth as he watched the guards, and when he was sure they weren't looking dropped his hand off his lap to squeeze her knee. "I love you, too, Darling." He whispered. "Don't forget that, please?"

"Never!"

He removed his hand and had to quickly blink away the sudden moisture in his eyes. He couldn't lose it now, he thought, he needed to be as strong as the other victims here, . . . they've all been here much longer than we have. One thing is for certain, he thought then, . . . if he did find a way out, he would do everything he could to get everyone out! . . . His heart went out to several of them because some must surely be in their fifties, or older, their long hair and beards were almost totally gray, . . . and how they were coping day in and day out, was something he couldn't quite understand. But he did, too, in a way because they were likely retired Military, and survival was something they learned from experience, . . . and discipline was something they were taught

However, they all had that same haggard, downtrodden and hopeless look on their faces, and especially those with wives here, . . . or at home not knowing what had happened to them? He was sure though that most of the women working the fields of Marijuana were the wives of someone that was here, with the exception of a few maybe, . . . and those working the cave. Some of those appeared to be quite young, and according to Pete were brought in by the Cartel. These girls were victims of urban abductions, leaving mothers and fathers to grieve over their losses.

The order was given to return their plates and spoons then and they got to their feet to join the line behind those in front of them. He urged Nora ahead of him, and once their plates and spoons were in the bucket headed toward the cave

*   *   *

After having heard Pot-luck's warning to watch for rattlesnakes and Grizzlies, Mitch and Reno left the campsite to once again head northward in the ruts made by the all-terrain surplus truck, . . . and as the sun topped the monstrous Pines and began to warm them up they both removed their ammo-vests again. As usual, insects began making pests of themselves again as well as causing them to constantly slap at face and necks in efforts to swat them.

But at least, they were able to ride for a while as the landscape was becoming more flat, rocky and timber strewn, . . . and the dead wood was literally everywhere, but passable if taken slow. The ground was becoming more like gravel, too, with less and less topsoil to show the truck's wide ruts, . . . and it was not long before Reno had to resort to finding the rubber marks on rocks again, or timber that had been crushed by the vehicle's weight.

It was mid-morning when Reno stopped his horse and reined it around in the narrow space between two large boulders. "We're coming into timber up there, Mitch, and from here the trail leads right into the thick of them, . . . so we better rest the horses here, I think."

"You can still follow it in the trees, can't you?"

"There'll be bent grass and brush in there to show us the way." He nodded. "And I've got the flashlight." He looked off down the rocky slope then. "The ground is breaking away down there again, we're probably going to be scaling another canyon before long." He sighed then and stared at the trees again. "Those trees are still about a half mile away, and uphill!"

"What else is new, be nice to find one of those roads up there." Breathed Mitch, also looking up at the trees.

"Yeah, it would! . . . But we've got some more walking to do before we get there, and a lot more rocks and grass to go through. You got your stick?"

He held up the dead length of wood. "This stick will never leave my hand again, brother!"

"I didn't think so." He laughed. "Well, come on, let's get it over with." He led off again and a short time later they were dismounting to lead the horses up the almost solid, boulder-riddled hillside, . . . and constantly beating the sparse patches of shoulder high grass as well as poking beneath and between the rocks for the coiled killers. Reno called a halt three different times along the way while he used the stick to discourage, kill, or toss one of the reptiles away from their chosen path of ascent until they were finally at the line of ancient, towering Pine Trees, . . . and here is where they stopped once again.

"I hate snakes, Reno!" He remarked as he looked back down the slope and shivered. "That truck rolled over one or two of them, too, did you see them?"

"Yeah, . . . but it never touched the ground all that much . . . . Okay, keep your stick ready, snakes live in the woods, too, come on, brother, . . . it went in right here."

It was well past noon now, and they were still following the debris of crushed grass and undergrowth left in the wake of the large truck. Broken limbs, thick with pine needles and cones lay in their path and were kicked or moved aside to make room for the wide-eyed horses to walk without spooking them.

It was steamy hot in the dense forest of Pines and quite dark, with only an occasional patch of sunlight filtering through to highlight their way, . . . but the path they had taken through the maze was just wide enough and making Reno think that the truck had to have come through this way as well, . . . and more than once! Mosquitoes, gnats and large flies constantly swarmed them, drawn by their sweat and exhaled carbon dioxide, . . . and the sweat was drenching them once again.

Neither of them had said a word since entering the maze of trees and except for an occasional nickering, or snort from one of the animals there was no sound at all save the constant buzzing of insects, . . . or a slap on the neck. The forest reeked of rotting leaves and undergrowth, but was tolerable until Reno's horse decided to relieve it's self in the most nauseating way, forcing Mitch to try and avoid the miss-hap in the almost total black of the forest-floor.

The heat and insects almost had them exhausted by the time they found the small clearing and the patch of luscious looking, large black berries, . . . and here was where they decided to stop again to sample the fruit.

After using their sticks again to check for snakes, they each began gorging themselves of the juicy berries.

"You ever tasted berries this good, Reno?"

"Not in a long time, if I have." He said as he peered at the dark trees that surrounded them. "But we're probably not the only ones that think that either, you recognize the smell?"

"Now that you mention it, I do . . . . I can see it now, too, several piles of it! . . . Think I just lost my appetite, too." He started scanning the trees then. "Wonder haw far these woods go?"

"I wish I knew." Sighed Reno. "But it don't matter, that truck went right past here. The bears are probably still too scared to come back!"

"Well that damn thing has got to stop somewhere, Reno, . . . We've been following these tracks since Sunday and here it is Tuesday . . . . Where in hell are they?"

"Take it easy, buddy, . . . we're just a little too anxious, we'll get there! . . . Besides, . . . just because that truck had to move a little slow, it was still able to move five times faster than us, . . . and it didn't stop to sleep. We'll find them, brother."

"Did you just have a birthday or something, Reno?"

"What?"

"I just wondered, because you're beginning to sound more seventeen, than sixteen." He grinned. "Just keep reminding me, else I'll lose it again."

"Oh," He nodded. "No problem, Mitch." He looked around again. "I don't know what it is, but you're right! . . . Sometimes, and especially today for some reason, . . . I feel like I know exactly what I'm doing, and what to do! . . . It's almost like I've been here before." Still grinning, he looked past Mitch as he spoke, . . . and his eyes grew very large. "Forget what I just said, Mitch, and don't move, buddy!"

They both heard the heavy puffing of the bear then as it entered the clearing and when it saw them it reared up to it's full height of what looked to be twelve feet tall to the frightened pair.

"Grizzly!" Breathed Reno as he gripped Mitch's arm. "We have to go, brother."

Neither horse had yet smelled the intruder and was in fact eating the half dry grass as Mitch and Reno moved around them to mount, . . . and at the moment they were in the saddle the bear opened its enormous mouth and emitted a loud, grunting growl. The unnerving sound instantly filled the small clearing with such suddenness that the startled horses squealed shrilly and bolted, all but unseating the boys as they leaped to a hard run into the trees.

They managed to rein them hard enough to steer the animals back onto the path left by the truck, and were several hundred yards from the berry patch when they finally regained control, stopping the hard breathing mounts in the dark of the trees. Dismounting painfully, they both pulled pine needles and twigs from where the slapping branches had deposited them in their clothing.

Oh, shit, Reno!" Gasped Mitch as he touched the welts on his face.

"I believe I did!" Breathed Reno. "Now be quiet, it might be following us." They both listened intently for any telltale sounds coming from behind them and when they heard nothing above the sounds of their horses' breathing, finally calmed themselves enough to relax a little.

"My God, that thing was a monster! . . . Did you see the size of that thing?"

"I saw the size of it's everything, brother, . . . now let's get away from here!" He led his horse back around. "Keep your ears open, Mitch, dad says a running bear makes a loud grunting sound when it's front paws hits the ground, you hear it yell, okay?"

"Don't worry about that! . . . But what if it's not running, you thought about that?"

"I'm trying not to, now come on, these trees can't last forever!"

"Lead on, brother." He fell in behind Reno's horse again, but this time at a much faster pace than before. They continued to follow the truck's wide trail through the dark of the trees for another couple of hours before finally seeing daylight ahead of them, . . . and a short time later were leading the horses out of the dark forest of trees and onto yet another very rocky and treacherous looking downhill slope.

They led the horses down through the soft dirt and shale and were cautious not to slip or fall, or to allow the animals to gain too much momentum as they also could slide into the man leading them and knock him down or worse yet, stumble and tumble down onto the rocks below. Either way both knew that if it happened it would be the end of their hunt, . . . for if they themselves were not mangled, or crippled by the falling horse, the horse could be killed and set them afoot.

Once on the bed of the deep arroyo, Reno stopped again and looked up at the sky, then checked his watch before looking back up the hill."

"Damn, Reno, you look like you've been in a fight or something, your lip is bleeding, . . . and you've got red welts all over your face."

"Then you know what you look like, brother." He grinned then winced as he touched his lip. "Damn trees tried to kill us!"

"It's better that, than being mauled by a Grizzly." Grinned Mitch then also winced and reached to rub his mouth and nose. "Not much better, I don't think."

"That truck went right along here." Sighed Reno as he followed the tracks with his eyes. "And right up the other side over there, you ready?"

"As I'll ever be!" He looked at his own watch then. "We wasted four hours in that jungle up there!" He followed Reno and his horse across the rocky floor of the mini-canyon and furtively watched the ridge behind them, half expecting to see a thousand pounds of Grizzly bear coming out of the trees.

"We'll make camp again when we reach the top." Said Reno loudly as he looked back at him. "We have to dry these clothes again."

"Might have to peel mine off!" He replied back. "Feels like they're glued to my body . . . . How far do you think we've come today?"

"Hard to tell, . . . three, four miles, maybe more . . . . Not far enough!"

"Twenty more to go!"

"How do you know that?"

"Pot-luck said that tall peak was twenty five miles away."

"We can't go by that, Mitch . . . . Mister and Mrs. Zee could be anywhere in between here and there . . . . But he did say one thing I believe is true."

"What?

""They will have a lookout somewhere between us and them."

"Then we'll have to be more careful!"

"That's an understatement, Mitch! . . . Okay, brother, meet you at the top." He started the climb toward the upper crest of the gully and tugging the reluctant horse up the slope behind him, once again forcing the animal's head low to prevent it's trying to rear.

*　　　　　　*　　　　　　*

It was afternoon by the time Michael and the other two men began work at unloading the third truck that had arrived overnight and ever since they had unloaded the Baxter's supplies yesterday, he had been curious to know why Pete had been avoiding him, . . . if he was? At any rate he had not been walking beside him so they could talk, . . . and as yet had not done so today. He had about resigned himself to the fact their friendship was over when to his surprise Pete suddenly appeared beside as he carried the heavy bundle of poppy.

"How ya doin', Mike?"

"Hello, Pete, . . . I had begun to think I made you mad at me."

"Naw, . . . them fuckin' foreigners been watchin' too close, that's all, . . . how's your wife holdin' up?"

"Pretty well, considering! Thanks for asking, Pete . . . . Tell me something." He left the question hanging as the other two came past them and went on to place his bundle down before coming back.

"Who was that man with the supplies yesterday, . . . the fancy one?"

"Hell, just another Colombian hatchet man, Mike, like the rest of 'em. He's usually th' one that delivers th' Baxters their share of th' wealth."

"From the looks of it, they don't spend any, either!"

"Hell, they can't spend it!" He laughed. "Somebody might wonder where they got it?"

"And the Cartel wouldn't like that, would they?"

"What do you think?"

Michael went on to grab another bag and come back. "Then tell me what good several million dollars is going to do them?"

"Not a thing! . . . It'll all go back to the Cartel as soon as they're done here."

"What do you mean?"

"I've been talkin' with Ramon Silva, . . . he's one of th' other guards, the friendliest one! . . . It seems th' Cartel will operate one a these places for a few years, or until they think it's time for the odds to turn against them, . . . then they'll change locations."

"What happens to all of us?"

"They won't leave any witnesses, Mike."

"I wish I hadn't asked!"

"Sorry, Mike . . . . That does include me, by th' way."

"Now, I'm sorry, Pete."

"Don't be, . . . I'm not goin' out without a fight!"

"That makes two of us! . . . Is all this slated to happen any time soon, you think?"

"This one's been here for three years, Mike." He sighed then. "It took six months and twenty workers to put together that mesh cover up there, and they have to constantly do repair on it! . . . It's gonna fall apart one a these days and some airplane will spot that dope field. It's gettin' pretty rotten!"

"Think there'll be any warning?"

"They'll come at night." He sighed. "We won't have time to prepare for it! . . . One morning, instead of poppy bein' on them trucks, there'll be men with machineguns."

"Pete, . . . you do know how to make a man's day!"

"I do what I can."

*   *   *

It took more than half an hour of lost footing, sliding and clawing at the loose dirt on the slope to finally make the crest, but they did and as they both stood beside their sweating horses and looked back down at the bottom, they could see where the truck had had a time of this one as well, . . . it had veered and slid it's way almost a hundred feet further along the embankment before rolling over the top.

They led the winded animals along the crest until they found the deep gouges in the rocky turf where the truck had come out and followed the ruts toward the North again for another hundred yards or more before finding a good spot between several large boulders.

"Looks pretty good to me, Mitch."

"Suits me, if it does you." They led the horses inside the grouping of rocks and unsaddled them, and taking time to use the large cotton towels Jimmi had supplied to rub them down, . . . and then watered them by pouring water into their rain-proof caps.

"I think we should use the rope and tie them to one of these big rocks for tonight." Sighed Reno. "They've been spooked a lot today, . . . might not take much to run them off!"

"Let's do it then." Said Mitch bending to remove the nylon rope from his saddle.

With the animals taken care of, they found wood for a fire and soon had a crackling blaze going and then, after retrieving their bag of meat that Jimmi had thoughtfully prepared for them, Mitch brought the turnips and they both sat down by the fire to eat.

"I don't know about you," Said Mitch as he chewed and watched the sun's last caress on the rolling sea of Giant Pines in the distant valley. "But I'm not up to sitting around in my skivvies again, . . . I'll just sit closer to the fire and dry them . . . . Wouldn't help much anyway as filthy as I am, I stink worse than the horse I'm riding!"

"I wondered which one of us would complain first?" Grinned Reno. "I haven't seen enough water to bathe in anyway, . . . and I thought there was lakes and streams all over these mountains?"

"I saw two or three large lakes below us a day or so back, . . . and old Pot-luck said there was a creek somewhere behind his camp. But other than that, zilch!"

"Well, we got them towels, brother." Said Reno. "And we got water in the canteens, what do you think?"

"Think we might need the water to drink?"

"You're right." Sighed Reno as he chewed more of the meat and swallowed. "We could be another two days away from Mister and Mrs. Zee! . . . Anyway, I think we should keep the fire burning all night tonight."

"What if the kidnappers are close enough to see it?"

"I think it's less of a chance than we've been taking anyway . . . . Besides, . . . I still have a bad feeling about that bear, and I want to be able to see it!"

"You don't think it followed us?"

"Dad says they have a history of it. Grizzlies are meat eaters and that one did see the horses! . . . Those berries are only treats anyway, like ice cream is to us! . . . He did say they mostly only eat something that's already dead, but they have been known to kill cattle and horses," He looked at Mitch then and shrugged. "And on very rare occasions, a man! . . . Who knows, maybe we intruded on his personal berry patch, he did mark his territory?"

"Stunk to high heaven, too!" Nodded Mitch.

"Anyway, I don't trust the damn thing!"

"You've got me worried now, too!"

"We've got enough fire power to kill it, I think!"

"And maybe warn the kidnappers?"

"Yeah," He sighed. "I guess you're right. "I guess a rifle is out of the question, which means," He looked back at his saddle. "We do it the Apache way."

"That's one big bear, Reno?"

"Maybe he's not following us at all." Nodded Reno as he looked at the darkening sky. He ate more of the salt meat from the bag and held his hands closer to the fire. "Well, it's already cooling off, Mitch, . . . I think we should get out of these wet shirts at least, don't you?"

Throwing the empty food bags on the flames, both got up to move their saddles closer to the fire and removed their shirts, draping them over their saddles to dry. Spreading their blankets on the ground as a mattress, they sat down again to wrap the cover blankets around their upper bodies.

"How do we sleep tonight, Reno, . . . one at a time?"

"Don't worry, brother, . . . if old Slew-foot gets within a hundred yards of us, the horses will wake us up!" He grinned then and reached to pull the longbow from behind the cantle, hiked his leg through it to bend it then hooked the cord's loop over the notched end of the bow, then removed his leg and tested the pull.

"This is the best bow I've ever pulled, Mitch, . . . it'll send an arrow plumb through old Slew's heart, guaranteed!"

"I hope so, brother. All I've ever heard about a Grizzly is how thick their hides are, and how hard they are to kill."

"Yeah, . . . Seems I heard that, too . . . . But it's either this, or the rifles?"

"We could be screwed either way."

"Beats being dead, my man!" Nodded Reno, and he had a serious expression on his brown face. "And old pal of mine, I don't plan on being dead!"

"I think I was right about you," Grinned Mitch, and when Reno frowned at him. "You're maturing far too fast for a sixteen year old high school graduate . . . . You are in your element here, buddy."

"Yeah, I do sort of like it up here." He sighed then and retested the bow. "Always have. But I'm not all that mature believe me, I'm shaking like a leaf inside! . . . It's just that we are here to do something we have to do, and if we don't, my God Parents could die! . . . And that don't make me a Daniel Boone by a long shot!"

"You're right." He sighed. "We could be the only chance mom and dad have, . . . but don't sell yourself short either, if not for you, I might have let grief get us both killed already."

"Mitch, we can pat each other's backs all night, but it won't change the fact that we don't know what we're doing, . . . or what we'll do when we find them . . . . You are the smart one, brother, so start working on that strategy !" He grinned and tossed Mitch one of the wild turnip bulbs. "Now eat your veggies, maybe the spirits will tell us what to do tonight?"

"The spirits are your department, Tonto, but you're on!" He grinned and bit into the large bulb.

*   *   *

Jimmi and the three guides slid and grappled their way down the steep embankment into Rattlesnake Gorge, and with their flashlights found the deep ruts left by the big all-terrain vehicle and followed them to the rock and dead timber infested slope, . . . and that's where they stopped.

"This is where the National Guard lost the trail." Said Jimmi as they shined their lights up on the rocks. "Maybe they did, maybe not, but one thing is for damn sure, . . . that truck didn't fly out of here, so let's look around. If you can't find where that truck went up, look for Mitch and Reno's tracks, they had their horses with 'em." He watched them spread out along the base of the steep wall of rocks, their flashlights urgently lighting up the huge boulders and tall grass, . . . and sighing, he began his own search.

He knew by the size of the ruts, and the axle width that the truck was large, . . . and the ruts had clearly showed it coming in this way, and leaving the same way. He also knew that there was not any vehicle he ever heard of that could crawl down a wall of rocks that large, let alone crawl up them again, . . . it just was not possible! . . . He remembered seeing dune-buggy type machines do incredible stunts in impassable places, but not one of them could have accomplished this. This truck would need a suspension system like on one has ever heard of!

However, he was sure of one thing, . . . every tire on every vehicle was made of rubber, and rubber leaves some sign of it's passing, . . . every time! He cupped his hands around his mouth and yelled at the others

"Look for burnt rubber residue on the rocks, tops and sides, . . . and watch for sn, . . ."

"Whoaaaa!!!" Yelled one of the men suddenly, and quickly turned and ran.

Jimmi saw the large snake as it struck, it's momentum carrying its entire length out of the cover of rocks and onto the dirt of the canyon's floor where it quickly coiled again, . . . but by then the intended recipient of the strike was twenty feet away with his flashlight on the killer. The next closest man quickly used his search stick to toss the serpent back up into the rocks before turning to shine his light on Jimmi.

"The only thing we're gonna accomplish in the dark, is snake-bit, Jimmi!"

Jimmi sighed dejectedly and walked back toward them. "Okay," He sighed as they all stood together. "That wall of rocks is where that truck came down here, and it also left that way, these tracks prove it!" He shined his light back at the slope. "But so help me, God, I don't know how?"

"Well, I don't know of a truck that can do that!" Voiced James Mason, the oldest of the group. "A half-track, maybe."

"Maybe it was lifted out by one a them big Army choppers." Suggested another, and when he got no response. "Just a thought, Jimmi."

"And it's not out of the question, jack, . . . but I don't think so. Something like that would require planning, and would have been seen by somebody . . . . Any more suggestions?"

"I got one." Said Mason. "We know that truck left here by climbing out . . . . If it did, there's got a be tracks up there at the top somewhere, . . . and our horses are already up there, so let's go around. Hell, it might be a mile out of our way, and rougher than a cob, but it'll beat climbing up that damn wall and gettin' snake bit!"

"Okay James, . . . that's also the smartest thing to do, thanks . . . . One of you shinny back up to the horses and toss us down a rope."

*   *   *

"Come on, Mitch, wake up!" Urged Reno, gently shaking him. "Mitch, wake up, man!"

"NOOO!" Sobbed Mitch and quickly sat up in his blankets. His eyes were red and his cheeks wet from the tears as he blinked wildly and looked around at the large boulders . . . . He blinked again as he finally focused on Reno. "Wha, . . . is it here?" He quickly stared past the licking flames at the darkness beyond the camp.

"The bear's not here, buddy." Smiled Reno. "And you can stop pretending now, I know all about what you're going through and how hard you've been trying to hide it! . . . And I want to tell you it's okay."

Mitch stifled back another sob and swallowed quickly as he breathed deeply of the freezing air. "Sorry, Reno, . . . I can't even think about them without wanting to cry . . . . I have to keep other things on my mind all the time, afraid I'll lose it."

"I know, I've been listening to your nightmares for the last three nights, brother. They were your own private grief so I didn't wake you, but you were yelling tonight and scaring the horses."

"I saw them die, . . . and I couldn't get there to help them! . . . It was so damn real, man!"

"It was a nightmare, brother, that's all . . . . Most dreams are based on fantasy, remember, you aced that subject? A nightmare is about some underlying, . . ."

"Underlying, unconscious fear, I know!" Interrupted Mitch.

"There you go, you have an underlying fear for the safety of Mister and Mrs. Zee, . . . you unconsciously believe they are going to die and it's natural, they're your mom and dad! . . . Well, brother, I have that underlying fear myself, I believe they're going to die, too, . . . if we don't get there in time. But we will, Mitch, believe me." He smiled at the look that came over Mitch's face then, and shrugged.

"What can I say, . . . I aced psychology." And as they both laughed, both horses snorted loudly and began nickering nervously as they pulled at their halter ropes, . . . their restless hooves kicking up small tufts of dirt as they stared wild-eyed into the darkness beyond the camp.

"Oh, shit, Mitch!" Breathed Reno as he reached back for the bow and the quiver of arrows.

"You think it's the bear?" He asked fearfully. "Maybe it's wolves or something?"

"I'd rather see the bear than a pack of wolves!" Said Reno nervously.

"Well where the hell is it?" Mitch got to his knees as he also began peering into the darkness, and a thick mist from his rapid breathing clouded his immediate vision and still, they could not see more than ten feet of the rocky terrain in the light from the fire. He slowly picked up the flashlight and turned it on, the beam lighting up the ground and rocks some twenty yards out.

"Can't see anything but rocks, Reno, . . . where the hell is he?"

Reno got to his feet and pulled on his now dry shirt, and then his ammo-vest for warmth. "Watch the horses, Mitch, they can't see it either, but they'll be looking where it is!" He saw Mitch look back at the horses then quickly moved the beam of light where they were looking.

"There, Reno, see it?" He gasped loudly and jumped to his feet. "Where did it go, I saw it?"

"It's behind the rocks out there, probably raised up for a look when you saw it." He pulled an arrow from the quiver and shakily inserted it on the bow. "Mitch, brother, . . . You might ought to grab your rifle and hold on to them horses, just in case . . . . And put on your shirt, you're freezing me to look at you!"

Nodding, he grabbed his shirt and pulled it on, then the vest and with the flashlight still focused where the horses were looking, pulled the Marlin from the boot and got to his feet to move slowly back to grab the animals' halter ropes. He saw them both turn their heads and look to the opposite side of the camp then.

He quickly focused the light beam where they were staring. "It's over here, Reno!" He blurted. "On your left, there, see it? . . . Damn, it's gone again, but I saw it!"

"It's circling us, buddy." Gasped Reno, slowly holding the bow ready and turning to follow the flashlight's yellow beam as it played on the surface of the huge boulders. "It's stalking us, Mitch!" He blurted in realization.

Placing the halter ropes in the crook of his arm, Mitch slowly levered a cartridge into the chamber, the sound causing Reno to look at him.

"Don't shoot that thing unless I miss, brother." He said nervously. "Or if I don't kill it! . . . And brother, if you have to, put every bullet you got in it, you hear me?" He grinned at him then. "We can dry our pants out later!" And when Mitch stared curiously at him, he shrugged. "I just pissed in mine."

"Then you're a little late!" He nodded. "Whoaaa!" He said quickly as the frightened animals moved their bodies around to face the danger. "I might not be able to hold these horses, they're too strong!"

"If that thing charges us, don't worry about the horses!"

"I know that's right!"

The large bear continued to circle the campsite in the darkness and each time it did, would move a little closer to them in the rocks, . . . and all the while trying to avoid the flashlight's beam of light, . . . possibly seeing the light as some form of unknown danger. Whatever the reason, it seemed to be a deterrent, and it appeared to be keeping the animal at bay or at least, keeping it cautious! . . . But after what seemed to them an hour or more, they could tell the beast had managed to close in on them because now, the bear's breathing was quite audible in the ice-cold stillness. They could also hear the occasional grunt as it walked.

The frenzied horses continued to give Mitch a problem as they tried to free themselves and run. His hands were frozen and almost numb as he gripped the ropes in one hand and the Rifle in the other. Heavy mist from the horses, and his own breathing was a constant thing, and he wrapped his arm in the ropes to make holding the flashlight easier because he couldn't see anything. The bear was now successfully avoiding the light altogether . . . . But they knew it was close, it's breathing was telling them so.

"Can you see anything, Reno?" He asked in a low voice, quickly cutting his eyes enough to see Reno crouched with the bow in his hands. "The horses are looking right in front of you now . . . . You think it's leaving?"

"Be ready, Mitch!" He whispered. "That's what it wants us to think, now don't talk, okay, you'll make me miss . . . . Shine your light in front of me!"

No sooner had he spoke, and the flashlight's beam was positioned when the grizzly charged, all twelve hundred deadly pounds of it, and grunting loudly with every leap. It's size did not seem a hindrance as it quickly covered the dozen or so feet between them in what seemed to be less that a heartbeat, it's eyes glowing bright red in the light's wavering beam

Reno's own heart leaped into his throat at sight of the monster, and his arm movement felt like a slow motion movie as he raised the bow with a quivering arm, pulled the cord as quickly as he could and released the steel-tipped projectile. The monstrous bear was only a lunge away from ending Reno's young career when the arrow buried it's self deep in the animal's thick breast, bringing a very distinct, and loud growling grunt from the beast as it's head suddenly dropped down into the rocky turf, the momentum causing its body to flip up and then over to crash into the large boulder in front of the fire, and bringing another painful grunt from the animal as it struck the rock and careened backward onto the rocky ground.

Terrified, and yelling shrilly, Reno picked another arrow and fitted it to the bow as the grizzly suddenly regained its feet, . . . and as the fearsome beast raised itself onto its rear legs to lunge forward again, he released the second arrow almost at the instant of the Marlin's ear shattering explosion.

All twelve feet of the creature's rearing height shuddered violently as it was struck, and then it just suddenly collapsed and fell backward, . . . the sound of its falling very distinguishable in the rifle shot's fading echoes. It had been sudden, . . . and it had been loud! . . . But then it was over.

The horses were squealing loudly and hauling Mitch violently off the ground in their frenzy, . . . and as terrified as he was himself, had dropped the Marlin and was hanging on to them for dear life!

Reno became conscious of his own yelling when the bear went down and closed his mouth as his own legs gave away, sending him to his knees beside the flickering fire.

Mitch finally managed to quiet the horses and with his heart beating in his own throat rushed to drop to his knees beside Reno. "You okay, Buddy?"

They looked at each other and then both broke out in tears, sobbing helplessly, . . . their relief coming from deep inside of them in gut-wrenching release.

"I've never been that scared before." Sniffed Reno after they had regained composure. "I think I would have died if you hadn't shot it . . . . Thanks, brother."

"I had to turn the horses loose to do it!" Breathed Mitch. "I could picture you being mauled, man, . . . and I guess everybody knows were here now!"

"If they do, I'm glad!" Nodded Reno. "They'd better get ready, brother, cause we're on our way! . . . Not bad for a couple of sixteen year old punk kids, huh, Mitch?" Sighing profusely, he sat back on his haunches and stared at the bear.

"And you know what, . . . we just took out the meanest killer that ever didn't carry a gun, all two thousand pounds of it!" He looked at Mitch then. "And you didn't hesitate under fire, old buddy . . . . You can't get more mature than that!"

"Thanks, Reno."

"What for, you did your job, we both did! . . . And I think them God blamed kidnappers better look out for us, because we are coming for them!"

"Damn right! . . . But I still hope they didn't hear the shot."

"Only one shot? . . . They'll think it's just some hunter, Mitch." He sighed then and reached to unlace his boots and tug them off his feet, then came the socks before standing up to unbuckle his belt and pants, . . . and when he saw Mitch's face; "What, . . . you think I was joking?" He looked down at himself to show Mitch the front of his pants, . . . and as they both laughed he pulled them off, under pants and all in the freezing cold and spread them across his saddle. They were still laughing as he wrapped his cover blankets around himself and sat down again.

"Yours don't look so dry, my friend."

"You're right!" Laughed Mitch, and followed suit.

*   *   *

Jimmi took the Army surplus radio from his pack, pulled the aerial out and set the dial before pressing the button. "Charley calling echo, come in echo, over!" He released the button, and after a few long seconds of nothing but static mashed it again. "This is Charley calling echo, come in, echo, over?"

"Go, Charley, this is echo, where are you, over?"

"North of the Gorge, made camp for the night, what's left of it, over."

"You find the trail, over?"

"No, sir, not yet. We hope to find it at daybreak . . . . Echo, those searchers didn't lie, we found no sign of the vehicle leaving the Gorge, over."

"What about the boys, over?"

"Couldn't find where they climbed out either, too dark! . . . We stopped looking when Drew nearly got snake bit. Over."

"Be careful out there, men! . . . Call again when you find the trail, I have a feeling those boys are in trouble. Over."

"You got it, echo, out!" He put the radio away and looked at the others before staring out at the large boulders surrounding them. He couldn't believe they found no tracks between any of the large rocks to indicate the truck's passing, . . . unless, he thought, unless it stayed on top of the rocks so as not to leave any! . . . If it did, it would need to change course some, because the rocks were more numerous west of them a ways. That would be the place to look! He looked at the others then.

"It's not long till mornin', guys, we better get some sleep."

"Jimmi," Queried James Mason. "What if we don't find any tracks tomorrow?"

"Come on, James!" He sighed then. "As far as I know, trucks don't have wings! No wait, . . . I apologize, James, . . . it's just that, . . . things like this just don't happen. There's not a truck of that obvious size ever made that can do what it appears this one did, and we all know it was not a half-track! . . . That damn thing came up that slope back there, and it did it on the rocks, . . . how, I don't know? . . . Damn thing should have broke apart being twisted like that!"

"Yes sir," Agreed James. "Unless it weren't a normal truck . . . . Them Army trucks got one hell of a Grandma gear system, put th' damn thing in gear at idle speed and it'll climb a forty-five degree hill all by itself. What I'm sayin' is this, . . . somebody with a whole lot a smarts, and a ton a money worked on th' thing . . . . And they done some very big alterations on it!"

"Has anybody ever told you, you make a lot of sense, James?"

"Well, no, . . . but I helped my older son build up a couple a dune racers, and them things could go just about anywhere and over some damn big rocks, . . . and it all had to do with suspension, transmission and overall drive-train! Expensive as hell, too, . . . but of course, pocket-change compared to what somebody spent on that truck!"

"I agree with you, . . . and here's what I think . . . . We know it drove out on them rocks, . . . and I think it stayed on the rocks after it got out and if it did, . . . it went farther to the west of us before the rocks played out! . . . We saw how thick the rock-field was out that way, because we had our flashlights and could see it, . . . now look around us here . . . . We are going to find those tracks a couple hundred yards out that way and when we do, we'll find those two horse's tracks right along with them! . . . Somehow, that Reno kid found the trail in th' rocks. I know because their horses were in that gorge with them, . . . and if he can read sign like that, you can bet your ass they're still following that truck! . . . We could learn a lot from that Apache Kid! . . . We call ourselves trackers."

*   *   *

The sun was just threatening to overpower the dawn when the restless animals woke them up again, causing both boys to sit upright on their bedding and wildly look around the small rock enclosure until finally their eyes came to rest on the ton of Grizzly carcass not more than six feet away from them. They stared as if mesmerized, a frozen mist emitting from their mouths and blankets pulled tightly around their naked lower bodies. Finally Mitch released his pent-up breath and glanced at Reno then sighing, reached for his underclothing and began to get dressed.

"Aren't you cold, Reno?' He asked as he got up to pull on his pants.

"What?" "Gasped Reno and turned to look up at him. "I'm freezing, man!" He threw off the blankets and grabbed his own clothing. "What's that smell?"

"The bear, I guess." Said Mitch as he buckled his belt.

"Too cold last night for that!" He looked around as he stepped into his pants and grinned. "Bear had something to do with it, though."

Mitch saw him look and looked also. "Man." He laughed. "Scared them more than it did us, huh? . . . I know they gave my arm a workout, my whole shoulder is sore!"

They were both fully dressed in fairly short order and after buckling on their weaponry, rolled up their bedding and tied them behind the cantles then picked up saddles and blanket and set about saddling the horses.

"Want to eat something first?" Queried Mitch as he slid the Marlin in the boot.

"Not with that smell, you go ahead."

"I'll pass, too." He coiled up the rope and looped it in place then both of them poured water into their caps to let the animals drink before drinking themselves.

"Talk about ice-water!"

"Got ice in mine." Said Reno. "And they were beside the fire! The other two is frozen solid, I bet." They replaced the canteens and led the animals out of the campsite and past the dead bear. "Won't anybody believe this, Mitch."

"We will." They led the horses out into the large rocks and threaded their way back to where the truck's deep ruts were evident and stood gazing at the towering, somewhat ominous dark blue and green mountain in the distance.

Sighing a cloud of icy breath, Reno climbed aboard the groaning saddle, followed by Mitch and still, they sat for a minute to stare up at the mountain.

"Wonder where they could be?" Muttered Mitch, and then breathing deeply of the cold, mountain air. "If mom and dad's as cold as I am, they must be miserable."

"Don't think about it, it'll just depress you." Reno turned in the saddle to peer at the surrounding thick, forested mountaintop above them, and then below them.

"That canyon appears to be a deep one," Mitch commented. "Could be a mile long or more, too."

"And there's smoke down there, . . . and more off yonder!"

"Moonshiners, maybe?"

"Maybe, . . . We should have brought your binoculars with us." Added Reno.

"Why, . . . you think it's them?"

"Mitch," He sighed. "I have no idea! . . . I do know that anything is possible in this God forsaken place."

"I thought you were at home here?"

"We've been at home long enough!" He looked back at the zigzagging trail of deep ruts then. "Tracks are still going toward that mountain there, that means Mister and Mrs. Zee could be anywhere between here and there! . . . Mitch, if old Pot-luck was right and it was sometime Thursday night when he saw that truck, . . . it could mean they got to where they were going before daylight on Friday."

"How can that be, Reno, . . . We had to walk most of the way, and it's taken us four days to get this far?"

"We haven't seen any campsites, Mitch, . . . and they wouldn't chance that truck being seen in the daylight. If they had stopped, we would have found signs of it . . . . Nights are pretty long up here, . . . they could have gone fifty miles by morning."

"They'd have to average thirty miles an hour for thirteen hours." Mused Mitch. "Is that possible with no roads?"

"For that truck, it might be. At any rate, I think we had better go slow and keep our eyes open from now on . . . . I also think old Pot-luck was right, . . . whatever and whoever these bastards are, what they are up to is not legal, . . . and they will have a lookout somewhere between us and where they are."

"If they do, he heard that shot last night!"

"We can probably depend on that!"

"How far to that mountain, you think?"

"I don't know, five miles, maybe more, can't tell up here. It's not the biggest one, but it's big enough. They wouldn't be on top of it anyway, airplanes could look down on them! . . . They'd be lower down, I think, in a thick cover of trees someplace." He sighed a heavy mist then. "I don't know what I'm talking about, Mitch, you know that!"

"It makes sense to me, now lead out will ya, we're burning daylight!"

"Yes sir!" He grinned then gigged the horse into one of the wide ruts, with Mitch close behind him.   •

*   *   *

Michael was awakened once again by revving engines and the whine of gears as the two large, single axle trucks entered the pre-dawn compound behind the barracks and once again, mentally tracked them on to the cave area where they stopped. He sighed heavily, seeing the heavy cloud of mist in the freezing air as he did then stared up at the dark, cobwebbed barracks roof as his thoughts turned to Nora and how thin she was looking . . . . But then again, so was he, along with everyone else in the slave camp. No one was getting enough to eat, no means to brush their teeth, or to take a bath, other than to sponge themselves when given the opportunity. The watery stew they were fed twice a day was hardly enough to keep up their strength, . . . and no one even dared ask for more.

But he thought he knew why they were kept hungry, with just enough strength to give a full day's work. Exhaustion was a good deterrent for those thinking of escape. He mentally placed the position of his barracks in conjunction with the other two, as he had been doing every night until exhaustion put him to sleep, . . . and then again every morning when the trucks came in. His barrack was next to the drying shed, and the drying shed was parallel to the pathway leading to the cave. The Baxter's house bordered the pathway on the East side and was shrouded in trees along the base of the looming mountain, . . . and facing the compound.

The next barrack abutted theirs on the West side, a solid wall separating them. That one housed those working the marijuana field and canopy repair. A carport of sorts was between that barrack, and the guard's quarters and housed the large all-terrain vehicle. The guard's quarters were at timber's edge where the downhill angle of the Mesa's rim plunged sharply down into the broken area of forested canyons and gullies below. The guards took turns sleeping, usually leaving only five or six on duty during the day, and only two at night in the compound, and two at night at the cave.

Pete was assigned to Michael's barracks and slept on a cot just inside the open-sided entrance. He stayed with them all the time, day and night, . . . and Michael was thankful for his alliance with the burly guard, however thin it might be because as long as they were friendly there would always be the chance for escape. He dwelled on this again as he watched Pete's sleeping form not ten feet away.

He thought again of the truck that brought them here, and because he was an engineer himself, still marveled at the vehicle's abilities and maneuverability. They had been tossed around in the truck's covered bed so violently that he had lain on the floor between the metal benches with Nora clutched tightly in his grasp for most of the night, their captured feet and tightly joined arms screaming from the numbing pain and lack of circulation.

He could tell there had been something different about it because he could hear the bumping and grinding the axles made beneath them as they were being so rudely manhandled by gravity. They had been moving quite fast at times as well! But as yet, he still had not been able to mentally estimate the distance they might have traveled that night, . . . but somehow he knew that it really did not matter.

He knew, even though to date he had not conversed with any of the other abductees, other than to acknowledge by nodding, that they were the recipients of the so-called bear killings Cato spoke of, . . . and therefore, him and Nora were here because a Baxter had insanely murdered two of them. He had no idea where they were, or what part of the San Juans they might be in, but he had not heard a helicopter, or a plane since their arrival, . . . nor had any of them seen the open sky above them, except through the tightly-woven camouflage. Pete was right, he thought, they were in hell and as of the moment, with no way out! Sighing, he saw the guard's approach and watched him shake Pete awake. Time for another day at the mine, he thought grimly, . . . and there was no mirth in the thought.

CHAPTER NINE

"By God, we know it didn't fly out a that gorge now, don't we!" Said Jimmi as they sat their horses and stared down at the deep, wide ruts, . . . and the prints of two horses were quite visible inside of them. "You're the man, James, . . . good thinking."

"Oh, no, Jimmi, . . . was me, I'd still be over yonder scratchin' my old head, . . . it was you had this idea! . . . But it don't really matter, we all want a piece a them Bastards!"

"Let's go then!" Nodded Jimmi and led the way through the rocks.

*   *   *

It was mid-morning when Mitch saw his horse's ears prick forward and it was followed by a nervous nickering that caused him to quickly scan the timber's edge some thirty-odd yards to the right of them, . . . and he was about to dismiss the warning when he saw the dozen or so shadowy figures slinking through the trees.

"Hey, Reno!" He called to stop him and once he reined his horse around, Mitch nodded toward the trees. "We're being stalked again."

The large gray wolves had stopped when they did and were now watching them from the shadows.

"Timber wolves, I guess." Sighed Reno. "Big ones, too."

"They look hungry to me."

"Wolves are always hungry, probably see us as riding a couple of large steaks! . . . As long as we're on our horses they won't try anything. Dad says wolves are afraid of people, . . . they won't attack unless cornered."

"Well I'm not about to corner them, let's go."

Grinning, Reno continued to follow the zigzagging ruts through the uneven field of large boulders and splintered remnants of rotting timber, while Mitch nervously watched the gray predators and followed him. It was noon or after when Reno called a stop and waited for Mitch to pull alongside.

"What is it?"

"Something doesn't feel right, brother." He said as they both sat and stared down the sloping jumble of rocks. The trail was quite visible as it twisted and turned its way down the steep decline.

"What are you feeling? . . . Do you think we're close?"

"I don't know, . . . but these ruts clearly go into those trees down there." He looked at Mitch then. "And tell me you don't smell smoke in the air?"

Mitch sniffed the air a few times and finally nodded. "Yeah, maybe I can." He half-whispered. "It's not all that prominent, but it's definitely there! . . . Where's it coming from?"

"From nowhere right now, I think . . . . It's just remnants of what was left in the trees, maybe, I don't know."

"Think we've found the lookout?"

"I'd say it's a pretty fair chance, brother." He sighed as he studied the trees. "If it is, we are real close, because I've got a strange feeling about those trees down there."

"What sort of feeling?"

"A weird one, . . . I don't know, it just don't feel right!"

Okay then, what should we do, . . . If he's down there, he's going to see us if we ride down that slope? . . . And we don't know where he is!"

"We'll just have to find him . . . . You're the tactical engineer here, brother. Put that brain to work."

Mitch sighed and stared at the monster trees for a minute and then also at the towering pines to the right of them. "All right, Reno, . . . if that lookout is down there, he'll be watching this slope, . . . and that would put him somewhere in the trees right close to where that truck went in . . . . We can't leave the horses up here to go look for him either, we'd have to stake them out and those wolves would appreciate that! . . . The racket would alert the lookout, too, if they attacked." He looked at Reno and shook his head. "If he's not down there, and we lose the horses, we're on foot!"

"Well, brother," Chuckled Reno. "I think you just covered all our options!" He sighed then. "What do you think?"

"God, Reno, . . . as much as I hate it, . . . I do not want to ride down that hill."

"That makes two of us, so what do we do, walk down, . . . he's still going to see us? . . . And what about the horses, like you said, we can't leave them here?"

"We'll have to turn them loose . . . . We'll tie the reins around their necks and run them off . . . . Like Jimmi said, . . . if they survive, they'll go home!"

"God, I hate this!" Breathed Reno as he looked back at the trees. "Okay, it's your show, how do we do it!" He dismounted as he spoke, and so did Mitch.

"We use the trees." They each took a full canteen and hung it around their neck, and did the same with the rifles. Reno strung the longbow and put it, and the quiver of arrows over his head and shoulder then stood and peered at Mitch. "We'll be in trouble if he isn't down there, brother, you know that!"

"Well I don't have a better idea." He shrugged. "I do know that we are still ten miles from that tall mountain off yonder, maybe farther than that! . . . So, before we do this, . . . if you think we should just take our chances and ride down there, we'll do it, . . . old Pot-luck could be wrong about it? . . . But if he's not, that could put that lookout right down there where we think he is! . . . Want to toss a coin?"

"Brother," Sighed Reno with a shake of his head. "You are confusing hell out of our logic here!"

"I know, but I'm just saying that if he's not down there, we'll be walking all that way with an extra fifty pounds of weight on our backs, that's all."

"Well I don't have a better idea." He shrugged then and looped the reins around the horse's neck and tied them to the saddle horn.

Sighing, Mitch did the same and both turned the animals around to face back the way they came then suddenly whacked them sharply on their rumps, sending them squealing into a startled gallop back along the rocky landscape.

"Okay, boss." Breathed Reno. "What now? . . . Our radio and flashlight are still on the saddle. We are now walking with no way to see at night, and no way to call for help!"

Mitch walked forward and peered down at the trees. "Where would you be, if it was you?"

"I'd be somewhere to the right of where that truck went in."

"So would I . . . . We'll move over in those trees and go down, Reno, . . . if we're lucky, we can come in behind him." They made the couple of dozen yards to the timber and once inside the mountain jungle began the downward descent, painstakingly working their way through the brush and trees and having to fight the constant entanglement of rifles and long-bow in the jumble of growth, as well as the snagging branches and up-thrusting dead wood they encountered, . . . and the way was literally all but blocked with the mess.

They were sweating profusely and having to fight the nagging insects as they slowly descended the treacherous labyrinth of trees and rocks, . . . and a half hour passed before they were finally at the bottom of the steep grade and once there stopped to listen, and to get their bearings.

"Which direction is that trail from here, Reno, . . . we could be totally off course?"

"It's somewhere to our left, come on." He led the way down the small trench of the ravine until they could look back up the rock-riddled slope, and Reno stopped there and nodded toward the right. "We go up that way now." He whispered and they slowly climbed up the small embankment and made their way through the maze of trees and much more of the brush and debris for yet another few dozen yards before they saw the cabin snugly nestled in the trees.

Reno stopped in the same instant, as they both heard the very distinctive rattle of telltale beads. They froze as they wildly searched the brush and leaves for the source, . . . and the blood was pounding in their ears by the time they saw the coiled snake.

"Back away real slow, Mitch." Breathed Reno and together, they put distance between them and the rattlesnake, . . . but they had also heard the gruff barking of a large dog at the cabin.

"That's all we need," Whispered Mitch. "What now?"

"Let's get closer to the house, it could just be another moonshiner."

"What about that dog, . . . we can't fight it, and the man in the cabin, too?"

"Let's look first, come on, . . . and be careful!"

The small cabin was made of logs and had been there for a very long time. But there was glass in the windows and they could tell it had a fireplace, able to see a chimney and a rack of wood next to the house. The large black dog looked to be a Mastiff, and it was standing at the front of the cabin and staring at the trees in their direction causing them to squat lower in the brush.

"What's the plan?" Whispered Mitch.

"I think I'll give the dog something to play with."

"Like what?"

"Rattlesnake!" Reno turned and made his way back into the trees, returning a few minutes later with the snake dangling across the forked end of a long, dead stick.

"Jesus, Reno!" Gasped Mitch as he moved past him.

"When I throw this thing at the dog, you go around the back of the cabin there, I'll be right behind you. When the man comes out, he'll have a gun." He stood up in the brush and moved out into the sparse yard of the cabin, and when the dog began his snarling, barking attack, used the stick to launch the snake at it before quickly following Mitch around the rear of the cabin. The dog went crazy then as the snake hit the ground and began striking, only to coil and strike again as the animal got closer.

"What is it, my friend?" Came a voice in broken English from the doorway, and when the man cautiously peered out around the door's facing enough to scan the rocky slope, he saw the snake. "Ahhh, caramba!" He blurted then looped the automatic weapon over his head and reached back inside for an axe before rushing out to kill the intruder.

He tossed the axe aside and squatted to lovingly caress the dog's large head, speaking to it in fluent Spanish . . . . And it wasn't until he stood up and turned back that he saw the two boys, and the rifles that were pointed at him. The dog saw them, too, and went crazy with rage.

Reno aimed the rifle at the animal and the man yelled, "NOOO!!" And stepped between them.

"Then shut him up!" Yelled Reno.

"Drop the gun first!" Said Mitch loudly. "Do it now!"

The Sentinel nodded and slowly removed the weapon from around his neck.

"Throw it away!" Ordered Mitch again, and after the man complied. "Put that dog on a short rope, now!"

While that was being done, Reno walked out a ways into the yard and looked at the roof, . . . and when he saw the tall radio antennae knew that Pot-luck had been right! Once the man had the dog tied, he went back to join Mitch, telling him to go into the cabin first to check it out.

Mitch went inside the one room shack with caution, and upon seeing it was empty, went back to nod at Reno from the doorway before moving back inside to stand beside the man's unmade bunk to watch as Reno pushed the man inside. He still had the Marlin trained on him as Reno told him to sit down, . . . and his insides were shaking so violently with fear that he could barely hold the rifle steady.

The time they both had been dreading was upon them now. They were forced to use deadly force, and the question still remained in both their minds, . . . could they actually kill a man? . . . It seemed so easy in the movies, such a natural, expected thing to do. Shoot the bad guys and save the good ones! As Mitch looked at the man, the reality of it all was like a slap in the face. This was the real thing, he thought, . . . and he had to stand up to it if he was going to save his parents. He was shaken from his thoughts then as the man spoke.

"Who are you?" Asked the dark eyed man in his broken English, his eyes flicking back and forth to each of them.

"Answer me!" He demanded. "Who are you?"

They looked at each other and frowned, . . . and at that moment knew that the man was not afraid of them, or the rifles they held, . . . and that knowledge had an unnerving effect on them.

Mitch cleared his throat loudly. "It don't matter who we are!" He said shakily. "What you are going to tell us does."

"I tell you nothing." He grinned. "Only that you will never grow old!"

"If you want to grow old, you will." Said Reno flatly.

"Your big rifles do not scare me!" He sneered. "You are nothing but little babies, you have never kill a grown up man before! . . . You will need diaper change!"

"A truck came by here five days ago," Said Mitch, ignoring the sarcasm. "Where did it go?"

The man shrugged. "I see no truck come by here, you are mistaken, Bambino!"

"Are you sure about that?" And when the man shrugged. "Reno, go kill his dog!"

"A good idea, it's getting on my nerves anyway." He started for the door.

"Wait!" Said the man quickly. "I will tell you something, . . . if you shoot dog my friends will hear, and they will come, . . . they are not far away!"

"Then I won't use a gun!" Grinned Reno and gave Mitch his rifle, and still grinning, he took the bow from over his head and arm, but it was not until he pulled the arrow from the quiver and fitted it to the bow that the man's eyes grew larger.

"What are you doing, what is this weapon?"

"Don't they watch western movies where you come from?" Laughed Mitch nervously. "My friend there is an Apache Indian, . . . you do know about American Indians don't you, the old west?" He looked at Reno again. "Kill his dog, Reno."

The man suddenly broke out laughing, slapping his hands down on his legs. "Kill my dog, I don't care!" His eyes grew darker, and more dead looking as he leaned a little forward. "But I tell you this, little Bambinos, . . . you do not know what happens to you now! . . . Do you ever hear of Colombian Neck-tie? . . . Huh? . . . First, the throat is cut." He used his finger at his throat as a gesture, moving it from ear to ear. "From here to here, . . . your blood is all over everywhere! . . . They will stick hand inside neck and pull out the tongue." He made a grimacing face as he stuck out his tongue and laughed. "It make one pretty good neck-tie for Bambinos like you!"

Reno's face went a little pale as he listened to the outburst, then he suddenly raised the bow and shot the man, the arrow's steel tip completely going through the Colombian's right shoulder. The man's face was a mask of complete and surprised shock for the fleeting part of a millisecond as he stared blankly at the arrow's feathered shaft, . . . and then he yelled shrilly as the intense pain took over, giving in to the arrow's penetration as he fell almost completely out of the chair, . . . and then screaming obscenities at them as he straightened up again.

Mitch stared at Reno in shock, not believing what he had done, and realizing that he was holding his breath let it out as he watched the Sentinel right himself in the chair. He realized at that moment that they might actually have to fight violence with violence to save his mother and father. And as he watched his best friend reload the bow, found a new respect for the half Apache. Breathing deeply, he moved forward to stand in front of the glaring, grunting man.

"You just got a taste of Apache Indian torture, Mister Colombian, . . . you can't even imagine the pain he can cause you! You could live for days before he's through! . . . Now, what about that truck, God damn you?"

"I see truck!" He said surlily, his pained eyes still on the arrow affixed to Reno's bow.

"Where did it go?"

"To compound!" He gestured with his head. "That way!"

"How far is this compound?"

"Five kilometers away," He gasped. "Then you will die!"

"You know what, ass hole? . . . We might die up there, but this is American soil you're on, . . . not yours! And Americans fight back, we don't take any shit from scum like you! . . . Now where is that God damn compound?"

The man gestured with his head again. "Take road, you will find it!"

"At last." Said Reno. "A road!"

"Now will you kill me?"

Ignoring him, Mitch turned to search the cabin, and seeing the wooden box went across the room and opened it. There was a coil of rope, one of wire, and a tied together bundle of white plastic ties, all about eighteen inches in length. He took the ties and the rope before closing the lid and coming back.

"We're not murderers, Sen'or!" He said hatefully. "We prefer letting American law take care of that!" He moved around in back of the man's chair and pulled a couple of ties from the bundle. "They will, too, you know, . . . they'll fry you like an egg in a hot skillet, . . . now put your hands at your side, man!"

"What are you to do, . . . I am hurting, I need doctor!"

Mitch grabbed the man's hurting arm and forced it downward, bringing another shriek of pain from him, and when he tried to turn in the chair to use his left arm, Mitch reached and placed his own arm across the bloody end of the arrow and pressed down on it, wrenching yet another shrieking groan of pain from him.

"Be still!" He said and looped the length of plastic around the man's wrist and the back of the chair and pulling it tight, then tied another one around the bend in his arm and the backrest, . . . and then did the same to the other arm.

Reno watched until the man was secured then shoved the arrow back into the quiver, shouldered the bow again and went to pull a curtain open along the North wall. The radio transmitter and receiver was larger than the usual ham radio he'd been used to seeing, and believed it to be much more sophisticated. The face of the set had a half dozen half-moon, plastic covered meters on it and several frequency dials, all with knobs below them. Shaking his head, he looked beneath the table at the batteries with their attaching wires before turning back.

"Found the radio, Mitch." He sighed. "This whole damn thing is about drugs!"

"Colombian drugs." Nodded Mitch. "I know." He got to his feet after strapping the sentinel's legs to the chairs'.

"You do not know what you do!" Rasped the man suddenly. "You can not win, you are children, not a man, . . . they will kill you!"

Mitch met Reno's worried eyes for a second then sighing, went to the bunk where he had seen the rumpled tee-shirt and held it up for Reno to see.

"He's got taste, at least." Nodded Reno as he admired Marilyn Monroe's almost nude iron-on. "Guess they don't have pretty women in Colombia."

Nodding, Mitch rolled it up tightly and inserted it into the Columbian's protesting open mouth and tied it behind his head.

"Mitch, we saw Rory Calhoun get loose from a chair like that, remember?"

"I remember." He nodded and picked up the rope. "But they didn't have me directing the film, brother." He looked up at the sagging log beam overhead then made a slip-knot in one end of the rope, shook out a noose and placed it over the man's bobbing head pulling it tight. He grinned tightly at Reno then threw the remaining rope up and over the beam and took out the slack before tying it tightly around the chair and the man several times, . . . then he knotted the end securely to the chair's bottom rung.

"I believe that might work, brother." Smiled Reno.

Mitch came around in front of the guard then. "Man, you know what will happen to you if you turn that chair over, don't you? . . . Yeah, you'll hang yourself, and it will take you a long time to die . . . . You'll start to choke as the rope gets tighter and tighter, . . . and as you choke to death, your tongue will stick out of your mouth! . . . In America, we call that a hangman's neck tie! . . . It just doesn't have all that blood!" He sighed and looked at Reno then, his face and worried eyes showing his returning fear.

"Here we go, brother!" He shrugged and then looked at the radio set. "What about that thing, do we call the lodge for help now, or what?"

"They'll be monitoring that thing at the compound, Mitch, it's a damn sophisticated system! . . . I'd say its probably able to monitor every channel that's floating around out there, picking up on the one that's transmitting."

"Then we'll need to shut it down."

"We can cripple the microphone, without it, they can't send." He went and disconnected the unit from the set and brought it back with him. "Now their open channel won't be disrupted, . . . at least on this end."

"Then let's go!" With a last look at the bound and gagged man, they left the cabin and immediately, the large dog began lunging at the chain that held it in tow, it's snarling barks loud in the stillness. They kept wary eyes on it as they continued across the yard's debris where Mitch bent to retrieve the man's discarded weapon and look it over.

"Ever see one of these?" He asked, turning it over in his hand.

"Nope, . . . but that clip must hold forty or fifty rounds."

"Can you read Russian?" He gave the gun to Reno who looked at the lettering.

"Nope, . . . but this looks more like German writing than Russian. It's foreign made for sure, and fully automatic. This thing's a killing machine, Mitch!"

"Good, we might need it!" He took it back and looped the nylon strap over his shoulder. "What's another pound or two anyway?" He shifted the Marlin up on his other shoulder and they walked another few yards before finding the overgrown road.

"Wow, no wonder no one can find a road up here!" They, as well as the road, were in the thick forest of trees again only this time, they were having to walk almost blindly up the wide, overgrown pathway and having to move low branches aside at times, . . . and at others, having to push their way past thick growths of ground covering bushes and new saplings, those that were not already laying crushed across the road. However, there was evidence of the passing truck because hundreds of the branches appeared broken, or were laying in the road and also, . . . much of the groundcover lay beneath the saplings having been crushed flat by the large tires.

*   *   *

They were in the process of unloading the last of the two trucks that came in before daybreak and until now Pete had, for the most part, stood to one side to watch them. But this time he fell in beside him as he carried his bundle past.

"How's it goin', Mike?"

"Come on, Pete, how do you think it's going? . . . We're give out already when we start, and dead tired when we quit!"

"Just bein' friendly, Mike, I'll let ya be."

"Come on, Pete, I didn't mean that! . . . You're the only person I've been allowed to speak to in a week, and I appreciate it!"

"Yeah," He sighed. "I am sorry, Mike, but there's nothing I can do."

"That's okay . . . . Tell me something? . . . It's freezing cold here at night, . . . what's going happen to us this winter, man . . . . Will they give us a coat to wear, or what?"

"They'll give you what you wore in here, a coat if you had one, . . . a shirt if that's all you had . . . . They put a fifty gallon barrel in the barracks at night and build a fire in it for warmth. That's about it."

He went on to deposit his load and come back. "They brought us here in a truck, Pete, . . . but it was not like any conventional truck I've ever seen, what kind is it?"

"That I don't know, the Cartel brought it in! . . . It's supposed to be able to go just about anywhere though."

"Believe me, it does! . . . You also said this place was overdue to be shut down," He continued on to shoulder another bundle and come back. "Is there any more signs of that coming about, . . . anytime soon, I mean?"

"No, but I'm worried a little, the guards have almost all stopped talking to me, even the friendly one!"

"Then maybe you should think about helping us break out of here, there's no way we can do it without you? . . . You have keys to the shackles and you have a gun. With a little planning, we might confiscate a few more."

"Mike, I've never wanted to get away from anything more than I do this place! . . . But, man, don't ask me to openly commit suicide like that. I can't do it! . . . At least not till I have to."

"Then I guess we won't have to worry about spending the winter here anyway, we'll all be dead! . . . You wait till the last minute, so will you."

He went on to leave his bundle and come back. "I've been awake when the guard comes to wake you up in the morning. That's the way it will happen you know, instead of waking you one morning, he'll bend down and cut your throat, . . . and there goes your have to scenario . . . . These are ruthless people, Pete, think about it, will you, . . . for all our sakes?" He sighed heavily as Pete stopped, and continued on to shoulder his load and come back, still keeping his head down as he walked.

He knew he could be putting his and Nora's lives in danger confiding in Pete this way, but he also knew that if he couldn't get her out of here soon, chances were good she would eventually be raped by those animals, . . . if they all weren't killed first! He wouldn't have a chance unarmed and alone and not only that, he had never killed a man before, . . . and he was not sure he could, even under these dire circumstances. But then again, if Nora was being threatened, he believed that he would!

He couldn't really blame Pete for not wanting to help because he was as afraid as everyone else here. He was just someone else blinded by the promise of money and led into a trap, . . . But what he really failed to understand about it was why Pete was given a job as guard, instead of just becoming one of the laborers, or why they didn't just kill him? If he still had the time, he thought, he might ask him about that! . . . If he decided to even talk to him again after this?"

*   *   *

Mitch and Reno were each walking in one of the wide, deeply worn tire trails on the seemingly ever-winding road along the mountainside, and each with their own impending dreads and thoughts as they used the newly procured sticks in search of the deadly timber Rattlers. They were both breathing a little hard from all the extra weight they were carrying, . . . but neither one desired to discard any of it for fear they might need it.

"I could use a rest, Reno." Said Mitch tiredly. "How about you?"

"Oh, yeah." He breathed and began relieving himself of rifle longbow and the canteen of water. "But I'm a little afraid to sit down anywhere."

"Clear a spot in the ruts." Said Mitch as he unloaded his own weapons. "I am!" He sat down heavily on the hard-packed surface, and as Reno did, both uncapped canteens and drank deeply.

"How far have we come?"

"Maybe a mile, I guess!" Sighed Reno and looked around at the seemingly impenetrable wilderness. "You would think we'd hear some sort of sounds coming from up there?' He sighed. "If they're even there! . . . That Bastard might have lied to us anyway, you think about that?"

"Could be? . . . At this point, I don't know what to think." Sighed Mitch.

"Exactly!" Agreed Reno. "But you really should have been an Indian, Mitch . . . . How did you come up with that idea anyway?"

"The rope? . . . He was a killer, Reno, and he's more than likely been in similar trouble before . . . . You were right, I think he would have found a way to get loose."

"We're going up against more just like him, brother."

"Colombian drug dealers . . . . Yeah, brother, I know. But why kidnap mom and dad, and all those other people? . . . What are they using them for?"

"A drug lab, maybe, I don't know . . . . But I have a feeling there'll be a lot of men with guns there, and I hope you're still working on a plan?"

"One plan at a time, buddy," He returned. "Great minds work at their own pace."

"Speaking of which," He sighed, getting to his feet again and donning his load. "We had better pick up the pace, we haven't even gone two kilometers yet!"

"Surely we have, Reno." He sighed getting up to shoulder his weapons. "A part of me wants to put this off as long as we can, while another wants to just run in there shooting right now! . . . And another part is afraid of what we'll find when we do get there! . . . All at the same time, too!"

"That makes two of us, brother! . . . But either way, I'm going to do my best to make the bastards pay for it!"

"Amen, old buddy!" He looked up the dark road then and sighed. "I'm on my way, Mom, Dad! . . . Me and Reno are coming for you!"

*   *   *

"Jesus Christ!" Voiced James Mason as he led his horse up beside Jimmi and his mount. "We been on and off these horses so much my back hurts!" He moved aside far enough to let the other two guides lead their horses over the crest of the canyon.

Jimmi watched them as they all made it to the top. "Ben, Joe, you two okay?"

"All but my feet, Jimmi." Grinned Ben Jamison. "Never been in and out a this many gullies in one day before, ain't used to it! . . . And Joe there's got a bad knee that's actin' up!"

"It ain't my knee that's hurtin' right now, Ben, it's my ass! . . . Be worth it though, we find those boys okay."

"Yeah, it will." Agreed Jimmi.

"This is some a th' worst country I ever seen!" Said Ben. "You been up here before, Jimmi?"

"I was ten years old, the last time . . . . Used to hunt bear with my father up here."

"Well, I can't figure how that damn truck, or whatever it is can climb in and out a these canyons like that, when a man has to claw like hell to do it, . . . it ain't natural!"

"We're not dealing with a natural truck, James, you said so yourself!" Reminded Jimmi turning to look at the distant bluish mountain ahead of them, barely visible over the giant pines.

"Where do you think it's going?"

Jimmi looked at James and shrugged. "If I had to guess, I'd say somewhere between us and Pole Creek Mountain, you can barely see it off yonder . . . . Wherever it was going, it's already there, though. And I think we can rule out Sunlight Peak, I doubt that truck has fins on it, the Los Pinos is fairly deep in the Summer . . . . No, I can picture that truck being somewhere in the Weminuche wilderness.

"That's a mighty big place, too." Sighed Joe. "When I lived in Denver, I worked for a loggin' crew in there for a few weeks."

"Come on, men." Nodded Jimmi. "Let's walk for a while and cool off the horses."

CHAPTER TEN

The marijuana truck was loaded and it's door closed, Michael and the other two loaders stood back with heads bowed as they waited for the final pallet of heroin to be placed on the ground behind the second truck. After the guard left the forklift's seat to join Pete, they closely watched them carefully pass each one-pound bag of the drug up to the two Colombians in the truck, then waited while the three bags were weighed again and placed into stainless steel containers, marked Transplant Organs before passing up three more.

The containers were filled to half way with the heroin then the container was fitted with a tight-fitting stainless steel separator plate, followed by hot ice from a much larger container in the truck. After that came the frozen plastic bags of what could have been donor organs, . . . but what Michael believed were probably an animal's remains. The container was then sealed, and another one opened.

It was coming on to meal time when the guard took the empty pallet away and they were ordered to a shower that had been set up in back of the cave, each taking their turn at being thoroughly rinsed in the cold water while standing on a cotton cloth spread across a plastic tub, . . . this was to make sure that every grain of the dope was accounted for and not carried away in someone's hair or on their bodies.

Michael stood aside as the inside cave guard ushered the women out, . . . and as he donned his toga and stood waiting for Nora, Pete moved in beside him.

"I've decided you're right, Michael, I'll help you escape, if, . . . if I can get my hands on one or two more guns and ammo, and it won't be easy! . . . We'll talk tomorrow."

"We all have to go, Pete, . . . everyone!"

"Out of the question, . . . three of us might make it, but that's all!"

"We can take the truck, we'd all fit?"

"Forget it, Mike, they'd kill us all, . . . I'm sorry." He walked away before Michael could respond and by then Nora had pulled on her toga and he moved in beside her.

*   *   *

"I feel like we've been walking for miles, Reno!" Said Mitch tiredly. "We should be there already."

Reno stopped and faced him, barely able to see his face in the darkness, the setting sun making it even darker in the cover of trees and before he could respond, the faint sound of clinking tin came to them causing them both to strain their ears and eyes at the darkening, fast fading road ahead of them. They heard the sound again and they both all but began to run up the overgrown trail with their hearts pounding.

They jogged up the winding road for several minutes before they saw the compound through the trees ahead of them and immediately stopped, to quickly move to one side of the road and go to their knees in the tall shrubbery. The late afternoon shadows were already darkening the area beneath the canopy, and they watched breathlessly as the heavily armed guards ushered the two small groups of workers into their assigned barn-like barracks.

"What is this place?" Muttered Mitch. "You see that cover over it?"

"That's why the airplanes can't see what's going on down here." Breathed Reno. "It's a camouflage."

"I didn't see mom and dad, did you?"

"They all look alike in them gowns, Mitch, . . . and they had their backs to us. But they're here, buddy, . . . and right over there is the truck that brought them here!"

"I see it." He nodded then tearfully looked back at the open-sided barracks. "Did you count the guards, Reno?"

"Twelve, closer to us there, one more in the doorway of that far barracks."

"God, . . . thirteen armed Colombian murderers." Sighed Mitch. "That should just about make the odds even, don't you think?"

"Well, I don't know." He whispered. "What's your plan, amigo? . . . wait! . . . All but four of them are walking toward us and that small house over there." They watched the eight guards enter the cabin and close the door behind them.

"Wonder what that's all about?" Queried Mitch.

"They must rotate shifts, or something . . . . That leaves only four on guard out here, plus the one in that last building."

"How are we going to take down five armed guards without waking up the other eight?"

"'We'll have to figure out something, brother." Sighed Reno. "And it's not going to be easy, whatever we do!"

"At least they're not turning on any lights, but why, . . . they've got wires running everywhere out there?"

"They're too smart for that! . . . A plane could spot it!"

"Yeah, wonder just how big that camouflage is?" Asked Mitch as he peered up at it again.

"Look to our right over there, buddy, see the plants?"

"What is that, marijuana?"

"It has to be, and from the looks of it, there's several acres of it under that cover!"

"That's it then, they use the workers to work the Marijuana field . . . . God, Reno, they're nothing but slaves here, . . . this is nothing but a Colombian labor camp! . . . How did they even get here? . . . Hell, don't people ever pay attention?"

"Easy, Mitch, they could hear us!"

"Yeah," He whispered, "sorry, Reno, . . . well, . . . it appears all we have to do is take out five murderous guards, then we can look for mom and dad, . . . piece of cake! . . . Wait!" He whispered quickly. "Two more are leaving." They watched as the guards walked past the last building and disappeared in the fast fading light. "Wonder where they're going now?"

"Toilet, maybe?" Whispered Reno. "Let's hope they stay gone!"

"That leaves three, . . . now, . . . how do we get across that open ground before they see us? . . . And can we even hope to take them out if we do?"

"We might not have to cross any open ground." Insisted Reno. "Come on, stay low, let's move back on the road I have an idea." Once they were on their knees in the tall grass of the old road, he took the quiver from his back and removed the arrows, then reached inside and brought out a small, very round hardwood ball and placed it in Mitch's hand. "Remember that?"

"Yeah," He muttered. "You use these on your arrows to knock down the bowling pins at the archery range!"

"Yeah, and you just saw three bowling pins on guard out there!" He unscrewed a steel tip from one of the arrows and gave the shaft to Mitch. "Screw that thing on this arrow."

"Good thinking, brother, and you're right, . . . those bastards do resemble bowling pins! . . . You know, this could work, . . . how many did you bring?"

"Four, I think, . . . here's another one, . . . and here's an arrow. Unscrew the point, but don't lose it, I'll put them back in the quiver."

A few long seconds later, all four arrows were equipped with the hardwood knobs. "Now what?" Breathed Mitch as he gave Reno the arrow and looked toward the now very dark compound, and unable to see the guards at all, he sighed heavily.

"I have a feeling this won't work either, it's pitch black out there!"

"Then we wait for the moon to come up! . . . WO!" He gasped as the flapping of large wings suddenly broke the silence, followed by a shrill cawing as the large crow flew down out of one of the pine trees above them and up over the canopy to disappear.

"I didn't need that!" Breathed Mitch, quickly getting up to move away and relieve himself. "Almost used my pants again." He whispered as he came back. "It's getting cold already, too, I can see my breath."

"Listen, Mitch . . . . That camouflage is going to limit our visibility even with the moon out, so it wouldn't hurt to pray a little, brother." He sighed then also. "And, Mitch, if this is going to work at all, we'll need a way to separate those two guards, so we'd best put our thinking caps on! . . . If one sees the other one fall, he'll start shooting for sure, . . . then we're screwed!"

"God help us, Reno!" He sighed. "No one else is going to."

*   *   *

Pete had not acknowledged him at all as he stooped to close Michael's ankle iron, nor as he left to shackle the others for the night, and Michael was still sitting on the edge of his bunk when the guard returned to sit down on his in the building's opening, . . . but he really didn't expect otherwise! But given that and all that Pete had told him, he believed that if he was in his unusual position and actually believed the inevitable was coming, . . . he would take any opportunity at all to leave this hell-hole! The only problem they might have, other than the obvious, he thought, . . . would be fitting everyone into that truck out there? Because it would be crowded and would bring up another very important question, . . . could the truck do what it did with all that extra weight?

There are always obstacles, he thought tiredly. However, if they could get past the guards and get everyone in that truck, . . . the Baxters, and any guards that were left would be on foot, therefore the truck wouldn't need to perform to its potential! He looked over at Pete then and knew they couldn't hope to do it without his help! He sighed and looked out at the fast fading compound watching as the guards stood and talked for a time before the eight waved and walked away toward their own barracks. However, as he watched their dark shapes leaving, his peripheral vision detected what he thought was movement at the distant timbered edge of the compound and causing him to quickly focus on that area where the road came in . . . . but he saw nothing else and by this time it was totally dark in the compound.

Sighing once again, he lay back on the bunk to mentally go over what he was sure he had seen, . . . because it brought to mind what Nora had said about Mitchell coming to save them. He mentally pictured the fleeting shadow over and over again in his mind's eyes until he was convinced that what he had seen actually did resemble the movement a man might make as he ducked back out of sight. He was also aware of the tricks darkness could play on a man's emotional state, and did not rule out the phenomenon.

Thinking on it again, that slight movement had so caused his heart to quicken that the memory of what Nora had told him flashed across his consciousness again. He knew it had been only a dream, but when he saw that movement in the trees, he had hoped it was true! He thought of Mitch then, something he had made himself not do until now. That boy was his life, next to Nora, . . . his every dream for the future of Zant Industries was centered around him. He knew that Mitch knew by now what had happened to them because Carl Spencer would surely have called him right away . . . . And knowing his son, knew he would want to come looking for them, a first reaction for anyone under similar circumstances.

Mitchell was smart enough to know that professionals had a better chance at finding them than would a sixteen year old boy! . . . And he was thankful he was safe at home. He grinned to himself then. It would be exciting though, he thought, his own son coming to save them from the bad guys, . . . the pride would be overwhelming!

*   *   *

It was devastatingly quiet in the dark of the trees, and freezing as the night progressed, . . . causing them both to hunker down close to each other for warmth as they continued to strain their more than tired eyes at the dark compound, They could not see a thing and what little light the brilliantly-lit night sky might have provided them was denied them by that canopy of camouflage. They knew the whereabouts of the two guards because they would periodically light up their smokes but other than that, nothing other than the much deeper shades of the buildings were detectable.

"I never mentioned this before." Whispered Mitch, and was almost stuttering from the cold. "But it takes a very intelligent person not to carry a coat with them in the summertime."

"Yeah," Returned Reno. "There's not many like us."

"Yeah, . . . You're keeping your hands warm, I hope? . . . Wouldn't want you to miss, ya know?"

"I'm trying, brother, . . . what worries me is that I could miss! . . . Setting all jokes aside, they are not bowling pins, and I have never fired an arrow at night before . . . . If I can't hit him in the head, he'll give the alarm for sure, Mitch. That's when you'll have no choice but to shoot him, . . . and you'd best be ready for that! . . . And another thing, . . . Dad always said that when an Apache was firing his rifle in a night attack, they wouldn't stay in the same place to shoot again because the enemy might see the muzzle flash, or follow the sound of his shot . . . . We'll have to be prepared to move fast!"

"You're not making me feel any better, Reno."

"You're welcome, now stop talking, they might hear us!"

They settled down again to wait, and the agonizing minutes turned into another couple of hours before the large, yellow orb began peeking over the tree-covered crest of the mountain, . . . and yet another hour before the brilliant glow from God's candle shown down on the camouflaged canopy, its rays filtering through enough to throw the compound, its buildings and the two Colombian killers into a dim but recognizable light.

"Okay, Mitch." Whispered Reno. "Here's my plan, and if you have a better one, believe me, I'll listen! . . . Look around and find yourself a good sized stick, a short one. Make your way up close to that large cover there and throw it up as far as you can, . . . when it falls on top of that camouflage, the noise it makes should bring one of the guards looking . . . . They'll be separated then."

"Well, I don't have a better one." He said and they both began feeling around on the debris for a stick of wood until they found one.

"Okay, Reno, but be ready. I can't throw it too far through those limbs."

"I'm as ready as I can be, brother, go ahead, I'll move up to the edge of the compound while you get ready. Watch for my signal . . . . As soon as one of them starts this way, I'll pop the other one first, and then this one!"

"Good luck then." Mitch moved across the road and up into the thick mesh of brush and trees and when he was within an arm's length of being right below the tall canopy he turned to watch Reno's shadowy figure move into place, silhouetting himself against the light in the compound. He watched and could tell he was placing the arrow on the bow, . . . and when he saw him raise his arm and wave, he drew back and heaved the short, dead block of tree limb high and over the canopy's top then quickly cocked the hammer back on the Marlin as the audible sound from the falling stick on the mesh quickly caused both guards to ready their weapons and stare at the dark marijuana field for several moments and then, after speaking to the man beside him, one of them began to walk slowly in their direction, his weapon held menacingly ready.

Reno waited until the first man was several yards away from the other one and raised the bow, pulled back the bowstring and stood up in the road, took careful aim and loosed the wood-tipped trajectory at its target, seeing it strike almost immediately. As the man went down, he was already loading the second arrow, . . . and when the first Colombian, curious at the sound from the falling guard's body, spun around to look, his head was met by Reno's second arrow, felling him in his tracks.

Holding his breath, Reno loaded again, expecting the third guard to exit the barracks at any moment and when he did not, slowly lowered the bow, . . . and with rifle on his shoulder made his way to Mitch's side where they both studied the compound for several long seconds before entering the marijuana field. They moved through the tall stalks until they found where the guard had fallen then moved out enough to take his arms and drag him inside the cover of the plants. Mitch quickly used one of the ties he had taken from the sentinel's cabin, and the cap from the man's head to bind his hands and gag him, . . . then they both squatted in the shadows to again scan the compound's wide open area, and it was then that they heard the diesel engines starting up, . . . and a few seconds later, the sounds of trucks leaving.

"What's that all about, you think?" Whispered Mitch.

"I don't know, brother, . . . but if we don't put that other guard down pretty quick, this will all be for nothing."

"Sure is a long way across there, Reno. If somebody sees us, we're toast!"

"I know that, now let's think, man!"

*　　　　　*　　　　　*

Michael had lain awake for what seemed like hours to his exhausted body as his mind continued to dwell on Pete, and the conversation they had, . . . and from there to what he had thought he saw in the trees, rethinking the vision again over and over in his overactive mind until he would angrily force himself to think of something else. But his thoughts would only take him back to Pete, and his own thoughts of escaping, but then, . . . inevitably back to the shadow in the trees again.

When he would close his eyes to try and sleep, they would ache in their sockets and if not that, his legs and shoulders would . . . . And he was freezing, the one blanket they were given to cover themselves was far from adequate. Normally, exhaustion would overcome the severe cold at night, but it had no effect tonight and disgusted with tossing and turning on the uncomfortably hard cot, he finally sighed heavily, wrapped the blanket around his shoulders and sat up, crossing his legs under him to warm his feet as he continued to feverishly review his thoughts.

He was still sitting there when the compound began to materialize again in the moon's filtered light, his eyes on the two guards some few yards out as they smoked and conversed in Spanish and making him remember the Spanish he had taken in college, . . . and of how different it had been compared this. He was able to pick up on only a few of the muffled words.

He heard the dull sound of something hitting the canopy then and watched the long sticks as they swayed back and forth, but thought it to be only a bird hitting the mesh, which happened quite often. But then he saw the two guards looking toward the marijuana field, and when one of them left he watched him for a second, . . . and had just looked back at the guard in front when movement caused him to look at the trees again in time to see the pale figure of a man as he stood up and raised his arms. His heart suddenly lurched in his chest as he actually saw the flying projectile a fleeting instant before hearing the guard grunt loudly, . . . and then seeing the wood-tipped arrow hit the dirt in front of his cot as the Colombian was propelled toward the barracks open side where he fell and lay still, his head almost inside the barracks.

Still in an overwhelming daze, he quickly looked back at the timber in time to see the figure raise the bow and fire again, this time seeing the second guard fall. In awe, he stared down at the wood-tipped arrow in the dirt of the barracks for a second not believing what he had just witnessed, . . . but then realization set in and he quickly got to his feet.

"My, God!" He said aloud. "It's one of Reno's arrows." He looked back in time to see the two figures pull the downed guard into the field then looked at Pete.

"Wake up, Pete!" He said in a low voice. "Hey, Pete, wake up, man!"

"What is it? . . . What do you want, Mike?"

"Come over here, Pete, wake up!"

Pete rolled over on his bunk and sat up facing Michael. "What did you say, Mike?"

"The time is now, Pete, . . . you're either in or out, which is it?"

"What th' hell are you talkin' about?"

"My son is here, Pete, look outside there!"

Pete turned his head to look, and like a man shot jumped to his feet to stare down at the Colombian on the ground.

"Don't just stand there, man, drag him inside!"

Pete looked back at him, then cursed and quickly went to drag the guard inside. "What did you just say to me, Mike? . . . Who's here, what happened?"

"My son is here man, his friend Reno, too! . . . We're getting out if here today, now get this iron off me, come on!"

Pete squatted and opened the shackle then turned to look at the guard again. "What happened to him, Mike?"

Michael bent and picked up the arrow. "This is what happened, Pete."

Pete looked at the knobby shaft for a second, still confused, and then; "Son of a bitch!" He gasped loudly.

You have no choice now, man, . . . we take this whole mob down right now, tonight! . . . What do you say?"

"God damn right!" He gritted, and then: "Wait!" They heard the trucks leaving and then Pete gripped his arm. "Here, Mike, take my keys, . . . there's usually two guards at the cave, I'll go take care of them."

"Better wait," Said Michael quickly. "If the boys see you run out of here, they'll shoot you, Reno's an Apache Indian, he'll cut you down with that arrow! . . . Here, you go turn Nora loose while I go out to meet them." Pete nodded and hurried toward the rear of the barracks.

Michael quickly unarmed the downed guard, taking his long-bladed knife and automatic weapon then stepped out into the pale light so they could see him, . . . and waved at them.

They had just gotten to their feet and were about to move out into the compound when they saw the toga-clad man step out of the barracks and wave at them, causing them both to hesitate and peer at him for a long minute before recognition set in.

"Dad!" Gasped Mitch excitedly. "Reno, it's dad." He had started to rush out into the open when they saw Michael motion for them to stay so they waited and watched as Michael turned back, . . . and then two other figures came out, one of which literally threw herself into Michael's arms.

"That's Mrs. Zee!" Breathed Reno excitedly, but wait, . . . that other one's a guard!" They watched as Pete left the barracks at a fast walk and then to disappear around the end of the last building. They saw Michael come out a little farther into the compound and study the buildings before cautiously waving them in and then, cautiously excited, they exited the marijuana field stopping just long enough to retrieve the guard's weapons before making their way past the iron pot and on into the waiting arms of Michael and Nora Zant!

Once the semi-silent reunion of hugs, kisses and tears were over they all four sat down on the two empty bunks to wait for Pete's return.

"You real sure about this guy, dad?" Breathed Mitch. "Because we're not out of this yet? . . . If he's not for real, he could get us all killed."

"I'm sure, son, . . . Pete was tricked into coming here. He's just as scared as we are, believe me! . . . Two years ago he was offered money to drive a supply truck here and they made him stay!"

"Then why is he a guard, and not a prisoner like you and mom?"

"I don't have the full story yet, I don't know!"

"Mister Zee, all these bunks look occupied, are they all okay?"

"They're just bone-weary, Reno . . . . They kept us all so starved and exhausted that nothing could wake us up until morning . . . . All except me, I guess, . . . I spent half the night, almost every night trying to think of a way to escape this nightmare, . . . Pete had just today agreed to help me." He looked around at the dark bunks then. "Some of these poor souls are very emotionally traumatized, and we have to take them with us!"

"This is not all of them either." Said Nora. "There's more in the next barracks."

"There's also eight more armed guards in that house on the end down there!" Said Mitch. "And what is that you're both wearing, it's freezing up here?"

"I call them Togas." Said Nora. "We all wear them."

"Our clothes are all in that house with the Baxters." Gritted Michael angrily. "And it will be my utmost pleasure introducing those Bastards to my family!" He sighed then. "It'll be dangerous, too, They're the meanest bunch you'll ever want to see . . . . And that's why I want to save them for last!"

"Here comes your man, Mister Zee!" They all stood up as Pete arrived with the other guard's weapons to immediately shake hands with Mitch and Reno and grin widely.

"I didn't believe Mike when he told me you was here." He nodded at Michael then. "All I can say, Mike, is that I never thought anybody could find this place! . . . These two boys made it look so easy, I'm ashamed of myself."

"Reno made it look easy." Grinned Mitch.

"It's not over though." Sighed Pete turning to look at the compound. "The worst of these guards are in their bunks asleep down there."

"We saw them go in." Nodded Reno. "So how do we get them out?"

"Oh, that's easy, I'll call 'em out, and we all take 'em down! . . . Hopefully without a shot being fired."

"Definitely without a shot being fired!" Said Michael. "The Baxters have four of the younger women in there with them, and they have been hurt quite enough!"

"How in the world do we get them out of there?" Asked Nora worriedly.

"They'll let 'em out come daylight." Said Pete. "And I'll escort them over here as usual just like nothing's wrong, . . . then I'll fire a couple of shots in the air, that'll bring th' Baxters running."

"It will also bring them armed, and maybe shooting." Said Michael quickly. "We'll have to do it another way, that or set a trap for them. At any rate, those eight guards come first! . . . . Nora, honey, you take one of these automatic weapons and stay here, if things go wrong, we don't want any of these people hurt." He kissed her longingly then nodded at Pete. "Let's go, big guy, . . . come on boys."

*   *   *

It took all of ten minutes to call out and disarm the groggy guards. Some were only half dressed, others with no shirts on, . . . and a couple were still in their underwear. All eight of them were quickly gagged and their hands tied before quickly marching them back to the barracks where they were made to sit on the ground and lean against the wall separating the two barracks.

"I can't believe they didn't start shooting!" Marveled Mitch, as he watched the glowering group. "They're not happy campers either!"

"It does seem strange." Reflected Pete. "Unless they weren't expecting what took place?"

"I think I know the answer to that." Sighed Michael. "I've been observing them, . . . and I believe they, everyone here, had become so lax in their belief that no one could find this place, that it had become just a routine job to them."

"That, or they're not used to being on the wrong end of one of these things." Grinned Reno as he raised the menacing firearm. "Can't say I blame them either!"

"Well after this, I hope I never see one again!" Shivered Nora.

"We're still missing a couple," Said Michael looking at Pete. "What happened to those at the cave, Pete?"

"I waylaid 'em, that's all, tied 'em up then lowered the forklift down on 'em! . . . They ain't goin' anywhere! . . . But what we do have in just a little while, is two delivery trucks comin' in, and we'd better be ready for 'em . . . . Most a these guys are hair-triggered as hell anyway! . . . Cartel soldiers, you could say."

"Sounds like another job for Tonto here!" Grinned Mitch.

"Ugh!" Returned Reno.

"Good idea." Remarked Pete. "There's usually two men to a truck, me and Mike will take two of 'em down, if you boys can handle two?"

"We'll do our best!" They nodded.

"Just remember this, all of ya, . . . and I'm serious . . . . These truck drivers work directly for the Cartel, they are responsible for delivering these drugs to a prearranged destination, . . . and calling them soldiers, mafia, or anything other than what they really are is like making a dry joke! . . . What they are is killers of the worst kind, seasoned assassins, and the best at what they do! . . . They don't deliver the drugs on time, or it's not all there, . . . they'll be marked for death themselves, and they know it!" He nodded at the captured guards then.

"These men here would kill you, and even enjoy doin' it, . . . but they gave up cause they didn't want to die! . . . The drivers know they're gonna die, they expect it. They don't speak a word of English, or understand it, so telling them to freeze, or drop their weapons won't work! . . . What I'm really saying is this, . . . be prepared to shoot and kill, you wound one, he'll still kill ya."

"If you're not one of these guys, how do you know so much about them?" Asked Mitch.

Pete shrugged. "One of 'em was friendlier that the others, and he speaks English."

"Okay, . . . why did they make you a guard, and not one of the workers, . . . or worse, yet, kill you?"

"You never did tell me the whole story there, Pete?' Said Michael. "If you don't mind, I'd really like to know?"

"I don't mind, Mike, . . . like I told ye, they offered me five hundred dollars to drive one of th' trucks in, paid me up-front, too! . . . Said it was only for one trip, and to me that was a lot of money, me bein' out a work! . . . But when I got here, a driver pulled me out a th' truck at gun-point and brought me up in front a th' Baxter's house and then called out Jesse . . . . I'd never seen a man that large or mean-lookin' before, and it scared th' hell out a me! Anyway, he came out and looked me over by walkin' around me a time or two then stopped and looked me in the eyes."

"That's when he told I should have turned down that job, because now I'd never leave here again! . . . And then he laughed and told me he was gonna beat me to death in front of an audience. He ordered the guards to wake everyone up and bring 'em outside while I waited to be killed! Anyway," He shrugged. "I was th' boxing champ of my Company durin' th' war, so I knew I wasn't about to just lay down and let it happen, so when everyone was seated around us, he came toward me with that mean look of his, so I took th' initiative and knocked the hell out of him, right on th' spot, . . . he went down, too! But he got up grinning and the fight was on!"

"I didn't whip th' ugly bastard, but he didn't beat me to death either!" He sighed then. "I don't know, maybe I made 'im respect me, if he's capable, . . . but when the guards raised their guns to kill me, he stopped 'em, said I was his new personal guard, . . . here I am!"

"That's an amazing story, Pete." Nodded Michael. "That's exactly the way of most bullies. He floored me with one punch the day I met him!" He shrugged then. "Murdered a good friend of ours too."

"He did a lot a that, Mike . . . . Until tonight, I believed him, . . . I really thought I'd never leave here."

Michael nodded. "So did I." He said moving to embrace Mitch and Reno again. "God, I love these kids, Pete!" He looked back into the barracks then. "And I know these people must have all given up completely by now."

"Yes, the poor souls!" Sighed Nora. "How will they react when we tell they're going home?"

"We're not telling them yet." Sighed Michael. "We haven't won the battle, and the way my insides are shaking right now, we might not!"

"You're just cold, Mike." Said Pete. "It's freezin' in here. Them guards all got coats in that Hutch down there, I'll go get 'em."

"I'll go get them, Pete." Said Reno, and moving out of the shadows he quickly looked around the compound and was gone.

"Thanks, Pete," Nodded Michael. "But it's not just the cold, man, I am totally scared to death here!" He looked at Mitch then. "I'm sorry, son, but it's true. Until now, I've only read about this sort of thing and never worried about it. Maybe because my world was so far removed from this one . . . . At this moment, I think I'm more afraid than any time since we've been here, . . . and there's no excuse for it, other than the fact I have never been in a fight with a man before! . . . I am your classic White-collar socialite and until now, I have never done manual labor in my entire life, . . . I used my brain! . . . Pete, my son has more bravery than I have ever had and I'm so proud of him I could cry!"

"Mike, . . . my friend." Laughed Pete shaking his head. "You are so damn wrong, man! . . . Don't you listen to this man. He's been after me to help him break everybody out a here for a week, and I didn't have the guts!"

"I know, Pete." Smiled Mitch as Reno came back with the coats, and between them helped Michael and Nora put them on.

"Got a couple for us, too, Mitch."

"When did you darlings decide to come look for us, Mitchell?" Asked Nora as they both donned the coats.

"I don't know, Mom, . . . I think we had already, because of the way I felt when you left you know, the omen? . . . It must have rubbed off on Reno, too, because he insisted on spending the night on Friday when you didn't call . . . But we convinced ourselves you got back to the Lodge too late on Friday, so we decided you'd call Saturday, and we went to the movies."

"They had a sneak preview showing of the Duke's new western at eleven-thirty." Nodded Reno.

"The Searchers." Said Mitch. "But I don't know, Mom . . . . I think we both knew we had to come the moment Sean brought the message we were to call Carl Spencer."

"Yeah," Broke in Reno. "When he told Mitch you'd been abducted, and that the National Guard had all but given up finding you, . . . well that was the clincher!"

"I couldn't have done it without Reno." Sighed Mitch. "He's the best tracker in the world, you know, . . . best friend, too, . . . even killed a Grizzly bear with his bow and arrow!"

"That's enough, brother!" Grinned Reno.

"You really did that?" Queried Pete. "I think I just found a new respect for you, little buddy! . . . Grizzlies are hard to bring down with a rifle!"

"Yes, and so did we!" Nodded Michael. "We love you, Godson, and thank you."

"My pleasure, Mister Zee, no thanks required."

"I think you both are more than wonderful!" Said Nora. "But I'm still worried about all of us here and now."

"So am I, Darling." Sighed Michael. "What time is it, son?"

"A little after two, dad, why?"

"The delivery trucks are due in any time between now and morning, . . . and if either one of you should happen to be hurt, I'd never forgive myself! Just watch yourselves, okay? . . . And Reno, maybe you can make use of those head-knockers again, just could even the odds a little!" He looked at Pete then.

"It's your show now, man, tell us the plan!"

"There's only one obvious plan here, Mike, we know where they'll be stopping the trucks, we just need to be there waitin' on 'em, . . . and that won't be no problem cause there's plenty a cover to hide in, and they won't be expectin' it!"

"There's always a guard there to meet 'em, sometimes two, but this time it'll be me, so they shouldn't be suspicious. They also know you don't start unloading till daylight, so, Reno, you'll be hidin' in th' trees on the rear truck's passenger side. When that man steps down from the cab, put 'im to sleep! . . . If the driver don't hear anything, he'll come on toward the first truck, and that's when you pop him . . . . Mitch, you just stay hid and keep that rifle handy, both of ya! . . . I'm gonna try and lure the first two drivers away from their truck far enough for you to cover them with your rifles. Now, . . . when I do, that's when Mike will step out from his hidin' place and tell them to drop their guns . . . . Maybe they'll give up, but I doubt it! . . . How many a them arrows you got left, Bud?"

"With the one I retrieved in here, I've got three, . . . the other one is somewhere in that marijuana field."

"Three'll work, . . . The second our two drivers clear their truck, maybe you can use the last one." He breathed a sigh then. "Anyway, that's th' plan, Mike, the only one we got!"

"Well I can't think of a better one, so we'll go with it! . . . Okay, . . . we're going to hear them trucks long before they get here, so let's just all try to settle down and get some rest."

"Lots a luck with that, Mike!" Sighed Pete.

"Your right about that, too." Returned Michael. "Okay, Mitch, Reno, . . . you boys best go bring that guard in from the Marijuana patch, be safer if he's here with the others . . . . See if you can find that other arrow."

*   *   *

"It's four thirty, Dad." Said Mitch. "And we haven't heard those trucks yet, do you think they're coming?"

Michael got up from the bunk and stretched, then yawned and looked out over the compound, "They haven't missed a day yet, son, . . . but we'd better get ready for them." He reached down for Nora's hand and urged her to her feet before pulling her against him to kiss her. "Honey, loop one of those machine guns over your head and keep an eye on these birds, . . . and stay out of sight!"

"Yes, Ma'am." Urged Pete. "And if you hear gunshots, don't panic, just stay hid! . . . We're gonna try and take 'em down without a shot, but it's not a guarantee."

"That's right, honey!" Agreed Michael. "You'll know what to do if anything happens."

"Oh, Michael, don't talk like that! . . . I'm frightened enough already."

"Me, too, sweetheart . . . . But this is reality time! . . . Just be prepared, that's all. It could be up to you to get these folks out of here."

"Of course, Michael, . . . I'll do what I have to! . . . Leave me the keys to their shackles though, just in case."

Pete gave her the keys and she kissed Michael again, then hugged and kissed Mitch and Reno. "I love you all so much." She sniffed. "Please be careful?" She stood back then and tearfully watched as they all left.

Pete cautiously led the way toward the drying shed, and all of them had their eyes glued to the dark porch of the Baxter house as they walked, . . . and as they rounded the shed, Mitch stopped and touched Michael's arm.

"What's in here, dad?" He whispered. "I see lights in there."

"Those are heat lamps, . . . look through the cracks, you'll see them."

"Drying the marijuana." He shook his head and shifted the Marlin in his hand. "Don't think I need to, dad."

It was a goof fifty yards down to the cave's large entrance and once there, Pete stopped to face them. "Th' first truck will stop right about here, . . . and Mitch, I'd like you to be in them bushes right over there." He pointed to a spot to the left of the road. "Mike, . . . you'll be on the right, right over there, and don't show yourself too soon, okay? . . . Reno, come with me, bud." He led the way up the old road to stop again.

"That second truck will stop close to these trees here, . . . it's usually offset to allow th' first truck to back past it when it's unloaded, . . . so pick your spot in them trees right there! . . . Now listen to me, man, . . . once you drop these two, move forward as close as you can to us . . . . You get a clear shot at that third man, use that third arrow! If you get 'im, it'll distract the other one enough for us to take him down. If you miss, it'll still be a distraction, and Mitch can take 'im out! . . . Either way, we got it to do! . . . Good luck, kid." He shook Reno's hand and walked back to join Michael.

CHAPTER ELEVEN

Mitch and Reno were at their assigned positions in the trees along the road, and both were watching Michael and Pete as they stood together in the narrow lane talking. Both of them were shivering a little from the cold, but mostly from the dread of what was coming, . . . and they both realized that they had been very lucky thus far to have survived this long, lucky that the guards had been so confident that no one could ever find the compound, that they had become lax in that confidence! But most of all, they thanked God that everyone was still alive and well.

They were only sixteen-year old boys, but they both knew how fickle Lady Luck could be! It had been easy so far, maybe too easy, . . . and not easy to believe that a single shot had yet to be fired, . . . and though neither young man would let it show, they were both severely frightened as both had Pete's graphic description of the truck drivers embedded in their thoughts.

They had seen men like he described in movies, and the damage weapons like those they found here could do, . . . and they also knew that the drivers would be equipped with these same weapons, and that both Pete, and his father could be killed if they were used, . . . and maybe them as well! . . . If that happened, these killers would likely kill everyone else here. That knowledge alone increased the pressure they were both feeling! To them, every life here depended on them doing their jobs well.

A light was always on in the heroin lab because being inside the mountain, the air was always damp and a heat bulb would keep the dampness evaporated away and keep the air dry. The drivers would know this and would pay it no mind because from the air, the light could not be detected, . . . and the light would be a good thing for those waiting to spring their trap! With the moon already behind the towering pines, its glowing light did not make it through, thus the cave's dim light would be all any of them would have to work with, . . . and would not make the job any easier.

"It's after five." Breathed Pete, sighing a thick misty fog. "I'm thinkin' we should a heard 'em comin' by now."

"They haven't missed a morning yet." Returned Michael as he continued to stare into the darkness. "Have they ever missed one?"

"None I can remember! . . . But there's always a first time."

"If we don't get this done, the Baxters will complicate things for sure!"

Pete looked at his watch again. "They'll be up anyway at six o'clock." He whispered. "If we have to shoot these guys, gunshots will bring 'em runnin' soon enough!"

"And then what?"

"If we survive it, I'll head up to th' house and wave 'em down this way . . . . We'll surprise them too, how's that?"

"You are sounding more and more like G.I. Joe, Pete! . . . Gung Ho!"

"Is it okay if I don't feel like him?"

"Pete, you are a brave man, . . . you have survived a war, beat hell out of a madman and lived to tell about it! . . . I trust your judgment, my friend."

"Well I hope you're right, . . . cause I can hear th' trucks!"

"I don't see any headlights."

"They don't use 'em, they got night-vision goggles! . . . Now make sure you can't be seen, Mike." He watched Michael hide himself in the trees then took a deep breath and checked the machine gun's breech, and the cartridge in the chamber, flipped the gun off safety and got Mitch and Reno's attention by waving and pointing at the dark road, . . . and then backed away a few feet to wait for the inevitable.

Reno pulled the bow from around his neck and watched the darkness intently and was, by now, able to hear the faint sounds of laboring engines as the trucks worked their way up the side of the mountain. Ten minutes later, his heart was in his throat and pounding as he saw the cave's dim light reflected in the large van's windshield. Taking two of the wood-tipped arrows, he clamped one in his teeth and loaded the other one on the bow.

The Diesel engines were loud now, and meshing gears growling as the first truck reached level ground and slowed as it idled past his position to finally roll to a stop several feet in front of Pete, who waved at them. The second truck came to a stop directly behind, and offset from the first one, as Pete had said it would, . . . and there sat for a minute before the driver switched off the engine, and still they sat for another minute before the passenger suddenly turned on a hand-held searchlight, causing Reno to quickly duck deeper into the underbrush. But the light was only a fleeting thing and scanned the trees quickly before being turned off.

After another minute, and evidently satisfied, the man looped the machinegun over his head and shoulder, as did the driver and they opened the doors. Reno slowly stood up again, raised the bow as the Columbian stepped down to the ground, . . . and as he closed the door, pulled the bowstring back and released the arrow. The solid crack of wood on bone sounded, followed by the sound of his head striking the truck's cab as he went down.

He quickly loaded the second arrow as the driver rounded the front of the truck, curious at the noise he had heard, . . . and when he saw the downed man, raised the weapon, but the arrow was already there and felled the killer instantly.

With a sigh of relief, Reno looked toward the first truck as the passenger was just getting out, watching as the killer stopped to look back toward the second truck, and unable to see the two bodies in the dark he closed the door and started toward the front of the vehicle.

Reno quickly reloaded the bow and moved through the underbrush with pounding heart. He could see Mitch's head and saw him raise his rifle, . . . and that's when he stopped and pulled the bow. There was only a small opening through the Pine branches as he released the arrow, but saw it strike the man at the base of his skull and spine with a distinct crack, pitching him forward to almost collide with Pete as he fell.

Expecting it, but unprepared for the man hitting him, Pete sidestepped him, but didn't see the driver crouch when the man was hit, . . . and he was just whirling back toward him in time to see the machinegun being raised, . . . and then the fleeting glimpse of movement as Michael clubbed the man from behind.

"God damn it!" He blurted, quickly bending to place both hands on his bent knees and breathing in great gulps of freezing air.

"You okay, Pete?" Gasped Michael as he rushed to his side. "You hurt, man?"

"Oh, no, Mike." He breathed. "Just my pride, man, thanks . . . . I wasn't prepared for that one fallin' into me like that! . . . And that other one had me stone cold dead if you hadn't stepped in, . . . you saved my ass that time, Mike!"

"Hey, I guess I did!" He grinned. "I started to shoot him, but thought about the noise and almost waited too late!"

"You got 'im though, . . . damn, I can hardly stand! I've been in close calls durin' th' war, Mike, but I can't recall one this close."

"Well, I knew that old rock over there had to be good for something, come on, I'll help you over!" He took Pete's arm and ushered him toward the large rock and sat him down.

Reno started working his way out of the trees when the man fell, and Mitch had almost shot the driver, but lowered the rifle when he saw his father hit him. He stood up before pulling the rifle's strap over his head and started forward just as Reno joined him, . . . and after several pats on the back, they were almost to the rock where Michael and Pete were talking when movement caused Mitch to look at the truck, and the driver as he was getting to his feet.

"Look out, dad!" He yelled, and with his heart in his throat, and an instinct he didn't realize he had, he pulled the Navy Colt replica from it's holster and fired, the lead ball's impact forcing an involuntary, agonizing grunt from the Columbian's open mouth as he was lifted slightly and thrown backward into the underbrush. The sudden explosion was deafening in the crisp mountain air and seemed to reverberate for miles before fading away.

Pete, Michael and Reno stood open mouthed as they stared at the killer's body, . . . then looked at Mitch who was staring down at the gun in his hand.

"God, Mitch!" Laughed Reno and slapped him on the back. "I never saw you do that before, brother!"

Mitch looked at his father and pointed at the body. "He was going to shoot, dad, I had to!"

"I know, Son, . . . and it was the most remarkable thing I've ever seen, thank you!"

"I love you, dad."

"Come on, Mike!" Broke in Pete urgently. "We have to hurry now. You three get out of sight, quick, I'll go bring th' Baxters, now hurry!" They all scrambled back into the trees along the pathway as Pete ran back up the lane toward the compound.

*   *   *

Nora found herself holding her breath as she watched her entire family walking away to a possible encounter with death! . . . She let it out in a gush of cold mist and did her best not to cry as she remembered what Pete had said about the Columbian truck drivers. Michael, and for sure not Mitchell or Reno had ever looked so much danger in the face before, . . . they could die out there, she thought tearfully! She was as patriotic as anyone else, and she knew that the price of freedom sometimes demanded sacrifice, and sometimes death . . . . But this was her family!

She lowered her head to say a short prayer and then to grip the stock of the automatic gun hanging around her neck as she stared hatefully at the dark shapes of the ten restrained guards, . . . and knowing full well they were staring back at her the same way. Stifling back a sob, she walked over in front of them and sat down on the foot of Michael's bunk.

"I don't know if you can understand me." She sniffed. "But this is my country, and you don't belong here!" She raised the gun then. "So I am going to make you a promise, . . . if anything happens to my husband and son, I will use this gun on you all, . . . I will blow your asses to hell!" She got up and went back to watching the Baxter's house.

Her heart gave a lurch when she heard the trucks coming in and waited breathlessly for the sound of gunfire that she feared would come, . . . and when there was none during the time she had mentally calculated, had begun to relax when the lone shot echoed loudly in the stillness, causing her to gasp loudly and unconditionally, . . . and moving back into the barrack's deeper shadows, she continued to watch the house. She was still gripping the machinegun when she saw the four nude women, all carrying their togas run down the rickety steps and across the compound screaming, . . . and her heart went out to them. She stood back as they ran past her barracks and into the other one and a minute later, three of the Baxters ran down the steps brandishing their guns and yelling for the guards, . . . and then hearing Jesse's fearsome voice cursing when they didn't respond.

She recognized all three of them as they started toward the barracks and raised the gun, mentally swearing to kill them all. She gasped again in surprise when she heard Pete urgently yelling for Jesse to come running and watched as they quickly turned and sprinted off down the pathway toward the cave.

Her relief was so overwhelming that she couldn't stand up any longer, and had to back up to the bunk again and sit down, . . . once again praying for her family's safety.

*   *   *

Rifles held ready, Michael, Mitch and Reno crouched nervously in the brush and trees along the side of the path and heard Pete call out to Jesse, . . . and a minute later he came running back past where they were waiting and stopped in front of the truck to wave back at the jogging trio and motion them forward, . . . and all the while his hand was on the machine gun's grip.

Jesse, Ethan and Benji Baxter all came to a sudden stop at sight of the Columbian bodies. "What th' fuck happened here, Pe, . . ."

"This is what happened, Jesse!" Grinned Pete. "And I'll cut all three of you in half if you try to raise them guns, . . . now drop 'em!"

"What th' hell are you doin', Pete, . . . put that thing away?"

"I'm doin' what I should a done two years ago, Jesse, . . . now drop them fuckin' guns, you piece a shit, all of ya!"

"If I was you." Said Michael in a loud voice, as he stepped out behind them. "I'd do what he says, . . . because it would give all of us great pleasure to kill you!"

"What's th' fuckin' meanin' a this, Pete?" He glared hatefully at Pete then. "Who turned this fuckin' Slug loose?"

"Well gosh, Jesse, . . . that would be me." He growled. "And if you'll look, there's two more with 'im! . . . Now, Jesse, I know you ain't got sense God gave a goose, but you are smart enough to know you will die if you don't drop them fuckin' guns!"

All three of them glared at Pete and then back at Michael and the boys before dropping their weapons on the ground.

"Pete," Growled Jesse. "You fuckin' Slug, why you doin' this to me, I saved your God damn life?"

"No sir, you tried to kill me, and couldn't! . . . And this ain't no fuckin' life, now shut up and walk!" He gestured with the gun as he spoke.

"Where to?"

"Th' middle a th' compound, . . . there's a few people would like to say hello, . . . now move!"

"You'll regret this, you turncoat!" Said Jesse nastily. "You'll fuckin' regret it!"

"Not before you do, you slime, . . . now move out!" He moved in behind them as they started the walk back to the compound, . . . and shaking his head at Michael, he grinned and jostled him as they both followed the trio.

Mitch and Reno both stopped to stare into the dimly lit cave.

"Drug lab!" Nodded Mitch. "It has to be, I can see the chemical canisters from here."

"Heroin!" Nodded Reno. "They cooked it, dried it, weighed it and shipped it right out of here, . . . a hell of a big operation!"

"Hell, is right!" Said Mitch and glanced back at the trucks. "Well, old friend, I guess we'd better check out and hogtie these assassin pigs, if any of them are still breathing, . . . wouldn't do for one to wake up."

"You got more of those ties?"

"A half dozen, maybe. You get their guns, I'll tie them up, how's that?"

*   *   *

Nora was watching as Michael and Pete herded the three men back into the compound, and as her heart pounded its relief hurried out into the almost totally dark yard to walk with them as they ushered them toward the old cast-iron cook pot.

"Okay, you can stop right there!" Ordered Pete, and when they complied, he turned to Michael. "It's a little dark out here, Mike, . . . think you could go open that drying shed's doors?"

Nodding, Michael turned to hug Nora. "Watch them, honey." He quickly backtracked across the compound and swung the shed's double doors out wide.

"Where's Mitch and Reno, Pete?" She asked, looking back toward the pathway. "Are they all right?"

"They're back at th' cave, Ma'am, they're both okay."

"Now ain't that fuckin' sweet, . . . Ma'am?" Sneered Jesse. "Her name's cunt, didn't she tell ya?"

Nora gasped then suddenly went forward enough to slap Jesse hard across his bewhiskered face, bringing a torrent of vile language from his cut lips. "Call me that again and I'll blow your balls all over your precious dope field, you ass hole!"

"But not before I knock your God damn teeth out!" Said Pete in anger. "Now you best shut your sewer and stand still!"

Just then, light from the heat lamps cast their yellow glow on the compound, illuminating the three men.

"You okay, Ma'am?" Asked Pete.

"Yes, thank you."

"What happened here?" Asked Michael as he came back.

"Nothing your wife couldn't handle, Mike!" He looked back at Jesse's snarling face then. "Where's your loco old man, Jesse, still in his beddy-bye?"

"Why don't you go find 'im, slug? . . . He's prob'ly waitin' on ya with a shotgun!"

"This garbage is all yours, Mike, . . . They give you any trouble, go ahead and shoot 'em, . . . it won't be a loss!"

"I have other plans for these animals." Gritted Michael.

"Okay then, I'll go wake up poochie-poo, wouldn't want crazy papa to miss th' party!"

"You go ahead, Pete, Nora and I can handle them."

Grinning, Pete nodded and hurried off toward the old house, but then took the sagging steps slowly one at a time, . . . and as he crossed the porch, the audible sounds of tired lumber was distinctly heard.

"Wake up, pop!" Yelled Benji suddenly. "Help!" He yelped then as Michael rushed in and hit him with the butt of the machinegun, sending him to his knees in a heap.

"Hey, now, . . . ain't you the tough Mother Fucker?" Sneered Jesse.

"He's tough enough to blow your stinking head off, you animal!" Shrieked Nora. "Now shut up!"

"Th' Cunt's tough, too, Jess!" Sneered Ethan.

"You shut up, too!" Growled Michael. They all looked toward the house then as they heard the burst of sewer language being screamed at Pete.

"It appears he found your old man." Laughed Michael, . . . and then they laughed again as the elder Baxter was kicked bodily across the old porch to tumble down the steps into the yard, and cursing all the way!

Pete came down the steps behind him as he tried to stand up, and was laughing as he kicked the old man in the ass, forcing him to his knees, . . . and then continued to kick his ass and groin until he began to crawl on hands and knees toward the others in his effort to get away. Still laughing, Pete followed and then kicked him in the groin one last time before the old man crawled among them to clutch at Benji''s legs and cry.

"Cock-suckers!" He screamed back at him, which only made Pete laugh harder.

"Michael," Said Nora getting his attention. "Most everyone in the barracks are awake now anyway, . . . isn't it time we let them up? . . . They must be frightened out of their minds by now."

"You have the keys, honey, go do it! . . . And explain to them what is going on, okay? . . . Tell them they're going home today."

"We might have a riot on our hands, Mike, they might just beat these ass holes to death, . . . and ya know what? . . . I wouldn't stop 'em."

"Did we miss anything, dad?" Asked Mitch as he pushed the two guards ahead of him and made them stand with the Baxters. Reno shoved the two Columbian assassins into the mix and all stood back to cover them.

"The other two killers are dead!" Said Mitch tightly. "Reno's arrow broke the other one's neck!"

"Both of those trucks were empty, too, Mister Zee!"

"Empty? . . . That ever happen before, Pete?"

"Not in my two years here." Pete sighed then and looked at Mitch and Reno. "Looks like you boys just saved all our lives, you'd got here tomorrow??" He shrugged his shoulders. "They weren't here to make a delivery this time!" He walked in front of Jesse then.

"Take a look at them two old boys next to ya there, Jesse, . . . know who they are? . . . They're assassins! . . . They was here to kill you old boys, and everybody else here. Yes sir, . . . looks like we just saved your fuckin' ass tonight!" He grinned widely. "Yeah them two weasel lookin' Mother Fuckers was here to murder you, Jesse. This little operation was closin' down, . . . and these old boys would not have left any witnesses."

"Fuck you, turncoat!"

"Looks like we just fucked you! . . . And look behind me there, old son, see 'em? . . . Them's all th' good people you been whippin' and rapin' all this time, and I know they can't wait to repay you boys for that kindness, . . . You nasty-assed Mother Fuckers!"

They all turned to watch the twenty three toga-clad slaves exiting the two barracks, and as Nora started back toward them, everyone of them came with her to stare hatefully at the captives.

"That's far enough folks." Said Michael loudly, just wait back there, . . . your time will come, I promise."

"Give me a gun, Mister?" Begged one middle-aged, long haired man, the heavy beard on his face all but totally gray. The man's eyes were filled with tears and his voice trembling as he reached his shaking hand toward Mitch's rifle. "Please boy, . . . They been raping my little girl over and over again for all these years, my wife, too!" He looked at the other men beside him and pointed.

"That man's wife, too, . . . and his wife, and his! . . . You got to let us kill them, we have that right!"

"Yes sir, you surely do." Agreed Michael. "You all do. But just because these men are inhuman, and deserve to die, doesn't mean you have to stoop to their level . . . . I've seen what you folks went through here, it was hell! . . . But now it's over, I'm taking you home, me, Pete here, my wife and sons, who by the way risked their lives to find us! . . . We're taking all of you away from here, you'll get the medical attention you need, your wives and daughters are going to get the help they need to get over this!" He looked back at Jesse and the others then.

"These men will get everything they deserve, too, to the fullest extent of the law, I guarantee that! . . . But you will get some payback satisfaction, too, before we leave here, I promise. But for now, please just stand back and watch." He looked back at the Baxters then before looking at Reno.

Okay you Baxters, it's showtime! . . . I want all of you to strip, right down to your nasty bare asses, and when you're done, I want you to fold your clothes neatly and deposit them under that old pot over there . . . . Do it now, damn you, because if you don't, this young man here will put an arrow through your shoulders! . . . Load it up, Reno! . . . I have a couple of things to do! . . . If they don't disrobe, shoot them!"

"You got it, Mister Zee!" He drawled then placed the arrow on the bow and pulled back on the bowstring pointing it at Jesse's leering face. "Get it done, jack-ass!"

Grinning, Michael turned back toward the others. "Now good people, while they are peeling off their filth, feel free to laugh, because it's not often that you'll ever see anything that funny! . . . Okay now, if you would, one of you could get ready to start that fire over there, but stand upwind, once those clothes start to burn it's going to be lethal.! . . . And now, I need a couple of you men to come with me, we have to bring out supplies, tables and chairs, . . . we are going to cook us up a decent meal, and we are going to eat it at a table like civilized people that we are." He looked at Pete then.

"Would you mind helping the boys make sure our guests shuck their clothing?"

"Not at all, sir."

"Thank you, and should Reno have to shoot one of them, help him load his bow again, will you?' He motioned at four of the other men then and they followed him toward the house.

"Mom." Said Mitch, looking up at the camouflaged mesh above them. "You and some of the ladies might enjoy doing something about this canopy. Burning sticks would sure let in some fresh air, not to say some nice sunlight come sunup?"

"Uh, son." Came one of the men at Mitch's elbow. "Some matches might help with that fire."

"Oh, here you go, sir." Said Pete, quickly giving him the box. "Wait for the clothes now, okay?" He turned back to the captives then, who were all in the process of tugging off their boots while holding onto each other to keep from falling. "Hurry it up, boys! . . . Don't be modest now . . . . That steel arrowhead sure looks sharp on that thing, don't it? I know I wouldn't want a get shot with it!"

"I should a let 'em kill you, you slug!" Mouthed Jesse as he unhooked the overall's shoulder straps.

"Why not, . . . you couldn't do it, SLUG!" He mimicked . . . . "Hurry up now, get yourselves naked, these good folks need a laugh! . . . And watch your filthy mouth, there's ladies present, and Jesse, . . . you don't move your sorry ass, this Apache Indian boy will enjoy puttin' that arrow in ya, he took out most a your guards singlehanded Anyway!" He grinned at Reno then, and nodded, . . . enjoying himself immensely.

"Hey, Jesse, very good! . . . Now fold 'em up and put 'em under that pot, shoes and all, you won't be needing 'em anymore."

Jesse reluctantly did as he was told, cursing the men and women who were laughing and calling him names, their jeers seeming to enrage him to the point of murder as he dropped his clothing under the pot and started back.

"What's wrong, Jesse?" Asked Pete. "It's right for you to abuse folks, but they're not allowed? . . . What if I just had you bend over and let somebody ram a stick up your sorry ass and rape you? . . . Would that be right, you ass hole? . . . I think some of these ladies might just enjoy that, too, don't you?"

"Oh, hell yes!" Voiced one of the women. "Please do it, Mister, Pete, I'm begging you to?" And that was choroused loudly by all the rest of them causing Jesse to look at them worriedly.

"What about you, Benji?' He laughed. "That sound like a good idea to you, . . . you did it to them, you rat's ass piece a shit! . . . Now fold them clothes and put 'em in the fire, Slug! . . . Move your fat ass!" Benji picked up his clothes and did what he was told without a word.

"Do it, Ethan!" Said Pete. "You, too, old man, else I'll kick you in th' balls again! . . . Hurry up, all of ya, and get back over here!"

Nora had been grinning widely as she hid behind Mitch to watch the show and then she sighed and hugged Mitch. "I'll see about some volunteers, honey, and some cooks."

*   *   *

Michael led the way up the steps and across the porch then stopped to face them before going in. "I want to thank you men very much for the restraint you showed back there, you have every right in this world to beat all of those men out there to death and you know what, . . . we would not have stopped you, because we want them dead, too! . . . But I don't want them to die right away, I want them to suffer, just like they made all of you suffer . . . . And what is left of them afterward, I want the law to have . . . . They are facing the death sentence for what they have done here, and with all your testimonies in court, it will be swift and sweet justice."

"I haven't been here but a week, but I have seen, and I know what you've been through. I don't know how long you've been here, and I don't want to know. What I want you to know is how sorry I am that this happened to you!"

"We want to thank you, too, for getting us out!" Said one of the men he had been working with.

"I don't deserve it." He said shaking his head. "It was my sons that found us. They're only sixteen years old, but they did something the National Guard couldn't do! . . . They deserve your thanks, and mine! . . . That being said, My name is Michael Zant, and I'm from New Mexico." He shook hands with each of them as they introduced themselves, . . . and then led them through the old house to the food-pantry, emptying it, and the freezer of what meat and vegetables they would need, and stacked it all on the porch while they returned for tables, chairs, linen and dishes.

By now, Nora and several of the women had pulled a couple of the long poles from beneath the canopy, set the ends on fire and had burned a wide opening in the canopy, and were all standing and watching a crisp, beautiful sunrise that most had not seen in more than two years, except through a tightly woven mesh.

Once the tables were placed end to end on the ground, Nora and the women took over, taking the supplies and using the tables to prepare the meal. A couple of the men had turned the iron pot over, dumping its contents on the ground and rolled the large cauldron off into the dope field, . . . and once the filthy clothing had all been burned, placed wood on the fire and used it to cook the food on.

Michael took the men into the money room where he stood in front of the money-bales and directed them to carry out everyone's own original clothing and place them all on the porch. Their hunting rifles were all in the old man's room in back of the house, . . . and after these were carried outside, Michael stayed behind and went back into the money room, picked up a large black satchel from the corner and placed it atop one of the bales before walking back out on the porch to watch as they all found their clothing and went back to the barracks to get dressed.

Smiling sadly, he watched them for a minute then sighed and went back into the dark room, tore open one of the bales and filled the large satchel with drug money before closing it up. It took both hands to lift and carry the heavy valise out into the hallway where he placed it against the inside wall beside the door then nodding his satisfaction, went out to retrieve his own clothes before going back inside to change.

*   *   *

With everyone once again dressed in their complete hunting attire, the women were back to their immediate chore of preparing the large meal. Michael put on his ammo vest and walked back out on the porch to watch them, . . . he also watched the Baxters as they cowered in front of the Marijuana field and tried to hide their privates, and grinning at the irony, watched the women again for a moment to marvel at the almost immediate change that had seemed to come over them, . . . and then had to smile as he remembered the old cliché saying that clothes make the woman!

All nine of the men were clustered around Pete and the boys, their hunting rifles across their shoulders, and thinking of that he saw his and Nora's rifles leaning against the steps and descended them to shoulder his own before looking down the pathway.

They dared not tarry here for too long, he thought, knowing they had been lucky this far. He also knew that the Columbians would be coming to check on things once the assassins failed to report back that the job was done. They might even be on their way here at this moment? . . . But they all needed food in them before they did anything else, and the truck had to be outfitted. So much to do, he thought urgently as he walked on out past the tables, and the working women to where the men were, and took Pete aside.

"They giving you any trouble?"

"Jesse is, . . . but all four are still cussin' us, . . . and the men are cussin' 'em right back, . . . but so far they ain't tried forcin' th' issue. What ya got in mind, Mike?"

"Time, . . . we're running out of it! . . . How much time do you think we'll have before the Cartel sends more men?"

"Hard to say, . . . but they would have expected the killers to call in on th' Baxter's radio by now! . . . They could already be on their way."

"I think so, too!" He saw Mitch look their way and motioned him over. "Pete, I'm going to have Mitchell radio Ames Bowman for help, . . . What I would like you to do is take the Baxters over to that whipping post and chain them up on it!"

"Any particular way?"

"Exactly the way they did these men when they whipped them!"

"That's what I figured you had in mind." He nodded. "You got it, Mike."

"That is Jesse's favorite position, by the way."

Pete grinned. "Your word is my command, Mon Capitan!" He left as Mitch arrived.

"Come on son, let's call Mister Bowman."

*   *   *

"How did you come to know these call letters?"

"We had a Walkie-talkie with us when we started out, Jimmi gave them to me."

"Had a Walkie-talkie?"

"Yes sir, . . . I left it on my horse when we ran them off! . . . I'll explain it later. Can you work this thing, dad?"

"Never seen one like it before, but maybe." He found the switch and turned it on, and on a whim, copied down the frequency setting on the dial before looking up at Mitch.

"Four point, one-one, nine Megs." And once the dial was set. "Code name echo."

Michael picked up the transmitter microphone and flipped the switch. "Michael Zant calling echo, over?" They heard only static, and a fluctuating ringing, so he flipped the switch again.

"Michael Zant calling echo, come in echo. Over?"

"This is echo." Burst an excited Carl Spencer. "Is this really you Michael. Over?'

"It's really me, Carl. We are all okay, Mitch and Reno found us and we are now in control of the situation here. Now listen closely, . . . Columbian Drug Cartel is responsible for all recent abductions. We are in the facility now. Heroin is made here, as much as thirty acres of marijuana is grown here, all dried and shipped from here along with the heroin, which is cooked, dried and packaged here. We have thirty-four men and women here. We have five children, all of them used for slave labor. We are all free and safe at this time, but fear Cartel will be coming soon. We will be leaving here at noon to start back."

"Authorities must be notified immediately. We will leave prisoners behind for them, eighteen in all! Two Cartel men, dead at drug lab. If posse does not get here before Cartel, they will kill all before information can be obtained! . . . They must get here by noon, I repeat, by noon today. Do you copy this, over?"

"Copied and recorded, Michael. What is your location, over?"

"In the mountains, Carl, . . . I do not know. Put planes in the air to fly north over mountains for at least sixty miles, repeat sixty miles. If they leave soon they will be overhead by noon, . . . tell pilot to look for smoke exactly at noon. Tell pilot to watch closely, Carl, we could be less than sixty miles out! Over?"

"Copy, look for smoke, copy that! . . . Is that all? Over?"

"No, . . . The Cartel is on the way, hurry! . . . Have ambulance ready for us, some passengers traumatized . . . . We will be coming back along the same trail that brought us here, and in the same vehicle . . . Now, copy this down, Carl, . . . fourteen, dot Three-three, dot one Megahertz. Could be the setting used by the Cartel to contact this operation. Over?"

"Message received, Michael, good luck. Over and out!"

"Okay son," He sighed, putting the transmitter aside. "Find something and smash this thing!"

The table was being set with food and plates as him and Mitch walked down the steps and on past the table toward the whipping post, and the men surrounding the chained up Baxters, . . . and the cursing the four of them were mouthing was loud and constantly obnoxious, until one of the abused hunters would punch one of them in the back with a rifle butt, . . . but all that did was bring another torrent of yelps followed by more cursing!

"Given the chance, they would beat them to death, Dad."

"And I'd love to give them the chance, . . . but we are better than that! . . . We stoop to their animalistic behavior and we become no better than they are . . . . But I do believe that if we were to turn them over to the

F.B.I. as is, . . . they would not nearly get the punishment they deserve! . . . For what they've done to these people, they should be flogged to death." He sighed then. "But a good whipping will have to do."

Pete looked around as they approached. "Did you get through?"

"We got through . . . . Whether the F.B.I. will get off their dead ass and get here in time is another story, . . . but right now the meal is ready, Pete, get the men over and let's eat, I'm starved, . . . and we have to be gone from here by noon!" Pete went back and told the men, who didn't have to be told twice it was time to eat and they all came to the long table and sat down.

After Nora gave thanks, they dug in, and it did not take all that long for the group of starving captives to eat their fill, and then to pack what was left for the trip out of the mountains . . . . When they were all done, Michael leaned over and told Mitch to go for the coiled blacksnake whip he had seen hanging from a nail on the porch of the Baxter's house, . . . and when he returned, he stood up and cleared his throat.

"Folks, . . . we have to leave this place no later than noon, and it is now after nine A.M., however, we still have a few things to do first." He looked at Pete then. "Pete, can you start that truck over there and pull it out here?" When Pete nodded. "We'll need all the rope you can find, too, just toss it in the bed. Make sure we have plenty of gas, too, and thanks." He watched Pete get up and walk away before looking back at them.

He nodded at two of the men then. "What's your name again, sir?"

"Joel McCreedy."

"That's right, I forgot . . . . Joel, I saw you whipped a day or so ago, how is your back, sir?"

"Still hurts like the devil!" He said, casting a hated glance at the Baxters.

He looked at the other man then. "Jack, . . . Carson, right?" And when he nodded. "I saw you whipped the day we got here, . . . why don't you come on up here with Joel." He looked at the other men then. "How many more of you have been whipped?" He watched three others get up to come forward and nodded at them. "Any more of you?"

"There was a lot more!" Grated McCreedy. "Eight or ten maybe in the past two years."

"Where are they now?"

"That Mother Fucker beat 'em to death, . . . a couple of their wives, too, I guess, . . . they were raping 'em! . . . At any rate, they disappeared . . . . A few of those here are their replacements, just like you and your wife . . . . You do need to let us kill the Bastards."

The law will do that, my friends, killing them would only make you as bad as they are! . . . But that does not mean you don't deserve satisfaction . . . . Now, I know some of your wives, and daughters have been raped by these animals, and I would like for those women to stand up also. You do not have to, ladies! . . . Only if you want to, . . . if you do not, your husbands, or fathers will do. Please just step on up here with these men."

The four girls from last night stood and came forward, along with two other men and he smiled at them. "Okay." He nodded. But then they all heard the rock-crawler's powerful engine roar to life and all turned to watch as the tall truck was driven out of it's shed and on to stop in the center of the compound.

Sighing, Michael took the whip from Mitch and held it at his side. "People, I'm going to leave it to you to do the right thing about these men." He looked around at the other bound Columbians then. "These men here do not worry us, the F.B.I. will be here at noon to take them into custody, as well as those in my barracks over there." He held up the whip then.

"This is what was used on you, men, . . . and I think it right that you should use it on them for what they done to you, you ladies as well! . . . Now I know you want to kill them, . . . but wouldn't you rather cause them a world of pain instead?"

"Oh, hell yes!" Nodded one of the man hatefully and reached for the whip.

Michael pulled it back. "Come on now, let's all go over and see how the Baxters feel about it, shall we?" He led the way across the compound with all of them on his heels, and when he came close to the captives, stopped the others while he went on to stand next to Jesse's ape-like hairy back and rear end.

"How are you feeling, Jesse?"

"Fuck you, Slug!" He gasped, . . . and then flinched as the frayed end of the whip was laid across his bare shoulder.

"You're about to have a ringside seat for the sport you enjoy so much! . . . I know you couldn't really enjoy the thrill of pain before because you couldn't feel it, . . . so I arranged for all these good men and women to explain the explicit sensations to you in person!"

"You go to hell, you Slug!" He growled angrily. "Let me loose and I'll rip your fuckin' head off!"

"Aww, I couldn't do that, you know why? . . . Because when Mister McCreedy here asked you to do that, you refused him! . . . Fair is fair, don't you think? . . . Sure ya do!" He moved around behind Ethan then and ran the lash across his, and then Benji's bare backs and buttocks, bringing jerking gasps of expectancy from them.

"I want you two old boys to know that this whipping is all your big brother's fault, and being his kin makes you as guilty as he is. It's true you didn't whip anybody, and maybe you didn't actually kill anybody, . . . but you did abuse these decent young ladies, and you got to pay for that!"

He looked at the old man then. "And you are the sorriest piece of no good shit that I have ever seen, . . . you are a vile, unloving, uncaring son of a bitch, . . . and I hold you responsible for your ass hole offspring being what they are! . . . If it was up to me, I'd let them slit your old throat, because you don't deserve any better . . . . All of you boys can blame your old man for what's about to happen, because he didn't teach you any better!"

He turned and motioned one of the four ladies forward and gave her the whip. "Now, ma'am, It appears to me that you should concentrate your revenge on their lower extremities, you can use this thing, can't you?"

"I don't know," She sobbed. "But I'm going to try!"

"Then wear yourself out, my dear and when you're done, give the whip to the girl behind you." He looked back at Jesse then. "Here it comes, Jesse!"

He heard the swish of the whip, then the crack, followed by Jesse's grunting scream as his testicles and buttocks were struck, and then struck again as the girl screamed obscenities at him with each strike. He walked over to the waiting men then. "She must have been Jesse's favorite."

"She was his choice." Nodded one of the other men. "Son of a bitch ruined my little girl, he did!"

"I am sorry, sir . . . . But every game has its rules, Mister Wheeler . . . . When these ladies are through, each of you will get a turn at them, . . . but only four lashes for each of them, okay? No more, no less and my friends you only have an hour, so make the most of it!"

He urged both boys toward the awesome-looking surplus truck then. "You boys climb inside and roll up the sides of that cover then gather up everyone's rifles, bundle them together and tie a bundle to each of those front rib-posts there. Stand them up and tie them securely, we don't want them to be flying around and hurt someone. He saw Pete returning with the ropes then, and once he tossed them into the truck's large bed, he motioned him aside and then to walk with him.

"Mister Pete Rhodes, you, sir have become a very good friend to me and my family, and I thank you very much for helping me retain my sanity this past week."

"It's me should be thankin' you, Mike, you made me a man again!"

"Oh, no, you did that yourself." He urged him closer to the house then. "Now, Pete, . . . right inside that doorway up there is a black satchel. Once we are loaded up and ready to go, I want you to take that satchel, and one of those trucks down there at the cave, and get the hell away from here! . . . And I don't want to hear any argument!"

"Why?" Queried Pete, stopping to peer at him.

"Because you don't belong here!"

"But you might need my help, the Cartel, . . ."

"If they are on the way here, you won't have it that easy yourself, . . . but I think you'll manage . . . . Go find that girl of yours and get married, man. I don't know how much money is in that bag, but it will get you started! . . . Consider it back pay, or wages received." He stuck out his hand and shook Pete's firmly. "I won't forget you, Pete Rhodes . . . . One other thing now, the F.B.I. should be flying over here at about noon, so before you leave, I'd like you to set fire to that first truck, . . . I told them there would be smoke marking the spot . . . . Oh, there's an open bale of money in that first room on the right, if you would bring it out and place it on the table, I'd appreciate it?"

He smiled and hurried back toward the whipping post then to watch the proceedings, and when the last man had had his turn, reached to take the whip from him. All four of the Baxters were hanging limply from their wrists, their backs and buttocks a bloody mess of deep lacerations, and checking each of them found them to be unconscious, but breathing. The old man, however was having some difficulty in breathing, his was a raspy sound and Michael knew the man could die. He also knew it would not be any great loss.

"Okay, folks . . . . If you'll all go back to the table over there, you can collect your back wages. There's a partial bale of money there, stuff your pockets with all you can carry, you earned that, and a lot more! . . . Don't weigh yourselves down too much, we're not home yet, . . . That Cartel could come looking for us!"

"Let the Bastards come!" Snapped McCreedy. "They'll see what Americans can really do! . . . Hey, where's my rifle?"

"They're all in the truck, Joel, I had the boys secure them. Now go ahead folks, there's your hard-earned wages right there, Pete just put it there!"

"Where did all that come from, Dad?" Asked Mitch as him and Reno walked up, each of them staring at the money.

"According to Pete, it's all marijuana profits! The Cartel brings it in to the Baxters every so often, there's a lot more in there, too! . . . Mitch, a few of the ladies are having a time holding onto their wages there, go grab a few of those togas to wrap it in. if you need more money, there's more inside the house." He placed a hand on Reno's shoulder then. "Son, would you please do these four killers the honor of moving them inside the barracks with the others?"

"Sure thing, Mister Z, . . . What about the Baxters, want them in there, too?"

"Reno, son," He sighed then and looked up at the clear sky above them. "I have never been this close to any violence before!" He looked at him and grinned slightly. "I've never done much of anything until now . . . . But the Baxters are the dregs of humanity, they deserve to wallow in their own hell for a while! . . . The authorities should be here in a couple of hours and if they are still alive, they'll find them . . . . If not, they'll die with what they've done on their minds, . . . and with the same helplessness as their victims felt."

"You going to be okay, Mister Z?"

He smiled at his Godson then. "It will take a while, son, but I will be . . . . Now, go ahead, when you're done get everyone in the truck. Cut the ropes up in ten foot lengths and give it to them, tell them to tie themselves to the bed's steel ribs, . . . otherwise they'll be tossed around like a salad! . . . Pack them all in there, son, we have twenty-three of them, . . . and we are not leaving anyone behind!"

"Yes sir, Mister Z!"

He had observed Pete talking with three of the girls as he talked with Reno, and as they were watching Mitch make bags out of the togas for them, he walked over to join them.

"Mike," Said Pete when he stopped in front of them. "These three girls here were all abducted off the street in Denver as they walked home from the movies . . . . If it's okay with you, they can go with me, you have plenty of witnesses to get the job done?"

"If it's okay with them, you have my blessing." He looked at the once, very young women and smiled. "Will you ladies be okay after all this?"

"I don't know." Said one of them shyly, and without looking up at him.

"Honey, don't be ashamed to look anybody in the eyes, none of this was your fault, . . . and no matter what anybody may think, you are still as good as any of them. Never forget that! . . . Good luck to all of you." He smiled at Pete then.

"Take care of them, man, they're precious cargo."

"Not to worry, Mike . . . . Remember, Mike, . . . the Cartel is usin' an old crop duster's airfield to distribute them drugs, and it ain't more than a hundred miles from here, two nights by truck!"

"You have any idea where?"

Pete shrugged and shook his head. "Across th' mountains north a here, maybe northeast. They took me there in a helicopter, and that was a two hour flight from Denver."

"I doubt they'll ever find it." Sighed Michael. "But I'll tell them. We're loading up now, Pete, . . . as soon as we pull out, take these girls and get away from here! . . . Be sure it's close to noon when you blow that truck!"

He looked around at the Marijuana field then. "There should be enough evidence here to open the Government's eyes to what's happening . . . . Good luck, my friend, . . . will you have any trouble?"

"Once I get to a well-traveled road, we won't, . . . if I can make it to State Seventy, look out Denver!"

Michael reached to shake his hand, and then the girls'. "Pete, . . . if you're ever in Albuquerque, look me up!" He turned and went back to help the boys load the passengers in the truck, arriving just as the women were being helped into the tall bed.

"Folks, you have all ridden in this truck, so you all know what those lengths of rope are for, tie yourselves in real good! . . . Okay, I need you men to listen to me now, . . . have any of you vets ever driven a truck like this?"

"Every day for four years." Nodded McCreedy.

"You know what you'll be driving on up here, can you handle it?"

"I'll figure it out!"

"Then get your wife settled in behind the driver's seat up there, and warm this rig up, it's time to go! . . . Mitch, Reno, get everyone tied down up there, and let the sides down, we have to go!"

CHAPTER TWELVE

Mitchell and Reno lowered the sides of the thick camouflaged tarp and tied it in place before climbing up and into the truck and taking a seat opposite each other on the end of the metal benches. Adjusting the automatic, confiscated weapons into their lap, they tied themselves to the bed's steel ribs, . . . and being the last two people on the more than crowded benches, and sitting across from each other, they were able to watch the trail behind them.

However, the swaying, heavily loaded truck had not gone a mile before they were both nodding off to sleep. Not even the constant scraping and slapping of thickly needled limbs being broken or pushed aside roused them until a half hour later when the truck stopped in front of the sentinel's cabin, and Michael told everyone to stay calm while he checked it out.

"It's okay, Dad!" Said Mitch loudly and yawning, untied the rope. "This was the lookout's cabin, . . . I'll take care of it!" He climbed down, and with the large dog once again going into a frenzy and lunging at the chain, cautiously opened the cabin door and went inside.

The Columbian was sweating profusely and glaring hatefully at him as he came in. "It's all over up there, man." He said as he pulled the knife from its scabbard, . . . and grinned when the man's dark eyes widened.

"I'm not a killer, don't worry." He cut the rope that threatened to hang the man then went to the jug of water, filled a tin cup and came back to remove the gag. After the man drank, he tossed the cup away and stared down at him.

"There is no more drug lab up there, and no more friends to help you . . . . And We do not have your Columbian neck tie! But I do want to tell you something, . . . if I thought you had anything to do with what my mother and father were put through up there, I would slit your God damn throat right here and now! . . . But like you said, I'm just a Bambino, and don't know what I'm doing! If you manage to get loose before the American

Government gets here, you had better leave my country, . . . because you are not welcome here!" He grinned again and left.

He crossed the yard, warily watching the huge dog and climbed back up to his seat. "Okay, dad, we can go!"

"Did you turn that man loose, son?"

"I gave him a drink of water!" He said and retied himself to the rib of the bed.

Grinning, Michael turned around and put his arm around Nora. "Let's go, Joel." He said, and the truck moved on out of the maze of trees and began to creep its way up the very rocky slope.

Mitch grinned at Reno then lay his head back between the tightly drawn tarp and steel rib and was instantly asleep again, but only for a second. His eyes popped open, as did Reno's when they heard the explosion, and they both stared back at the forest of trees below them.

"Relax everyone!" Shouted Michael, wanting to be heard above the whining engine. "Pete just blew up one of the trucks, must be noon!"

They watched as black smoke began rising above the trees, looking almost gray in the distance as it drifted up toward the trade winds at the Mountain's crest.

"There's a helicopter up there, too!" Shouted Reno, as he looked skyward. "Three of them, . . . looks like the posse's here, Mister Z!"

They were at the top of the grade now and already having to utilize the unnatural abilities of the renovated truck, as McCreedy worked the gears and steered it over the treacherous field of boulders and rotten timber. They were on their way home, packed like sardines in the bed of an Army Surplus Truck, eight people on each metal bench, five children on the truck's bed between them, and all tightly strapped to the bed and ribs of the heavily constructed steel cage supporting the canvass cover.

Four other adult men sat cross-legged between the benches, each with roped around them and anchored to rings on the bed of the truck. Twenty five victims of circumstance all crammed together in a common cause, and each thankful they were still alive. But even at that, they were all forced to hold to each other, or to hold on to the iron ribs of the cage to keep from being jostled to the point of injury.

Michael hugged Nora tightly, thankful for the heavy seat straps that held them firmly in their seat, and relaxed a little as they hit a fairly smooth section of the rolling landscape, then cast a glance across at McCreedy.

"How you doing, Joel?"

"So far, so good, Mike . . . . I just can't believe this truck!" He said loudly. "Was never one in th' war like it, I'll tell ya that! . . . They didn't have power steering either! . . . Hey, look at that?"

They all watched the dozen or so vultures as they scattered away from the bloated carcass.

"My Lord!" said Nora. "Is that a deer?"

"Could be a horse, Mitch said they turned theirs loose up here."

"Looks to me like a bear!" Said McCreedy. "Big one, too!"

"Must be the Grizzly, Reno killed."

"Hold on folks!" Said McCreedy, slowly stopping the truck to change to a lower gear. "Going down a canyon wall here. Looks wide and deep, so grab onto something."

"Just don't push it, Joel, we'll be okay."

The sudden descent caused the two boys to wake up again, each grabbing the steel rib for support, . . . and once they started up the other side, were thankful for the heavy tail-gate. But at last they were out of the wide canyon and into the darkness if thick timber, forcing McCreedy to switch on the headlights, as well as the six spotlights across the top of the cab.

"Would you look at that!" Said McCreedy. "I can barely see the trail through here for the brush, but I can see a half mile ahead of us!" He upped the speed a bit then, and they were moving quite fast as they entered the clearing, . . . each seeing the black bear and half-grown cubs running from the large blackberry patch in fear . . . . And then they were in darkness again.

*   *   *

Jimmi heard the call on his radio and stopped the other men while he took the Walkie-talkie from his saddlebag.

"This is Charlie, echo, come back. Over?"

"Good news, Charlie, Michael and Nora Zant are found and well, . . . I repeat, Michael and Nora Zant are found, and well. Over?"

"That is great news, Echo. The boys okay? Over?"

"They are on the way home with twenty six abductees, twenty one adults, five children. Over?"

"I repeat, are the boys okay? Over."

"Yes, Charlie, the boys are with them, they took down the whole operation. Turns out it was a drug lab run by drug cartel from Bogata. Over?"

"Are you talkin' Columbia, like the country? Over?"

"One and the same, Charlie. Must have been some operation. F.B.I. are air-lifting fifty marines in there as we speak! . . . You men can come home now. Where are you anyway? Over?"

"That's hard to say, echo, twenty five, thirty miles out. Over?"

"Well, come on home. Over, and out!"

He sighed and put the radio away before reining his horse around and leaning on the saddle-horn to grin at the others. "You heard it, boys, let's go home."

"Man, I wish I had been there!" Said Ben.

"Got a hand it to them boys." Sighed Mason. "Stayin' with it this long, and actually pullin' it off, . . . unbelievable!"

"They are extraordinary kids, all right. Come on, men, we'll use our old campsite tonight, I need some shut-eye."

*   *   *

It was close to dusk when the truck finally crawled out of the deep arroyo onto semi-level ground and continued on over the rock-strewn, and very uneven side of the tapering hillside. The deep ruts were still evident, but not as prominent beneath the covering of crushed dead timber, . . . and as McCreedy slowed the truck to a crawl again, Michael spoke to him, causing him to stop the truck.

"How far have we come, Joel?"

"Well, according to the odometer, fifteen point nine miles, . . . but I'm a little leery about going any faster!"

"So am I! . . . Tell you what, . . . we are all tired and hungry, why don't we stop for the night? . . . We've waited this long to get home, one more night won't hurt anything, besides, . . . it's pretty hard on those riding back there."

"Suits hell out a me! . . . Pardon the language, ma'am."

"Mister McCreedy," Laughed Nora. "Compared to what I have been subjected to these last few days, that sounded like music!"

"Amen, Mrs. Zant." He turned to look back over the seat. "Leona, honey, . . . are you okay?"

"Fine." She responded.

McCreedy sighed and faced forward again. "God, I'd like to whip them animals all over again!" He looked at Michael and Nora then. "She must have been raped two dozen times in th' past two years by that filth, . . . may never be the same again neither . . . . Well! . . . Do we want to hide the truck, or stay in the open, . . . I see a gap in those trees yonder?"

"Then by all means, let's get out of sight! . . . I don't think we're out of the woods yet, Joel, . . . I just don't trust these guys."

"Yes sir, the only good Columbian is a dead one, as far as I'm concerned! . . . Well, here we go." He turned the wheels and headed for the trees where he stopped the rig beneath the branches of ancient Pines and switching off the engine. "Watch for Timber Rattlers, Mike, they're plentiful."

Michael unlatched their nylon restraints and climbed out onto the low steel step below the door then reached into the open storage bin for the flashlight he had seen there and directed its beam on the thick ground cover before stepping down to help Nora out, and together walked to the rear of the truck.

Mitch and Reno were already out and standing off to the side while Joel helped the women down as soon as the other men untied their restraints. As the other women stepped down, Nora was there to offer them comfort.

Michael watched for a minute then turned to look back at the rock-littered trail they had just come over, walking to the edge of the timber to stare at it. He had felt relief at hearing Reno say there were helicopters over the compound, but not as much as he should have. He had been reading about the murders in Columbia for years, drug dealers fighting over their territory, murdering entire villages as a warning to others. It was a war zone. So how were they able to slip into the United States and set up an operation of this obvious enormity? Evidently all the drug dealers there had joined forces, and were now powerful enough to accomplish it, but how? . . . They could not, without some powerful help from someone already in America, someone with clout of their own to assist them.

He also knew that this one operation was only one of many that was probably operating in the United States, and no large organization can continue to operate at their desired level without demonstrating their power over those that want them destroyed. This was not over yet, he was sure of that! . . . They could not, would not let them escape without some form of retaliation, he was sure they would come after them. It would be too late to salvage what was left at the compound, because of the authorities there now, . . . but they could surely come after them to use as a statement of power!

He'd had a thought when they stopped at that cabin earlier, that the man there could just be their downfall. He hadn't known about him being there, well he did, because they had stopped there on their way to the compound, but he had forgotten about it, and the boys had failed to tell him he was there. If the Cartel assassins were to find him, they would surely know the trail they took, and that was what worried him now. That, and the safety of everyone here because more of them could be killed if it came to a fight, and no one would even know they were in trouble. Why didn't he remember about that sentinel? . . . He could have told Carl about him . . . . But he didn't!

"What are you thinking about, Dad?" Asked Mitchell at his elbow,

"What? . . . Nothing, son. I just don't think we're out of danger yet, that's all."

"Thinking about the man in the cabin, huh?"

"How did you know that, son?"

"Because I was, too, . . . and so was Reno. We forgot to tell you about him."

"Well, I knew he was there, too! It's not your fault."

"What should we do?"

"Just keep your eyes open." He sighed. "If we have to, we have the firepower to fight them off, . . . but that's not really what I'm worried about, it's you boys, and your mother, . . . and these good people here! They are so close to being free of all this, and if one of them is killed after all they have been through? . . . I don't know, son, . . . I'm just worried is all. Now come on, keep this to yourself. Get Reno to help keep watch."

They went back to where the others were all standing on the plush carpet of debris and pine needles, and almost all of them were moving around and groaning, or gasping in pain from cramped muscles. They walked in beside Nora then, and he placed an arm around her waist.

"Honey, why don't you take the flashlight and see if the ladies, . . . you know, . . . and watch for snakes, okay?"

Mitch quickly picked a dead length of stick. "Mom, here, . . . take this."

"What on earth for?"

"Beat the grass with it, in front of you and on both sides of you, if there's a snake there, you'll hear it!"

"Thank you, I think!" She frowned then went to ask the women if they needed some privacy and led them off into the trees while the men and smaller boys made use of the underbrush on the truck's blind side.

"I'll get the supplies, Mister Z." Said Reno as he snapped his trousers.

"Thank you, son, bring the water, too! . . . Okay?" He looked around at the underbrush. "I wouldn't want to sit on the ground in here for obvious reasons, . . . but, if it's all right with you men, we can spread blankets out there in the open for the ladies to sit on, . . . we can use the smaller rocks to sit on. But either way, I think it's best we don't make a fire! I know it means eating cold food, but we don't know who might be following us."

"How would they know already." Queried Jack. "They weren't there?"

"Jack, those trucks that came in this morning were empty, . . . and the drivers were not the usual drivers, and they all carried these machine guns, so what does that tell you?"

"I'm sorry, Mike, . . . but I don't know what you're trying to say?"

"Okay, . . . Pete was friendly with one of the compound guards, . . . and it seems that these Columbian drug dealers set up their drug labs in different places every two to three years. Once a new one is set up and running, they send assassins back to close up the old one, leaving no witnesses or evidence behind."

"You mean they were, . . ."

"Yes sir, . . . they were here to murder everyone at that compound and I suspect, guards and all!"

"That still don't mean they know about it yet, . . . does it?"

"No sir, it don't! . . . But the Columbian Drug Cartel is probably the largest crime organization of this kind in the world! It was built on discipline, ruthlessness, murder and terror, . . . and it's safe to assume they have hundreds of these assassins world wide and all very disciplined killers. If they had been allowed to complete their job today, they would have radioed their superiors when they were done, . . . and they didn't! They will send more men to check things out, why? . . . Because they rely on secrecy, they leave no witnesses, and they leave no trace they were ever there. A failed assignment means death for that assassin as well."

"Would they try anything with the F.B.I. there, . . . wouldn't they have given up and gone home when they saw them? . . . Hell, I know I would!"

"They never give up, Jack, . . . they never quit unless they have no clues, no informants, no leads, and no way to right the failed assignment! And just so you all know, . . . All that I just told you, I read about in college."

"Man, won't this nightmare ever end?" Blurted one of the other men.

Reno came back with the supplies then, and the blankets and they all went into the rocks to clear a spot for them to eat.

"Would there be any witnesses, Mike . . . . They're all in custody now, aren't they?"

Michael stood up, looked at Mitch and Reno then shrugged. "All but one, Jack." He sighed. "And I forgot about him, so I didn't tell them about him."

"The man at the cabin!" Breathed Reno. "We forgot about him, too."

"Why didn't we kill him, we were right there?" Asked another of the men with obvious anger.

"My sons are not killers, gentlemen, none of us are! . . . Many of you have killed, but that was war, so please, . . . not one of us here is to blame for any of this. The Cartel may not have found him at all and they may not be after us at all! We just have to be careful!"

"He's right, men." Spoke up McCreedy. "Them two boys there saved all our ass's back there, we'd all be dead now if they hadn't!"

"God, . . . you're right, of course. I'm sorry, Mike, . . . boys. I'm just not in my right mind, I guess."

"No need for any apologies!" Said Mike quickly. "Now here comes the ladies, topic over!"

It was getting dark in the grouping of rocks, but not so they couldn't see each other. The sky was brilliantly lit, by the trillions of visible stars, and the combined luster presented each rock to them in a pale, grayish blue translucence. Each person there was of a darker tone, but recognizable as they ate, and all were gazing up at the sky, and the mountain's ghostly beauty as outlined by the starlight.

"Where are you from, Joel?" Queried Michael, suddenly breaking the silence.

"We're originally from Houston, Texas . . . . Leona and I were childhood sweethearts! . . . We got married just before I shipped out." He was silent for a moment. "We bought a Summer Cabin in Ouray five years ago, came into these mountains on the first day of every hunting season, for the first two years anyway! The last time was three years ago . . . . That's when we met Jesse and his brothers!"

"Where were you hunting?"

"Oh, not too far from Sunlight Peak, . . . rode all night in that same damn truck over there!"

"What about you and yours, Jack?"

"Minnesota, we were regulars at the Mountain-view Lodge at Silverton for the last ten years or so, . . . never missed a year till two years ago! We always loved these mountains . . . . There was thirty people, all working on that damn Camouflaged cover when we arrived, and that's where we were put to work!" He sighed then, and his wife reached to hug his leg against her.

"Took all of six months to finish th' damn thing! . . . Then them damn Columbian Sons of Bitches came with trucks loaded with Marijuana plants, and manure. We must a planted thirty acres of th' shit!"

"Forty, Jack." Said Joel. "It was forty acres! . . . And we've been harvesting the shit ever since! . . . All but five of us here tonight worked the field, and all but a few of the women. Rest of you worked the cave!" He reached out and touched his wife's hair. "Leona just worked, . . . at times I don't know if she even knew it!" He cleared his throat then.

"Until recently there was always thirty people working the field and cover repair, . . . till Jesse beat some to death! . . . They weren't replaced neither, not till that crazy old man murdered a couple of them, that's when they brought you and Nora in, Mike. Guess they were afraid the Cartel would find out about the murders, . . . because they were warned against it!"

"They were all four scared to death of the Columbians, anyway, a day or two before Jesse beat those people to death, he must have made one of the Cartel assassins mad and I don't know what happened, but the Bastard held that machinegun on Jesse and made him get on his knees right there in the compound and beg for his life! . . . Course Jesse took it out on the workers after he left, Crazy son of a bitch!"

"You hear that, Mister Z?" Asked Reno, and they all began to listen to the distant drone of the aircraft.

"Helicopter." Said Mitch. "Down below us there, see the lights?"

"They got a spot-light!" Said one of the other men, speaking for the first time. "You think it's them?"

"They're lookin' for something, that's for sure." Voiced Joel.

"Maybe they're Revenuers." Said Mitch. "Looking for Moonshine stills."

"I think you're probably right, son. At any rate, we had better all sleep in the truck tonight, too many snakes around anyway . . . . We won't be too comfy, but body heat will keep everyone warm."

"I believe you're right." Agreed Joel. "But I think we should keep an eye on that Chopper for a while, see if it comes this way?"

"I don't think it will." Sighed Michael. "Cato, . . ." He had to clear his throat then. "Our guide told us they never fly helicopters, or light planes this high up, winds are too tough up there, . . . down drafts and such! . . . Above that, they couldn't see anything anyway!"

"Wind ain't blowin' right here!" Said Jack. "It can damn sure get this high with no problem!"

"If they got a Choctaw, even the winds won't stop it!" Added Joel. "I've seen them things fly in a hurricane!"

"Military Chopper, . . . why not?" Sighed Jack. "Sons a bitches seem to have the upper hand in this country! . . . They can get anything they want."

"How did you boys know about that man in the cabin, son?" Asked Michael.

"An old prospector told us there might be one." Said Mitch. "His name is Pot-luck! . . . Said he was a sniper in the war."

"How'd you come to find that guy?" Asked Joel. "Hell, I thought prospecting was a lost art?"

"It's a little embarrassing, Mister McCreedy, . . . but I was so sure my dad and mom were dead, that I guess I just lost it, . . . I couldn't even stand up!" He sniffed then, obvious to all, to fight back a tear.

"His horse saved his life, Mister Z, Literally!"

"What?" Gasped Nora and reached to rub Mitch's leg. "Poor, Darling, what on earth happened?"

Mitch cleared his throat. "Pot-luck called it the Granddaddy of all rattlesnakes, Mom . . . . I had my horse's reins wrapped around my arm and, . . . I didn't see the snake."

"The horse did!" Said Reno. "It reared backward when he saw it, and pulled Mitch back as it struck, . . . it hit nothing but air! It must have been eight feet long because it took three of us to carry it."

"And this, . . . Pot-luck was the third man, I assume?" Mused Michael.

"Yes sir." Replied Mitch. "Reno was going to throw the thing over a cliff, when Pot-luck yelled at us! . . . We ate our first rattlesnake Chicken that night."

"My Lord!" Gasped Nora. "You ate the thing?"

"Tasted a little like chicken, Mom, . . . wasn't bad at all."

"Anyway," Said Reno. "He told us that the enemy always has a lookout . . . . That an operation like kidnapping would make the bad guys very careful."

"And he was right!" Added Mitch. "He also warned us about going to sleep in our sweat-soaked clothes at night, they would freeze and make us sick!"

"That was Pot-luck!" Sighed Reno. "Rich, too, had several large bags of gold nuggets buried in his tent. He's one strange old man!"

"Smart, though." Chuckled Michael. "Sounds like someone I need to spend some time with, . . . I might learn something about real life."

"That chopper went on South." Commented McCreedy. "Guess the boy was right."

"I think so, but until we get back to Keyah Grande, we can't rule out being hunted."

"I hope to God, I can lay my scope on 'em!" Grated Joel, and that comment brought unanimous agreement from everyone else.

"Them copters got weak points, too, even th' Choctaw." Said yet another man. "Deer rifle will bring 'em down easy, if you know where to hit it!"

"How do you know that?" Queried Michael.

"I was in th' war, too! . . . Bellies on them things are thin as paper."

"The Columbians might have thought a that, too!" Came back Joel. "Same as they did that truck over there."

"Point taken." Returned the man. "Bastards seem to know more than our Government does anyway."

*   *   *

They were all strapped in and vigilant as Joel steered the truck back out to the vehicle's original ruts, and were immediately back into a treacherous landscape of rotting trees, a conglomeration of different sized boulders, and periodic clusters of ancient Pines, . . . all of which tried to unseat the truck's occupants in passing. The unique spider-like capabilities of the converted surplus truck was becoming even more evident to them, and appreciated as it crawled slowly over and off one obstruction after another, and going in and out of mini-canyons and gully-type depressions that even an experienced climber would have trouble scaling.

They stretched their legs again at mid-day, once again hiding the large vehicle in a grouping of Pines and Fir Trees, and eating a light lunch before leaving again. The mixture of engine and meshing of gears prevented them from hearing much of anything that happened to be occurring outside of the truck, therefore it was essentially out of sight, out of mind to all but Mitch and Reno, who were in their place at the rear of the covered bed.

Both had spotted one or two low-flying copters during the day, but had kept it to themselves so as not to panic anyone and besides, all of them had gone in a different direction. There had even been a Piper-cub flying low over the treetops in the valleys below them, but none of those turned toward them either. But later in the afternoon, a copter had come close enough for them to see the dark green color before it veered away and dropped from sight, . . . and it was this one that unnerved both of them.

Fighting down a sudden feeling of doom, Mitch turned to the man next to him and had him pass the word to his father that they should find a hiding place.

Michael turned around to peer at him over the seatback, and seeing him nod, touched Joel's arm. "Better find us some cover, Joel, we may have company!"

McCreedy saw the frown on Michael's face and quickly began looking for someplace to hide the large truck, . . . and not finding any trees close enough, or thick enough did the next best thing. He turned the truck sharply down the slope and over the crest of another deep, wide gully-like depression where he used the truck's lowest gear to help it crawl its way down into the small canyon and across the rocky bottom to stop as close to the tall, rock wall as he could, partially hiding them beneath a jutting portion of the wall. He killed the engine and quickly looked at Michael

"It's the best I could do." Breathed McCreedy. "Did you see something?"

"No, . . . the boys did, Joel! . . . Check for snakes out there, we'll have to exit on your side!" He unbuckled their harness and together followed Joel out and down to the rocky canyon's floor to quickly scan the high gully's crest and the cloudless sky above them, seeing nothing but high-flying Eagles, and several large crows.

"What did they see, Mike?" Insisted Joel as they got down.

"I don't know, Joel, come on, we need to get everyone out of the truck!" They hurried back to the rear of the vehicle and found Mitch and Reno already helping the women down as they approached, and Joel hurried past them to lift his wife to the ground, . . . and as the men and children came down, Mitch looked at Michael and nodded at the sky.

"We were seen by one of the helicopters, Dad. It saw us and veered off out of sight!"

"Any markings on it, son?' Asked McCreedy. "Any identification?"

"No, sir, none that I could see! . . . It was a plain, solid green helicopter, course we only saw one side of it!"

"It's got a be them." Breathed McCreedy.

Okay," Said Michael. "A couple of you men get back in and hand down those rifles, . . . and Mitch, break out those other two machineguns we confiscated." He turned to Joel.

"You men were in the war, Joel, it's your field of expertise, tell us what to do, man?"

"We need to get away from this truck!" Yelled Joel as the rifles were passed down. "Come on, Jack, get the women and head for some cover down th' ravine there, . . . anything we can hide behind! . . . Go on now, run!"

Mitch passed down the other two automatic guns and jumped to the ground, and the four of them followed the group, each watching the sky above the ravine as they went, . . . and shortly after, they were all grouped beneath an overhang in a cluster of large rocks.

"Watch for snakes, people." Warned Michael as he ushered Nora and the boys toward several large rocks. "They like to sleep where it's cool!" Mitch and Reno had already grabbed dead sticks and were gouging beneath the rocks and slapping at the tall grass.

"Stay back!" Warned Reno as he used his stick to pick up a large Rattler, causing the women to cringe and clutch their rifles to their breasts as he tossed the reptile some several yards up into some higher rocks.

"That's all of them!" Said Michael. "Okay folks, Joel there, and a couple of others here were in the war in combat situations." And as the two boys sat down behind the rocks, he nodded at Joel again. "You tell the rest of us what to do, men, we'll listen!"

"Just stay down!" Said Joel loudly. "Get on the ground, anything, just stay out a sight!" As they all complied, he looked at them and sighed. "Listen up, good people, . . . this is America, land of the free! . . . We went to war on foreign soil to protect it and now we might be doin' it again, right here in America . . . . I just want you all to know, that even after all the hell we've been through, it is still worth fighting for! Now if these sons of Satan do find us, I want you to take those big gins a yours and blow the Bastards back to hell! . . . We're all hunters here, we know how to kill animals!"

It was so sudden that it startled them all when the low-flying, dark green copter suddenly swooped down over the canyon walls above them, the displaced air from long props loud in the hot confines of the crevice, . . . and then it was gone as suddenly as it had appeared.

"You're right, son." Breathed Michael. "No markings at all."

"Do you think they saw us?" Gasped one of the women.

"It's hard to tell, Ma'am." Soothed Joel. "Just stay down."

"There was a man standing out on the landing gear, Mister, Z."

"I saw him, Reno, . . . and they may have spotted the truck."

"Tell ya what we'll do, Mike." Said Joel loudly. "If they did see the truck, or even think they did, they'll come back to look for us . . . . When they do, that copter's going to hover right up there above us while the spotters make sure! . . . When it does, them old German guns you got there will throw out lead like a hard rain throws down raindrops and Mister, four machineguns, each spitting out thirty rounds a second, all at the same time, well, . . . that would sure even the odds a bit!"

"Just spray the belly!" Offered Jack.

"You can count on it, Joel, . . . thanks, Jack! . . . Nora, boys, get ready to do it, make sure these things are ready to fire and please, . . . don't get hurt?" They each checked the long clips and found them fully loaded, then made sure a round was in the chamber and the safety was off. "We're ready, guys."

Time passed slowly for them as they waited, each of them were laying almost on the ground as they watched the canyon's high rim, . . . and sweating profusely, as there was no wind movement at all on the floor of the crevice, only sweltering hot sun. The heavy clothing, they were wearing contributed greatly to that heat, drenching their inner clothing to allow the sweat droplets to run down their bodies and still, they waited for what seemed an hour before hearing the chopper's approach.

"I hear it!" Said Mitch. It's coming, Dad."

"Me, too!" Said Reno.

They all could hear it coming this time, the popping sounds the props made was quite loud as the large copter slowly moved over the deep gully. They could see two spotters this time, one on each side as they stood out on the landing gears and each with a safety harness as they leaned outward to search the ground below them.

Raising the MP 40's, they waited as the copter drifted almost on top of them.

"Now!" Said Joel, and all four of them pointed the weapons upward and fired, as did twenty deer rifles, and the noise was ear shattering as the sudden deadly bursts of gunfire sprayed the aircraft's hull and both spotters with just as deadly accuracy. The spotters were hanging limp in their harness, and the copter had almost immediately burst into flames as it veered from sight, . . . and a few long seconds later, the explosion shook the ground beneath their feet, and was followed, by a wall of flames and billowing smoke that must have shot a hundred feet in the air.

"Them sons a Bitches won't be back!" Yelled Joel. "Way to go, people." But he had no sooner spoke, when he grunted loudly and was thrown backward into the hot dirt of the ravine.

"NOOO!" Screamed Leona as she scrambled to reach her husband. But only hit in the shoulder he had already began crawling back to cover.

"I'm okay." He grunted. "Get back Leona!"

But seeing her husband shot seemed to shock Leona McCreedy back to reality because she freed herself from Joel's grasp and reached out to drag his rifle back to safety, . . . and at the same time as another searching bullet from the hidden sniper careened off the rocks above her head. She helped Joel move in closer behind the rocks then raised the rifle and scope to look for the shooter.

"Locate that sniper, People!" Yelled Joel. "Use your scopes, find th' Bastard and kill 'im! . . . Mike?' He yelled, getting their attention. "Watch the rim up there above you, that's where they'll show themselves. You see 'em, spray hell out of 'em! We'll take care a th' sniper!"

All four of them placed their backs against the rocks they were hiding behind and strained their eyes up at the rocks and foliage along the crest of the canyon's wall. The only thing going for them at the moment was that the sun was sinking ever lower in the West, . . . and was behind them as they watched for the killers.

They were all sweating in the terrible heat and having to constantly wipe the perspiration from their eyes as they searched the rocks when suddenly the sniper fired again and as he did, Leona fired, striking the rocs at the point of the truck's descent into the canyon, . . . and as the man attempted to change position, at least nine rifles had him in their crosshairs and fired.

"Son of a Bitch!" Snapped Leona hatefully when they saw him fall then she smiled as Joel pulled her back against him and kissed her. With the help of the other women then, she dressed and bandaged her husband's wound by using the bottom of her blouse.

"Get back to your posts everybody." Said Joel. "They ain't gone, they just ain't all got here yet! . . . Mike, you see any better cover anywhere?"

"This is it!" Said Michael, still not taking his eyes off the ridge above them.

"Then watch the rocks everybody." He grunted. "You see movement, shoot it! . . . . We can't let th' bastards stop us now!"

"You just lay back there, Joel." Said Jack. "We'll do this. They won't stop us!"

Michael took his eyes off the crest long enough to wipe his forehead and check his watch. It was after five P.M., he noted and cast a look back at the truck. The setting sun had begun to allow the high cliff's shadows to creep across the floor of the ravine toward them, but the heat had already done its work as their clothing was soaked and sticking to their skin, . . . and thirst had become a major problem. Their eyes and heads were hurting, their eyes burning from the salty sweat, but there was nothing wrong with their ears. The chopping sounds of yet another helicopter was heard by all of them.

"Guess that sniper was the only one to get out a that first copter." Commented Joel. "Must have lowered 'im down with a rope. We'd known that, we could a drove out a here! . . . Okay, we got more coming, folks, get ready for 'em . . . . Mike, they're still gonna shoot us from that rim up there! . . . Wo! . . ." They were forced to duck again as more shots were fired from the distant rocks, ricocheting the bullets off the surrounding boulders and walls of the ravine, the noise echoing across the mountains to quickly die away. Everyone's eyes were glued to the rocks as they tried to find the sniper, and even Michael turned for a quick look.

"Look out!" Cried Mitch, and fired the MP 40 as the two Columbians stood up on the rim above them, spraying the area before the two could fire their own weapons down at them. The two jerked wildly as they were struck multiple times then both pitched outward, arms flailing to fall into the ravine's soft dirt.

"I guess Joel was right!" Breathed Reno as he stared at the bodies, and the man with a sling on his arm. "Recognize that one, Mitch?"

"Guess he wasn't all that smart after all!" He nodded, and when he saw his mother and father looking at both of them with questioning eyes. "The man from the cabin, dad . . . . I guess I should have killed him!"

"No, son, that would have been murder, it would have been justified, but it would have been murder! . . . Those men there are different, you killed them in self defense, and to protect the rest of us."

"Good job, Mitch!" Voiced Joel, and the rest of them joined in to praise him. "They had us dead to rights, son." He nodded.

Bullets began hitting the rocks again, as well as the wall they were crouched under, and they could tell that there was now more than one sniper shooting at them, . . . but this time they drew return fire from all nineteen rifles, the copper-coated projectiles chipping away at the snipers' cover of rocks, causing two of them to hunt better protection, except that one of them was felled before he could make it, . . . and the other was limping as he made cover again. The third man also stood up to run, but before they could train their sights on him, . . . they heard the loud, crisp order to drop their weapons. All of them quickly looked back up at the ravine's high rim, and the four Columbians that were standing there!

Michael's heart sank at sight of them. They had all four turned to watch the others flush out the snipers in the rocks, taking their eyes away from the cliff. He had the sudden feeling they were all about to die, . . . and if they tried to raise their weapons, he was sure of it!"

"Place the guns on the ground, my friends." Said the well-dressed man in his white, narrow-brimmed Panama hat. He was dark-skinned and had very white teeth as he grinned at them, . . . and his mouth was framed in a black mustache and trimmed goatee. The shirt was pink, his jacket white and his pants navy-blue. The three assassins were all in black and holding machine pistols trained on them.

"That's right, my friends." He nodded as they all placed their weapons on the ground. "You will not need guns any longer! . . . You have fought bravely, and killed many of my people today, . . . but now it is over. No one can fight the Cartel and win, . . . your American Government as well will know this when I kill you, . . . Adios!" He turned to nod at the assassins then, but before they could fire, rifle shots rang out and all three of them plunged headlong into the arroyo to fall atop the first two unfortunates.

Mitch and Reno quickly grabbed the 40s and was raising them to fire when Michael stopped them. They saw the well-dressed Columbian raise his arms and lace his fingers behind his head as he turned his back to the ravine.

"Hold your fire, Joel." He yelled. "Something's going on here . . . . Just don't shoot!" They were all holding their breath, as well as their weapons trained on the rim when the three men walked into view.

"You folks okay down there?" Grinned Jimmi. "Hi'ya Mister Zant, Nora, . . . hey boys, I see you made it?"

"Jimmi!" Yelled Mitch. "Dad it's Jimmi!"

"And James, too!" Laughed Reno. "And. Ben! . . . What took you so long?"

"We'd a been here sooner," Laughed Jimmi. "But we got called home . . . . Wouldn't be here now, we hadn't heard that explosion a while back, you sure done a job on that copter!"

"Yeah, it was making a pest of itself!"

"I believe it!" He looked at the Columbian then and ordered him to his knees, and that's when they heard the shooting, and then the second helicopter as it left.

"That would be Joe Burton, folks, . . . I guess he missed! . . . He'll be along in a minute. Why don't you all come on up out a that hole in the ground, got a nice warm breeze up here?"

"If you don't mind, Jimmi, I think we'll drive out!" Grinned Michael. "Meet you on top in a bit." He looked at the others then. "Load up, folks, let's climb out of here."

*   *   *

Not having the room to turn the big truck around, Jack pulled away from the overhang, straightened it up, . . . and after looking at Michael and shrugging, put it in low reverse gear and slowly crawled backward up the forty-five degree incline and over the crest where he stopped.

"Good job, Jack." Said Michael smiling. "Joel couldn't have done it better."

"Yeah, thanks, . . . I like this thing!" He opened the door and got out, as did all of them by the time Jimmi and the other men ushered their prisoner toward them.

"Is this the same truck we been tracking?" Asked Jimmi, coming forward to look it over.

"Yes sir, it is." Nodded Michael as the Guide squatted to check out the suspension, as did the other men, . . . and while they were inspecting the rig, Michael and most everyone else had walked out a ways to view the still smoking wreckage of the first attack helicopter.

"I'll be having nightmares about all this for a long time." Sighed Nora as she hugged Mitch.

"Is it over now?" Asked one of the other women, her haggard eyes taking in the twisted metal.

"Oh, honey," Said Nora sympathetically. "Yes, it is over, . . . we're all going home now."

"Thank, God!" She sighed. "I can brush my teeth again, . . . and I want a week long shower!"

"That makes all of us, darling!" Said Nora, squeezing Michael's arm tighter.

"Mike?" Said Jack as he came up to hug his wife, and stick his hand out. "Things are liable to get hectic from here on in, so I'm thankin' you now." He shook Michael's hand then reached to take Mitch's hand in a firm grip, and then Reno's.

"I have never know any young men like you two, . . . thank you so much! . . . We will never forget you, any of you!" He looked around at the others then and nodded at them.

"It's been a pleasure, Mike." Said Joel as he came around Jack and his wife to shake his hand, and then the boys. "Me and Leona will never forget you either, . . . and you boys sure taught me a lesson." He grinned. "You did something we were all too much of a coward to do, and saved all our lives doing it! . . . Thank you so much."

"How's your shoulder, Joel?" Asked Michael, placing a hand on the man's shoulder.

"Mike," He sighed, reaching to pull Leona against him. "If I had known getting shot would cure my Leona, I'd have attacked one of them assassins bare handed! . . . She's okay!" He said and kissed her.

"Thank you all." She smiled.

"Well." Sighed Michael and looked at the others. "We still have a ways to go, folks, we best get back to the truck."

"Mike." Said Jimmi as he walked back to stop at the truck. Jimmi shook his hand and then Nora's before looking back at the rig. "I've never seen anything like this thing, it's fantastic!"

"Yes, . . . it is." Agreed Michael. "But I wish we'd never seen it!"

"I can understand that!"

"We lost the radio, Jimmi." Said Mitch as he shook the guide's hand.

"And your horses!" Grinned Reno also shaking his hand.

"They'll come home."

"Where were you when you knew we were in trouble?"

"Yeah, and why were you out here?" Added Mitch.

"Told you I was coming after you, . . . but I had to wait for Mister Bowman's approval. Anyway, when Carl found out you were on your way home, he ordered us back, we were on our way home."

"All the way back to Rattlesnake Gorge." Voiced James Mason, coming up to shake their hands. "That was some explosion!"

"That's diesel fuel for ya." Said Ben also coming to shake their hands. "Stuff burns hot!"

Michael looked around at the other hunters and saw them all milling around and knew they were still not out of the woods. He had to get them all back to the lodge where they could get medical help.

"Load up, folks." He said loudly. "It's getting dark now, and we have a long way to go yet!" While they all climbed back into the truck, Michael turned to Jimmi. "What are you going to do with our Cartel man, Jimmi?"

"That Son of a Bitch should be shot, Mike, . . . but he's full of information our Government might like to know, so, . . . I'm gonna make th' Bastard walk every step of the way back to the Lodge! . . . You'll likely get there ahead of us, so tell them we'll be there sometime in the morning . . . . And by the way, I don't think this truck can bulldoze Pine

Trees! . . . There's no easy way you can make it through, . . . so, if it was me, I'd head right off down into that valley there, there's a road down there, just follow it south and you'll hit one-sixty, take you right to the Lodge. "Well, we'd best head on back ourselves, Mike, Nora. I'll radio ahead and tell them what happened here," He laughed. "The great F.B.I. will need to investigate, ya know! . . . See ya at th' Lodge!" They waved and went back to their horses.

"Son." Began Michael, putting an arm around his waist, and once again stifled a sob as he became emotional. "You, too, Reno." He pulled him to him in a hug as well, . . . and then pulled Nora in. "Thank you both for saving our life!" Both boys were in tears now as well, . . . and all of them clung to each other and released their week long ordeal with fear.

"We love you Mom and Dad." Sobbed Mitch.

"And dear, God, we love you, both of you very much!" Cried Nora as they all pulled away then to wipe their eyes.

"I can ask you now, Reno." Said Michael. "I know your father very well, so how in the world did Nakito and Lisa ever let you do something this reckless?"

"They didn't, Mister Z." He shrugged. "Mitch and I are on a Laguna trail ride! . . . They wouldn't have let either of us come, otherwise!"

"In other words, you lied to your parents?" Michael grinned and shook his head as he ushered them toward the truck. "Well, . . . I have never seen an Apache mad, . . . but we'll be with you when you tell them the truth."

*   *   *

"Michael, . . . Nora!" Beamed Ames Bowman as they entered the large dining room. "My, God, I'm glad you're all right!" He shook both their hands. "I was in the office last night when you got here and I didn't want to bother you." He walked with them across the semi-crowded room to seat them. "Catherine and I haven't slept a wink, to speak of since we got back! He sat down with them then and smiled at them. "Carl came to my office and told me you were all here, . . . said he'd already told Catherine, . . . She was already sound asleep when I got there, Probably won't wake up until dinner."

"What about McCreedy and the others?"

"They all left for Durango in an ambulance about an hour ago, Michael. Two F.B.I. Agents are with them to take their statements . . . . They'll all be okay, my friend, thanks to you and those boys!" He shook his head. "When Carl told me they had gone to find you, I was scared to death for them, out there all alone like that!"

"Ames, if any credit is given for any of this, it belongs to my sons, both of them . . . . We'd all be dead now, if they hadn't come!"

"Did the F.B.I. find that awful place?" Asked Nora.

"Yes, my dear, smoke led them right to it! . . . Everyone there is in custody, fourteen Columbians, and two dead ones, I'm afraid . . . . I'm also afraid Senator Oates and Special Agent Hallmark will want to speak with both of you, . . . it seems they have questions concerning the four naked men they found whipped and chained to a post."

"Seems to me that would speak for it's self!" Grinned Michael. "He'll get his answers when he reads the statements made by the victims we brought home, . . . because he'll get none from me." He looked across the room then. "Is that Mister Hallmark with Mister Oates?"

"Yes sir, and that other poor excuse for a man is ex-F.B.I. Agent Ron Howard, still trying to argue his case, I guess! . . . When you radioed Carl that you were coming home, He came and told me he called Mister Howard to tell him, but his aide told him the case was closed and Howard had left for a long weekend. So I called Washington. Senator Oates is a friend of mine, and he is a friend of J. Edgar! . . . By Ten A.M. yesterday, the Sheriff's Department helicopters were out on the front lawn with eighteen armed deputies, by Ten-fifteen, a National Guard copter arrived with thirty more soldiers, and right behind them, Senator Oates, Mister Hallmark and twenty Agents! . . . They left immediately for the mountains! . . . All except Oates and Hallmark, of course, but he got their butts in gear!"

"We saw the copters flying in as we were leaving . . . . What about Jimmi and his prisoner?"

"Jimmi radioed in about an hour ago, they'll be here soon. In fact, that's what the Senator and Hallmark are waiting on, they want that Columbian in Washington right away for questioning!"

"Do you know if they found that other helicopter, the one that attacked us?"

"I'm afraid it was too late by the time Jimmi told us about it . . . . They're out there looking right now, and also bringing in the bodies from where you were attacked. That must have been a war-zone out there?"

"That, and more, Ames! . . . I won't forget it for a while."

"Nor will I!" Sighed Nora

"And the truck?" Queried Michael. "What about it?"

"Confiscated, of course!"

"Well, Ames, I have a feeling that if they see that other helicopter, they'll never catch it." He grinned then. "By the time they put something in the air that can, it'll be gone, . . . and as far as the witness Jimmi's bringing in? . . . It wouldn't surprise me if he never makes it to Washington. These people can obviously get to anybody they want, any time they want! If they can put together an operation like we just left, right under our Government's nose, then they had better keep watch on all the prisoners! . . . These guys are for real, and they are brutally vicious."

"God, I hope you're not right!"

"But you know I am. We lost thousands of young men in the last war, but that was only the first part, . . . act one! . . . We're still at war here now, . . . only this time, it isn't on foreign soil, foreigners are bringing it to us, at home, . . . and in the form of Heroin, Opium, Marijuana and who knows what else? And Ames, I don't think we'll ever win this one! . . . Now if you'll excuse us, Ames, we are starved, and you can tell the Senator that I will have a detailed account of everything that happened at that compound by dinnertime tonight, . . . he can ask his questions at that time."